CROCUSES

HATCH

FROM

SNOW

CROCUSES HATCH FROM SNOW

JAIME BURNET

Vagrant PRESS

ADVANCE PRAISE FOR
CROCUSES HATCH FROM SNOW

"Personal and touching, *Crocuses Hatch from Snow* captures a true sense of Halifax that anyone who has lived there could attest to, but may not be able to name. Reading this book gave me back the sensation of walking through Halifax neighbourhoods at dusk. We are able to see into Burnet's characters' minds as if they were living rooms with lights on and curtains drawn open. We feel what they feel: their fears, desires and heartaches, and the ways in which systemic racism has played into the realities of their day-to-day existence, reverberating into the major events of their lives."

–REBECCA ROHER, award-winning author of *Bird in a Cage*

"Deftly told through diverse and interwoven stories, *Crocuses Hatch From Snow* is a heartfelt investigation into what a space can mean to those who live and love within it."

–TIFFANY MORRIS, Mi'kmaw sensitivity reader and author of *Havoc in Silence*

Vagrant Press is an imprint of
Nimbus Publishing Limited
3660 Strawberry Hill St, Halifax, NS, B3K 5A9
(902) 455-4286 nimbus.ca

Printed and bound in Canada

NB1423

Editor: Stephanie Domet
Editor for the press: Whitney Moran
Cover illustration: Jaime Burnet
Cover design: Jaime Burnet and Jesse Walker; Interior design: Jenn Embree

This story is a work of fiction. Names characters, incidents, and places, including organizations and institutions, either are the product of the author's imagination or are used fictitiously.

Quote from "The Butterfly" by Margaret Avison from *Other Canadians: An Anthology of the New Poetry in Canada, 1940–1946*, edited by John Sutherland. Montreal: First Statement Press, 1946.

Library and Archives Canada Cataloguing in Publication

Title: Crocuses hatch from snow / Jaime Burnet.
Names: Burnet, Jaime, 1986- author.
Identifiers: Canadiana (print) 20190154179 | Canadiana (ebook) 20190154187 | ISBN 9781771087902 (softcover) | ISBN 9781771088435 (HTML)
Classification: LCC PS8603.U73786 C76 2019 | DDC C813/.6—dc23

Nimbus Publishing acknowledges the financial support for its publishing activities from the Government of Canada, the Canada Council for the Arts, and from the Province of Nova Scotia. We are pleased to work in partnership with the Province of Nova Scotia to develop and promote our creative industries for the benefit of all Nova Scotians.

1

October 11, 2007

*T*he excavator's head hovers over the remaining half of a large blue house as if it doesn't know what to do, or doesn't want to do it. But the man pulls its reins and the machine complies, sinking its thick teeth into one hundred years of brittle history.

Three women stand on the sidewalk, watching their home of three generations come apart. Wood shingles crack, old windows smash as they hit the sidewalk. Ada, the youngest, stands with her back to the wind as it blows knots of unbrushed hair against her cheeks. Her arms are wrapped around her grandmother, Mattie, who is a foot shorter than her and swathed in a scratchy wool blanket. Ada's mother said it was too cold for the old woman to be outside for so long, but Mattie said she had to see this. Really, Joan thought it was a masochistic desire that shouldn't be indulged. But in the end they all went.

Joan makes a fist and breathes through the hollow to warm her fingers as she watches the excavator punch through what's left of the roof. She remembers her father re-shingling the house fifty years ago, working up on the roof at dusk, hammering down asphalt shingles after he'd finished with the cedar shakes. He stumbled in as she and her mother were sitting down to dinner, holding his bloody hand in a dirty handkerchief. He'd sliced off the tip of his thumb cutting a shingle and wanted help finding it. They searched with flashlights in the damp night, pawing through leaves. Joan thought she found the thumb but it turned out to be a slug. Mattie found the nub eventually, though by then Ian had decided he didn't need it. He said to throw it out. Little Joan couldn't sleep, thinking of the piece of thumb in the trash bin. She stayed awake all night, imagining it lying among eggshells and coffee grounds. In the morning she dug it out and her mother helped her bury it in the backyard with a shake for a headstone. Joan can see her memories cracking apart as the shingles hit the ground. She didn't want to watch this.

But Mattie doesn't mind. She'll miss the old home she came to as a newlywed and watched her daughter and granddaughter grow up in, but the neighbourhood is changing. Sports bars and chain stores with bright plastic signs have transformed it into a parade of shoppers and late night drunks. She doesn't want to know what the young man with the baritone bellow thinks of the ass of the girl ahead of him, her heels clicking fast as she tries to put more sidewalk blocks between them. And the ghost of her love, who has stayed with her at the house for the past year, will come with them to the new place across town.

As the excavator's rusted teeth chew away at the top floor where Ada and her grandmother slept, Ada says goodbye to the creaking stairs and wheezing iron radiator, which she is convinced was poisoning them all as it heated the house through layers of lead paint. She'll miss the high ceilings and backyard with the clawfoot tub full of lavender and goutweed. But the new house will be better. Her grandmother's knees need a rest from those stairs and her mother needs the money.

And Ken—Ken doesn't like pulling apart these old homes. He sits in the cab of the excavator, working the shovel, gingerly sliding its teeth on either side of the wall and drawing it toward himself, feeling a little sick as he hears the wood splinter. The same way he feels when his daughter cracks her neck, giving him nauseous shivers. "Kiah, I swear to God, if you keep doing that you're gonna paralyze yourself." He's heard the chiropractic horror stories. His best birthday present last year was a gift certificate from his kids for a massage. Not at the spa they send their grandma to on her birthday, but the physio clinic where he didn't have to be embarrassed by Enya and plug-in waterfalls. Kiah wanted to send him to the chiropractor, but there's no way that can be good for you, he's always said. He needs to relax, not feel like he's in some mafia movie where he's about to have his neck snapped in one quick twist.

The gold radiator tumbles through the broken floor and down the stairs, and he thinks of his mother's stories. Houses flattened to the ground with not enough warning to move the couch out of the living room, or even to box up family photographs. As frustrating as it might be to watch your house be bulldozed for a Starbucks, it can't compare to being evicted and relocated, the buildings and roads of your entire bright village erased.

"It must make you feel a little better to be tearing down white folks' homes," a crew boss joked to him once.

"Not really," Ken said.

Because as these people get pushed out of the south end to make room for sleek condos with minimalist furniture stores selling ceramic stag heads, and cafes serving six-dollar coffees on the ground floor, Ken and his family will be pushed farther north. The family who lived here has to move somewhere, and the north end real estate market is real hot these days. The north end of the city has "culture" and "soul," young non-Black agents tell their non-Black clients, which is a code meaning that there are enough Black people around to make you feel cool and worldly without ever having to talk to any of them.

Some of Ken's neighbours have already been pushed off the peninsula and begun what is often a northward migration, back to the Bedford Basin from whence they came. Others are making space for themselves in Spryfield, old Scotian families who wouldn't say they're from anywhere but here settling beside young migrant mothers who call to their kids in Kreyol and are answered back in English.

So no, Ken thinks, it doesn't make him feel better. But today his job is to flatten this house. He pulls on the lever and another wall collapses. A window smashes on the sidewalk below and the crew boss shouts to the onlookers to stand farther back. Ken pauses to watch as two women try to lead a reluctant old lady away from the spectacle. Slowly, she concedes and is taken by each elbow.

The woman keeps her neck craned back and her eyes on the house as she's led down the street. Maybe this was her home, Ken thinks. He gives her a wave from the cab of the machine, though he's sure she can't see him. She waves back.

"Yep, say goodbye to the house, Mum," Joan says. "Bye bye, house."

2

⚜

October 12, 2007

Ada's hand probes the corners of her soft bag and finds: book, spoon, penknife...pen? No, a piece of stale licorice. Many, many receipts, like a little pile of dried leaves. And some actual dried leaves—maple, the reddest ones. But no pen. She hadn't had time to scrawl down her dream this morning as she usually does, head lying still on her pillow, barely able to see her own writing as her stiff sleepy hand moves along the horizon of the page, recording her dream in inked loops and lines. Her mother was up early, still unpacking boxes in their twelve-days-new house, and that meant Ada had to be up unpacking too.

The walk to the café, across from the art school on a cobblestoned cul-de-sac downtown, is longer from the north end of the city than it was from her old house in the south, but only by a few minutes. You can pretty much walk from anywhere to anywhere in Halifax in under half an hour, it's like some kind of geographical law. From the house on Queen Street, Ada would walk along Barrington, through a downtown that big-city people find quaint. A few lonely high-rises reach above old brick and stone buildings like children growing taller than their parents. The ground-floor shops sell vintage dresses, silver sand dollar earrings, donairs and poutine, second-hand books, tobacco, dildos, and lollypops stuck in the headdress of a wooden chief. There aren't as many stores to stare into on the walk from the new house, but past the cop shop the road rises up the hill toward the Citadel, and from there Ada can see the ocean.

Now, sitting at this small table with a mug of milky coffee, the dream is leaving her. She just needs to remember the main part and she trusts her subconscious to fill in the rest, once she finds a pen. The old man at the counter—not so old, sixty maybe—with loose skin and long, grey eyebrows that grow into the hedges of his sideburns, has a pen in his breast pocket. But he doesn't seem to like Ada. When she comes in and orders coffee from him, he looks at her out of eyes that sit in a tilted-back head, skeptically appraising. But she wants that pen.

How did it begin again? she thinks. You were there, help me out. What did you say? No, it wasn't what you said, it was something you did. Oh! Teeth. You were collecting my teeth. Okay. Teeth. I can remember that. And now to get the pen.

Ada weaves between the tables and up to the counter.

"Excuse me, I wonder if you've got a pen I could borrow for a minute?" she asks as she stares at the man's pocket.

"What will you use it for?" he asks, eyeing her from under knit brows.

"To stir my coffee," she replies. And he smiles. Pen in her hand. Teeth. Teeth. Teeth.

She slides back into her seat and opens her book.

I am sitting in the kitchen and she sits across from me at the table. She made us dinner—these very tall sandwiches made of layers and layers of bread with all different kinds and colours of jam between. I lift mine up, holding it sideways like an accordion, and move to take a bite. I put my mouth on it and taste sweet tartness. I move my lips and tongue around but I can't bite. I see myself from outside my body and discover that I have no teeth. I try the sandwich again. Nope. I try to explain to you that I can't eat your dinner, but I can't talk either. You see the problem and start to look around the kitchen for my missing teeth.

Ada pauses her frantic scrawling as she notices that, again, she is addressing her dream journal to *you*. Since she met Pan she hasn't been able to speak about her in the third person for long. Even her inner monologue is addressed to Pan. She worries. She'll try again.

She looks on the floor, inside teacups, in the fridge. Aha! She finds a tooth. My tooth. They are like Easter eggs, precious and gleaming coyly from nonsensical locations. On top of a can of apple juice in the fridge. In the bowl of a dirty spoon in the sink. On the ledge of a picture frame. I think she is about to bring them to me so I can put them back in my mouth, but no—she puts them in her own mouth, one by one. Do you need a second row of teeth? Are you a shark?

You again. She gives in.

No. You swallow them, my ivory teeth. Polished and ground down flat like piano keys. Not like yours—ridged still, at thirty-two. How is that possible? Do you eat only soft foods? You do eat a lot of soup, you told me once. But you swallow them. And with each swallow a spot, shiny and hard, appears on your face and spreads to join up with others. They are smooth and cold and they are forming a shell. It covers your cropped dark hair. It spreads down your beautiful neck. And now it has covered your head entirely. You blink at me from your enamelled head and I blink back at you with my eyes and blink with my toothless mouth, opening and closing. I should be angry, I think. You swallowed my teeth. But instead I pull your cold, hard face to mine and kiss you on your smooth forehead.

And that's all. Grateful to her subconscious, Ada folds her soft book shut and looks up. And there's Pan, standing a few steps inside the door to the café, watching Ada with a closed-mouth smile. Ada smiles back and Pan's lips break apart, exposing her ridged teeth.

So strange, Ada thinks. But I'd like the feel of them on my tongue. Rough little pebbles.

Pan moves toward Ada with her casual gait and sits down like she means it.

"Hi," Ada says, kissing Pan with her blinking eyes.

"Hey, Ada."

Pan gulps Ada's coffee with her elusive lips.

Your lips are dry, Ada's inner monologue runs. They crave my licking. They tell me so, from across the table. Kiss us. Kiss us. Wet us with your tongue. Don't you hear them?

"Sorry, what?" Ada asks, distracted by her own narration.

"I asked how you were," Pan repeats, her tongue soft on the backs of her teeth, the corner of her mouth lifting in an amused half-grin.

Ada tells her about her day, a list of activities she offers as proof that she can do more than sit around and daydream of Pan. Nightdream of Pan. Jerk off thinking of Pan.

They've never kissed. Only in Ada's head, many times. Her imagination is so convincing, she forgets sometimes that it hasn't really happened. It has taken her so many modifications to reach this height of fantasy. In an x-ray, the points at which Pan has embedded herself in Ada's body would glow like silver stars and lines. A connect-the-dots of her obsession.

It's a tendency she's always had—forming crushes on remarkable strangers. Ada still sees some of her old favourites around the city, but they don't send heat coursing through her limbs like they used to. Don't thrill her like Pan does. She still has a fondness for them, though. Keeps them in a cubby in her heart, next to the goth punk she listened to at sixteen.

The blue-haired boy with an upper lip twice the size of his lower used to make her body-drunk when she would pass him on the sidewalk. Once, when she caught his eye leaving a bookstore, a flush bloomed in her cheeks so deep that it didn't recede until two hours later while she sat on a dock in the harbour with her face to the wind.

The girl with the yellow umbrella was another consuming crush, and the person with the thick, jewel-red eyeglass frames. Colour seems to draw her—these three cover the primaries. Especially in an ocean city, where mist coats the streets grey, bright colours have the power to cut through her daydreams.

But Pan was different. The reverse of how someone usually catches her eye. She saw her first nearly a year ago in this, her favourite café, its walls painted golden yellow and decorated with green leaves, red berries, and blue birds that hold up a large chalkboard banner painted on the wall above the counter. Pan, in the corner with her black coffee, black-framed glasses, and ink-smudged newspaper, always wears grey. Nothing but grey. That day, a grey sweater zipped up over a darker grey

T-shirt with faded black pants—grey on the thighs, white on the knees. A woven scarf wrapped around her neck, also grey. Ada couldn't see her shoes, but did later when she followed Pan out as she left the café and saw that they matched the cobblestones perfectly.

Pan camouflages herself in this city. But in this bright place her greyness makes her conspicuous. And now not even the grey city can swallow Pan in all her layers of smoke and slate. Ada's eyes turn to her wherever she is. A heliograph flashing on the periphery.

"Do you want a coffee or something?" Ada asks.

"Nah, I'll just drink yours," Pan grins. "How are you healing up?" she asks, hunching her shoulders, her rough-knuckled fingers encircling the ceramic mug.

"Not bad," Ada says. "But they're really tender. I bumped one in the shower yesterday and almost cried."

"You have to be careful with them. They're hard to heal. I ended up taking mine out after a couple of years. You can't say I didn't warn you."

Pan did warn her that nipple piercings were hard to heal. But Ada's running out of things to pierce, and nipples seemed a logical progression from septum, which came after navel, now housing four curved barbells—a jewelled compass in the centre of her body, and that was after her lip. So she had Pan pierce them both. Twice. The first ones three months ago, angled inward with the curve of her body, and these ones, pierced two months later, crossed over the first ones in Xs. And now they're having coffee before she has Pan pierce her nostrils—both.

Not all piercings hurt, but her nipples fucking did. Especially the second set. But then, it's a question of hurt. And in this case it was a hurt that Ada wanted, so in that way they felt incredible. Pan's needle puncturing her tender flesh. The grip of her gloved hands, the hot push of steel. Her nimble fingers sliding the delicate bars through the wounds, lubricated by a slight seeping of blood from the holes, creating two small kisses on either side of Ada's heart.

Ada likes when she brushes them by accident and the pain comes gently back to her. It's an echo of what Pan inflicted on her, a fond reminder. She smiles with her secret.

Should I tell you that I went and saw your show at the gallery across town? Ada wonders. Because I did. Of course I did. You must have figured I would. Ada had fallen in love with a print Pan had up in her room in the tattoo studio. "I just fell in love with your print," Ada had said, and was sorry immediately after, face red and eyes shut tight.

"I went to see your show."

It escapes out through her mouth before she can consider it further.

"Oh yeah?" Pan grins.

Pan always grins, never smiles. A smile is more open, vulnerable. Pan's grin is a grin because it's a smile backed by confidence. It's sly, though not quite a smirk. It's boyish and way too charming.

"Whadja think?" she asks.

Ada had thought many things. The stark lines sliced out of linoleum, void of paint, are burned into her head as negative images. Secret pictures like songs played backward. The shapes abstract and spell out a message of desire, captured in sharp highlights and insinuated with shadows. But all she can think to say is, "I liked it."

Ada smiles and shakes her head, trying to dissolve the inarticulacy gluing her tongue to the roof of her mouth.

"They were beautiful," she says. "Really raw and disarming, because they felt tender too."

Pan grins again, this time looking a bit modest. Bashful, even, glancing down into the usurped mug.

She talks about her art, shoulders hunched up around her ears, hands on the mug, shifting slowly on her elbows, side to side. Ada is mesmerized by the line of her jaw, how it curves down into her neck. Soft hairs catch the sunlight coming in through the window and illuminate that delicious contour. Trace me with your fingertips, it says. Slide your cheek against me. Bury your face in me, Pan's neck tells her, where you can smell my smell the best.

When Pan stops speaking she looks a bit embarrassed, as if she's just professed her greatest passions to a toddler, endowing her with imagined maturity. Ada is younger than Pan is, but she's not a child. Though admittedly, the nuances of Pan's artistic vision are lost on her when all she can think of is running her tongue along Pan's collarbone.

Pan looks down at her watch, strapped into a thick leather cuff on her wrist.

"We have to go," she says. "Get you pierced before my next appointment."

She drains the last drops of coffee and Ada follows her out the door.

3

December 13, 1947

Mattie heard her whistling through the brush before she saw her. The sharp wind blew the notes back to her high and clear while the magnetic pull of the river drew her to its edge. Little birds hopped from branch to branch alongside her, resting lazy wings.

The narrow path was muddy from the previous day's sleet, so Mattie mounted its banks, one foot on each side, and walked along. The water pulled her by the chest like a fishing line with its hook caught in her ribs, tugging, coaxing. Or was she pulled by the whistle in the wind?

You can get pregnant by the wind, her grandmother told her, if the right idea's floating on it. That's why you keep your legs together and hold your skirt down when it blows in from the ocean. You never know who's sent their thoughts inland from the boats. You could wind up with a fisherman's baby growing in your belly, or even the child of a thoughtful fish.

The red mud squelched under Mattie's boots and she hiked her skirt higher to keep the hem dry. That story was for kids. The cold air between her sweating thighs in their cotton stockings was a refreshing breath, and she breathed in deep.

The sun glinted blue-green on the oiled feathers of a blackbird as it bobbed between branches up ahead, whistling its wind song.

And then the bird turned its head, and she was a girl.

"Oh!" said Mattie. "Hello!"

The whistling girl stepped around a bush, emerging in full height in front of her.

"Gee, you're tall," Mattie said.

"And you're not very ladylike, are you?" said the girl, as Mattie stepped over to the left bank of the path and lowered her skirt. "Well, I'm not either. Came out here to drop my dress in the river. Drowned the damn thing."

"I thought you were a blackbird," Mattie said. "The sparrows were following your whistle."

The girl laughed. Her thick black hair was cropped to a bob that curled around her ears. Her bangs arched across her forehead, like her face was the moon and her hair was the night sky.

"What sort of stupid sparrow would come to the song of a black-bird?" she asked. "Haven't you seen them fight? If I were a blackbird I'd eat those titchy things up mid-swoop."

She stepped closer, and Mattie's eyes swept over her round face, her shining hair, her muddy shoes.

"Is it because you're Indian that you can talk to the birds?"

The girl raised an eyebrow.

"My mother just told m-me, uh…" Mattie stammered, feeling stupid. "I thought maybe you could talk to animals. Animal spirits?"

The girl stared.

"Your…ancestors? In the birds? I thought maybe you could… talk."

The girl put her hand on her hip.

"Should I call them then? My animal spirit friends?"

Mattie stared, nervous.

"Don't be daft!" she laughed, startling Mattie, who dropped the hem of her skirt in a puddle. "I was whistling Betty Hutton."

"'Doctor, Lawyer, Indian Chief'?"

"That's the one."

"I love that song!" Mattie smiled, singing a line about the chief and his tommy-hawk and waving her finger in the air.

The girl stared. "Maybe I don't like it so much after all," she said.

"Sorry, I'm an awful singer," Mattie said, sheepish.

"It's not your singing."

The girl's stare conjured waves of heat to Mattie's face. She tried to calm herself by examining a nearby tree branch, but the pull of the girl's eyes kept drawing her back.

"Listen, don't tell anyone you saw me here. Or that I drowned my dress, all right?"

"No," Mattie said. "I won't. I promise."

"What's your name?" the girl asked.

"Mattie," she replied with a wave.

"Maybe I'll call you Sparrow," the girl said. "Since you were dumb enough to come to my song."

Mattie looked for a smile in the girl's eyes, and finding it, nodded.

"Sure," she said, half of her mouth crooked in a grin at her teasing. "I'm a sparrow."

"I mean it," the girl said. "Don't tell a soul."

"I promise," Mattie said, and the two girls parted.

When she got to the riverbank, Mattie could just see the white dress as it floated on the water's muddy surface, out toward the ocean. It looked the way she imagined those white whales would look, the belugas she herself had never seen, but had heard of from kids at school who'd sighted them off the coast of the Bay of Fundy. Those ivory ghosts would never come this far up the river, but the dress was a whale for Mattie that day. She stared with narrowed eyes as it swam steadily away from her, trying to keep it in her sight. They look like corpses, a fisherman's son had told her. No, said his kid sister, like fat angels. Mattie watched the whale and remembered her grandmother's warning, imagined what it would be like to feel wet whale skin against her own. To slide along each other underwater. She closed her eyes and saw the girl's face, her smooth cheek, and touched her own warm cheek with her palm. Flushed from the teasing, must be.

AS SHE WALKED BACK TO the school, Edith could still feel the fabric of the dress against her skin, tight under the armpits, the matching white stockings pulling at the hairs on her legs. She thought of the wretched thing, now soaked through with red water, and grinned. The wind whistled softly through a gap between her front teeth. Enough, she had told herself. Enough of dressing up to be shown off, for the Department of Indian Affairs and newspaper photos, pretending they were being taken care of by compassionate sisters and a kind father.

Some of her boldness dissolved as she thought of the nuns. A cold ache spread across her chest, as if she had been buttoned into her suffocating dress and was sinking into the frigid river, drowning along with it. She was nervous for what awaited her, in case the nuns had noticed she'd gone missing.

After escaping the school grounds, it had occurred to Edith to bolt, just run into the woods. But she would have been brought back by the Mounties. It had happened to many others, including one of her younger cousins. Joe, a clever boy she whisper-bragged about to all her friends when word spread one morning that he had made the classic escape the night before, out the window on a rope of bed sheets. And in the same way she shared the pride of his escape, Edith felt his humiliation pulsing through her veins, burning in her ears along with her furious anger when he was caught. Her own belly ached as he was fed nothing but stale bread at supper, when he was released briefly from the soap closet, blinded by the light. So full of rage was she as she watched the nun shave off his hair that she bit through her lip to keep from screaming. She had remembered the taste of her blood as she made her way down the red mud path, out toward the water. The nuns knew where her parents lived, and she had nowhere to run but home. So she stuck with her original plan—drown the dress.

Oh, why had she spoken to that girl? Edith scolded herself. She was sure to tell on her.

Somehow Edith slipped back onto the school grounds and blended in with her friends, still outside for recess, without the nuns noticing. She glowed with relief. Susan and Dorothy hadn't even had to cover for her, as the sisters were distracted by the wailing of the smallest of several Marys at the school, all but the eldest of whom had been renamed. This one, now called Margaret, had slipped in the mud and, from the sounds of it, broken at least one finger.

"I can't believe you did it," Dorothy breathed under the wind. "You're so brave."

"She's nuts," said Susan. "They'll just make you wear another dress, probably even smaller."

Edith wouldn't have had to wear the chafing, strangling thing in the first place if her parents hadn't taken her to the Resi. The Shubenacadie Residential School. Edith's father kept her away for as long as he could, until an Indian agent threatened to throw him in jail. "I trust you'll do the right thing," the buttoned-up man said as he stood in the doorway of their home, as if her father truly had a choice. "Why would you deprive your child of an education?"

Edith knew her alphabet and how to spell her name and the names of her brothers long before the agent came rapping at the door. And she could mix *lu'sknikn* dough and bake it golden nearly as well as her mother did, later missing the dense warmth of it in her mouth as she sliced loaf after loaf of dry bread in the kitchen at school. She had learned to split ash to weave baskets, and the medicines of sweetgrass, juniper, sage, white spruce, alder, golden thread. She loved peeling the moss from rocks and unthreading those delicate gold roots. But to the nuns this was not an education. It was witchcraft. So they stamped it out. Or at least they tried.

IT WASN'T UNTIL TWO DAYS later that Edith learned the dress hadn't drowned. Someone had pulled it out of the river by Princeport before it could escape out to Cobequid Bay, out to the ocean. The label in the collar let them know where it came from. They brought it to the school, thinking a student had fallen into the water. The nuns only needed to look at the embroidered number to know whose it was.

For a week after she was strapped, Edith could barely sit down. In class, she lowered herself slowly onto her hard wooden seat, keeping her face as still and blank as she could. She cried silently into her pillow after the nun shut the lights. And though it stung, she cleaned the wounds carefully with soap to prevent an infection. Sickness could send her to the infirmary, from which some had not returned. Edith had seen other kids beaten unrecognizable, lips split and blooming red, eyes swollen closed as if bitten by blackflies. When a beating had gone that far, such that it might have caused a complaint from a doctor and an investigation, the children tended not to recover. "Tuberculosis," the nuns would say. With so many having perished this way, it seemed a likely enough explanation.

4

October 22, 2007

It's been a year since Leona died, and Ken still can't bring himself to change their bed sheets. He left them as she did, rumpled and musty, with the weight of her sick body impressed into the old mattress and feather pillow. No one's allowed to lie there. His kids know not to sit down on her side of the bed when they come in to talk to him. Every night, Ken slips in beside her impression, careful not to disturb the sheets.

"Let me wash them, son," his mother asks every few months. "She wouldn't want to see you living like this."

But Ken won't allow it.

He thinks of her face. The high, creased forehead where he planted firm kisses when she worried. The smooth nose she nuzzled into his neck on Saturday mornings before Kiah and Shawn woke up. The full cheeks that dimpled when she smiled. He thinks of her body. The curve of her back as she knelt down to tie Shawn's shoes until he hit seven and finally understood what to do with those bunny ears. The soft swell of her twice pregnant belly under the giant cotton underpants she insisted on buying because it was like giving her butt a hug. Her butt that could make those giant undies and even her shapeless pastel nursing scrubs look good.

He forgets how the sound of Leona sucking her teeth, her tut tut tutting at everything she had an opinion on—from Kiah's short skirt to that crack in the ceiling to the carpet that needed vacuuming—would make his ears itch. He forgets the deep crease between her brows when he did something dumb like forget to pick up groceries for dinner, or the clenched muscle of her jaw when he cracked a beer and retired to the couch after returning from an eight-hour shift and she from a twelve, when there were kids to feed and laundry to be done. A blessing of memory, how the hard things soften and the sweet things shine.

In Ken's memory of their rocky first year, the sound of Leona's *NowYouListenUp* voice telling him what's what and to straighten out and that he won't know what a good thing he has until he loses it is drowned out by the sounds of Prince's "Let's Go Crazy," Leona's favourite song that summer. In Ken's mind, he sees her finger pointing in his face as just another one of her funky dance moves. But he can't deny the effect she had on him. Before Leona, all he cared about was looking good and acting tough. And she had no patience for this. He started to get pushy, picking fights with guys on the street after a few beers, and the finger-pointing would start. This was the standard beginning of most of their arguments that year. Inevitably it would lead to one of the boys Ken had been hassling calling back that his bitch had him whipped, and Leona would shout that she was nobody's bitch, and Ken would say Lee, this is the last time you shame me, and the beer would take it from there.

Ken was born the year before his family was pushed into the sterile housing project on Gottingen Street, with no grass or gardens and no good places to play. His parents had owned their own house out on Bedford Basin's southern shore, painted yellow between red and blue neighbours. The brightness of Africville. His father knew everything about keeping the house up—how to fix a hole in the roof, build kitchen cupboards, replace a broken window pane. But then their belongings were packed into dump trucks, carted into Halifax, and unloaded into the Square. And weren't they just too telling, those trucks? Especially considering how the suits that ran the city had surrounded the community with all the things it would later use to justify its destruction. A prison. A slaughterhouse. A goddamn fecal waste depository. An infectious diseases hospital. And the town dump. It was a racist cliché. It was too absurd. And yet, there it was. There they were, dumped out into Uniacke Square, ushered into identical houses. They were renters now, just barely able to pay up at the beginning of each month. Though Ken's father had been heard to remark that it was nice to finally be hooked up to the water and sewer systems he'd been paying his damn taxes to for all those years.

So that's where it came from, the anger. That and centuries' worth of other shit. But for Ken, it was particularly this. Particularly that, though Leona disputed the science of it, Ken swears the stink of the slaughterhouse is his one memory of his first year of life. Particularly that falling asleep to the sound of his parents arguing over money is his strongest memory of years two through twelve. Particularly that, as soon as he hit thirteen and surpassed his dad's height seemingly overnight, he couldn't walk down the street without being hassled by some cop.

Eventually, Leona showed him how to channel his anger out. She was twenty-one and a nursing student when he finally, finally asked her on a date, which thrilled Ken's mother—Betty began not so subtly suggesting marriage after their second. Though Ken didn't really care about her education back then. It was that smooth skin, those dimples, that laugh, those legs. Back when they were in high school, he'd watched her walk down the hall a thousand times on those perfect legs. But there was no way some skinny tenth grader in a neon orange cap turned backward—the hall monitor calling after him to take it off and show some respect or she'd take it off for him—was going to get Miss Young Gifted & Black to turn away from her group of girl geniuses on their way to biology.

He was just smooth enough to keep it under wraps when he finally managed to talk to her. To convince Leona, with her straight spine, loud voice, and curly hair that shook when she shouted, that he wasn't just looking to get some. Of course he lied about his age. What high-horse textbook-totin' grown *woman* was going to go with a nineteen-year-old kid living in the Square, his buddy Ray asked.

"Who you callin' a kid? I'm a man, man!" Ken protested, popping Ray on the shoulder. "We ain't in high school no more. Age ain't nothin' but a number."

But he took note. Went to the barbershop. Got a slick fade and shaved the hair shading his top lip.

"And trim your damn nails," Ray told him. "If you don't know why, I ain't telling ya."

Knowing well his friend's lack of prowess with ladies, Ray decided to give Ken a well-manicured hand up. He asked his older brother to ask his girlfriend where Leona was hanging out these days. Expecting his brother to come back with the name of a club, Ray went through his personal inventory of dance moves and pick-up lines. He did a spin, a couple of snaps, a hip pop and some shoulder shrugs in the bathroom mirror. As research. He was a good friend. Ray decided he would recommend shoulder shrugs and a subtle head bob, along with a compliment about Leona's eyes. Everyone knows that one's surefire. No ladies have hangups about their eyes, and telling a woman you think she has a beautiful mouth right off the bat is too much too soon. She'll know you're thinking about blow jobs.

When Ray's brother told him the only place he knew of where Leona was hanging out was with a group of folks meeting about the million-dollar construction of a dog park on Africville land, Ray's lady-killer instincts got fuzzy. Ken couldn't pass as cool with smooth dance moves in a circle of people talking politics.

"Man, Leona don't go to clubs. She goes to meetings. Just like in high school. Debate team. Yearbook. You should've signed up to cut and paste photos of football heroes three years ago if you wanted to get close to this girl, 'cause my friend, you don't know shit about this park business."

"I don't know shit? What makes you think I don't know shit?"

"Kenny." Ray passed him the joint. "I know for a fact that everything that goes through your head comes out through your mouth and into my ear. You never said nothin' about the park so I'm left to deduce that it's not on your mind."

"And I'm left to deduce," said Ken, staring at his friend through the haze, "that you don't know shit about me."

"Now don't get crazy on me. Settle, man."

"Don't you think I hear my folks talking about it, on and on? First thing in the morning, at the dinner table, on the phone. I hang out with a bonehead like you to escape that shit. I don't talk about it to you 'cause it's above your intellect."

"Big talk, Kenny," Ray said, waving away his friend's insults along with the creamy smoke. "I do know you, know you well enough to know you get awful *sensitive* when you've got your eye on a girl and your pride on the line. So I'm willing to let this one slide, and I'll do you the favour of accompanying you to this meeting. Maybe I'll even let your bashful ass sit beside me so some of my *intellect* can rub off."

At the meeting, Ken's blood thrummed so hard through the tiny vessels in his ears that he could barely hear the debate, let alone the whispers of his friend, who prompted him with practical questions and fiery outbursts, but to no avail. Ken sat still, aside from the occasional nod in support of what seemed like the predominant opinion of the group. Once Ken saw enough heads nodding in agreement, he'd nod a bit himself. By the time the meeting finally ended and it seemed like folks were splitting up to grab a drink or go home, Ray managed to subtly herd Ken in Leona's direction.

"I liked what you had to say tonight," he whispered in Ken's ear as he gave him a gentle shove toward her.

"I liked what you had to say tonight," Ken said to Leona's glowing bare shoulder, shrugging through the neckline of her purple sweater. She turned and cocked her head. He adjusted his gaze.

"Well thanks," she said with a half smile. "Haven't seen you at one of these meetings before."

"I keep pretty busy, but I know what's up. You know. Stay informed, much as I can. It's important stuff, right?" Ken slid his sweating palms into the pockets of his jeans and nodded his head in agreement with his own question.

"I sure think so," Leona said, her teeth ready to break from behind her smooth lips in an amused smile.

"Maybe, uh," Ken's eye snagged on her mouth. "Maybe we could talk about it over a drink sometime?"

Leona's lips parted to reveal a grin that Ken couldn't tell was pleased or mocking him in his barely concealed bashfulness.

"Maybe," she said. "You old enough to drink?"

"Old enough to drink? I'm more than old enough to drink. I'm twenty-one!"

"Twenty-one, huh?" Leona's cheeks dimpled. "You must have flunked kindergarten twice, Ken, cause you've been two grades behind me my whole life."

Ken let out a chuckle of disbelief, like he'd been poked soft in the gut.

"That was just a test," he said, recovering his wit. "Just wanted to see how close you've had your eye on me. Nice to know you've been paying attention."

LEONA BROUGHT HIM UP TO speed, brought him out to protests. After they were married, when Kiah was four and Shawn was two, they fought to stop the government from allowing a truck road to slice through Africville land, and to have their Baptist church rebuilt. That was sixteen years ago, and the government still hasn't followed through on its promise to build the church. Without Leona, though, Ken can't bring himself to care. It feels like too much of a lost cause.

So he works. Gets up at the same time every day. Toast with butter, coffee with cream. Ham and cheese in a Ziploc bag in his hand. Keys, wallet, phone. Always early, never late. Pulls the levers that pull down the walls. Takes things apart to keep it all together.

You need money to keep it together. The demolition jobs pay pretty well, but when you're renting your house, supporting yourself, your mother, a disillusioned eighteen-year-old son, and a daughter in university, money can be tight. Ken tries to talk to Shawn, asks him to work harder at holding down a job, but the boy doesn't care. Any place that will hire him is embarrassing, he says. When he got the job at McDonald's, all his friends would come in, bug him for free Cokes, sit down and crack jokes about him for hours. They had nothing better to do. And Ken sympathizes. In a segregated city full of well-off university students, who's going to hire his son? "I can't support you forever," he's told him. But he doesn't know how to motivate the boy. What can he say that isn't some empty slogan? Shawn reminds Ken of himself at that age. So why can't Leona be here to inspire him?

It had been so easy with Kiah. That girl knew she was going to university since she was seven years old, and in high school she had the grades and got the scholarships to help her along. Her dedication floors Ken. How she can sit upstairs in her room working on a paper or studying for an exam for hours is beyond him. But then, he also can't comprehend how Shawn can sit in the basement, marathoning video games. Same drive, different goal. Ken knows his son has the ability—he just can't quite replicate his wife's magic to redirect it.

By all accounts Leona was magic. When she started working as a nurse at Camp Hill, the older patients who couldn't remember their own children's faces on bad days were somehow always able to say her name.

"Unforgettable, that's what you are," her favourite, a flirtatious eighty-seven-year-old would croon to her while she checked his feet for swelling. It had been her and Ken's wedding song, their first slow dance as a married couple. Later it was their excuse to stop doing the dishes for five minutes and dance in the kitchen, or kiss against the refrigerator after Kiah and Shawn had gone to sleep. Once or twice it was Ken's backup plan when they'd each stomped off to separate rooms after a fight and he hadn't yet mastered how to say outright that he was sorry. The last time Ken heard it was at her funeral, and he can't stand to hear it anymore.

At night, Ken crawls gingerly into bed and tells Leona about his day. He talks softly, careful not to let his family hear him carrying on half a conversation with the empty room. They would worry. But Ken's all right. This is what keeps him going steady, allows him to sleep. The sleepless nights for months after she died were wearing him down. His mind was getting hazy, like a cocoon was being woven thicker and thicker around his head. He had spent so many years lying down beside the same woman, listening to her smooth voice, feeling her warm hand heavy on his chest, telling her all his wants and worries, hopes and insecurities. He couldn't tell them to anyone else and they were keeping him up at night, floating around unsaid. So he talks to her. Tells her he loves her more than anything. Breathes in the scent of the sheets, rests his own hand on his chest, and falls asleep beside his wife.

5

November 6, 2006

The first day Ada saw her she was completely absorbed. Pan emitted a pure, low hum that radiated through the floor, up the metal tuning rod legs of Ada's chair and into her body. She was captivated by the slow lowering and raising of Pan's eyelids as she read. Pan blinks less than most people. And her hair was a bit longer then—she let the strands by her temples grow so that they fell in front of her ears in loose curls and rested on her cheeks. Her slow blinking eyes behind the thin frames of her glasses like lazy fish in small glass bowls.

Ada was fascinated. The way Pan held her book like a fan, the gentle lean of her body in the rigid chair. The near indiscernible movement of her lips as her eyes absorbed the words on the page. When Pan finally looked up from the book and checked her wrist for the time, lifting herself out of her lean, Ada shut her book too. She dropped it twice before she got it, finally, into her bag, just as Pan was pushing herself out through the door and into the cool air. Ada left her pot of tea half finished. She rushed out of the café. And there Pan was, calmly loping across the cobblestones, her granite-grey shoes blending in with the wet floor of the city.

It was November and a chill rain had tapped silence into the streets. The sidewalks still held its dampness and the air its cold. Ada followed, past the bike shop, the sushi place, two cafés, and a bookstore. Pan turned right and Ada followed her uphill until she slid through a door beneath a hanging sign that advertised ink and body piercing. Ada went in through the door behind her, Alice tumbling down headfirst after the waistcoated herald.

She was caught off guard when she entered the room and came face to face with Pan, standing behind the counter. Pan grinned and Ada's stomach dropped.

"Hi," she said.

Ada can't remember what sounds she made in response, but they were fumbling enough to prompt Pan to help her along with a gentle, "Do you have an appointment today?"

"Nope, just uh...looking."

Ada looked around. Yes. She would like to make an appointment. All she could think about at that moment was the slow, slight pursing and pressing of Pan's lips as she read in the café and how she wanted to press her lips against them now. And so she said, "Lips."

Fuck. Ada blushed hot and closed her eyes. But Pan interpreted her slip.

"Did you want to get your lip pierced?" Pan helped her along, seeming amused. "Because I have some time now if you want."

Pan would touch her lips right then if she asked for it? Yes. Ada did want.

She filled in a sheet of paper and gave Pan her ID. Ada's tiny image looked out knowingly from her little window in the plastic card, from Ada to Pan and back, smiled and shook her head. Ada thought she saw her tiny self wink as she slipped the card back into her wallet.

Once they were inside the small room, Ada inched onto the tissue paper–covered table while Pan adjusted her gloves. As she studied Ada's mouth, Pan asked, "Where do you want me to pierce you?"

Oh God, Ada thought. My heart. My cunt. Ada wanted to feel Pan's warm hands between her legs. She was so wet, sitting on that crinkling paper. But she did not lie back on the table and moan for Pan's touch. She held herself together.

Ada asked Pan to pierce her top lip, vertically.

"I've only done one like that before," Pan said. "But I think I can handle it."

So Ada put her trust in Pan's marksmanship.

As Pan pressed a purple dot into the dip below Ada's nose and another in the centre of her top lip, Ada could feel her pulse throbbing in her ears. Pan doesn't use clamps. She likes to pierce freehand, she said, and Ada thought that sounded poetic.

She exhaled as Pan pinched her lip between two fingers, warm through the latex. Pan's own lips parted as she placed the tip of the needle on the higher of the two marks.

"Ready?" she asked.

Ada could feel Pan's warm breath on her face and taste its coffee scent in her open mouth. She made two small sounds in affirmation and Pan counted one, two, and on three, pushed the sharp steel down through her skin and out through her now angry lip. As the needle slid through, Ada could feel a whimper rising in her throat but it caught and she made no sound. She breathed out hard as Pan took her hands away to pick up the jewellery from the tray, leaving the curved needle in. Pan told her in a soft and sure voice that the worst was over. She just had to slip the jewellery in and then Ada would be done. Ada lifted the tip of her tongue to touch her swollen lip and tasted blood, sweet and metallic. She knew that she wouldn't be done with this for a long time.

Pan fitted the bar into the hollow of the needle and fed it through the tender path, then twisted a silver bead on the end. Her fingers played on Ada's mouth, warm and smelling like a dentist's. Ada wanted to bite them, tongue them gently. Suck them. Pan dabbed around the holes with a cotton swab, looking intently at her work as Ada focused her gaze on Pan's eyes, not a foot from her own.

Behind Pan's head, Ada noticed a beautiful print hanging on the wall.

"Oh my god," she said thickly. "I just fell in love with your print."

Ada wandered back to her mother and grandmother at the old house, lightheaded with adrenaline. The wooden shakes her grandfather had shingled the outside walls with so many years ago, coated in lifting chips of light blue paint, were falling off in places.

Ada's journalist mother, practical and wound tight, has black hair cropped bluntly just below her ears and a mouth red with dye and fish scales. That's what Ada heard lipstick is made from, anyway. Joan, whose only form of adornment aside from lipstick is the string of small shells that hangs from the arms of her glasses, was unimpressed with her daughter's skewered lip. But she only got out an "Oh Jesus Christ" and a "Why would you do that to your pretty face?" before she gave up. The dull pain and warm metal resting against Ada's skin were preoccupying her thoughts, tangible reminders of Pan's touch. Joan could tell that her admonishing couldn't compete with whatever was filling her daughter's head and making her hum.

Mattie told Ada that she looked like a trout and asked who had caught her. She was sitting at the kitchen table, wearing her flannel robe and eating yogurt with a spoon, which was impressive considering her arthritis. This was when she was just beginning to get sick—misplacing her hairbrush often, forgetting Joan's birthday. It was also just before Mattie started seeing Edith.

The way Ada first came to know of Edith was this:

At around four one morning, Ada was sitting awake in her bed, supposed to be sleeping but not. "Supposed to" according to normal hours of sleeping and waking as dictated by daylight. Because humans are not naturally nocturnal. But she didn't have any good reason to be sleeping at 4 A.M. She had no classes to attend the next morning, having finished high school, and had recently quit her job.

The grocery store Ada had been working at had a no-visible-modifications policy, which she was well aware of. The seventeen-year-old redhead who worked the till next to her had recently had the hideously rendered kanji for what she said was *luck* scratched into her wrist and was consequently fired. Her name was Erin and her parents were from Ireland. The sloppy, probably backward or completely made-up symbol was surrounded by a bright green shamrock.

But the warning of Erin's lucky Japanese clover was nowhere to be found in Ada's undependable brain when Pan's latexed hands were hovering by her mouth with a needle in their grip, and so she quit before she could be fired, not willing to sacrifice the silver kiss to Super Grocery.

So, free at that point to sleep or not sleep at 4 A.M., Ada had chosen to not sleep and instead to listen very quietly to Icelandic art rock while contemplating how to ask Pan out for coffee. Mattie's room was beside hers in the old house and their beds were pushed up against either side of the same wall. If the house were like a dollhouse with a removable roof, you could see that they really only slept a foot apart from one another.

A soft thump against the wall Ada was leaning on reverberated in her chest and the scene floating above her head of she and Pan swimming naked inside a coffee pot broke apart and settled on the sheets of her bed.

With her newfound alertness, Ada heard a moan coming from the other side of the wall, and wondered whether her grandmother was having a bad dream. She decided to wait for another moan before going in to wake her. She wasn't so sure the first was a moan of discontent. Ada turned her music down, and then off, and still heard nothing.

And then, when her mind was starting to conjure the coffee pot back up from the sheets and reassemble it mid-air, another moan made its way through the plaster, this one higher and shorter. And then another, a second after. Another. And then a loud, open-mouthed, body-heaving moan, and finally a series of closed-mouth mm mm mm mm mms and a breathy sigh.

Ada sat still in the silence, leaning against the wall with knitted brows.

Then Mattie began to giggle. She went on for a while until she laughed herself to sleep. And on her side of the wall, Ada smiled with the thought that at seventy-four, her grandmother was still getting her rocks off.

6

November 6, 2007

The family that moved in next door over a month ago still hasn't come over to introduce themselves. It's rude, Ken thinks. His mother agrees.

"Probably afraid of us," she says.

"Bunch of racists," Shawn says as he picks at the fish cake on his plate.

Betty sits up straighter.

"Might be. Eat that fish cake. It's not every day I make them and you'd better enjoy them."

"Or at least pretend you do," Ken says, nudging his son.

Kiah glances up from her textbook to look at her skinny brother, pushing a perfectly fried fish cake around an untouched serving of salad.

"Y'know, if you don't want to be a beanpole forever you should eat that."

Shawn sits back and glares at his sister.

"Yeah, and if you ever want a boyfriend you should lay off the second helpings."

Kiah's face burns.

"Okay, enough of that," Ken says, exasperated. "Thanks for another nice family dinner, guys. You're both excused."

"Thanks for the fish cakes, Grandma," Kiah says, closing her book. "I'll be upstairs."

"Have a good night studying alone in your bedroom, Kiah," Shawn says with a sarcastic smile.

"At least I'm not playing video games alone in the basement," she says, trying to channel the heat from her cheeks out through her eyes, hoping her brother will burst into flames.

He scoffs through pursed lips.

"You're both excused," Ken repeats. "Put your dishes in the dishwasher."

He closes his eyes and reaches his arms up and back, stretching the muscles in his aching shoulders. He may not be on the ground, picking up broken boards and shovelling chunks of concrete like some of the guys on the crew, but sitting in the cab and pulling those levers is straining. He and Leona used to trade massages at the end of their work days—a back rub for him and a foot rub for Leona, who was on her feet for twelve hours in a row. He misses her hands.

"I'm going to go lie down," he says. "You all right, Mom?"

"'Course I am," she says. "Going to watch my shows."

"Sounds good. Shawn, make your Grandma some tea, okay?"

"Sure," Shawn says, mashing his fish cake with his fork.

But when the kettle starts whistling on the stove, he's already left the house to meet up with his friends. Ken gets up so his mother won't have to and takes the kettle off the element. He fills the brown teapot with boiling water and two bags of orange pekoe. The tea steeps while he loads the dishwasher and scrubs the stuck-on bits of fish and potatoes from the frying pan in the sink. The TV glows in the living room and the tense, crime-thriller soundtrack creeps into the kitchen.

"These shows are crazy," he says as he brings a cup of tea to his mother. "So violent."

"I like them," Betty says, taking the tea and balancing it on her knee. "Thanks son."

He sits beside her on the couch and stares for a while at the screen. Same music, same detectives, same dead girl as always.

"You think the neighbours are actually afraid of us?" he asks her.

"Oh, I don't know," she says, after a long pause. The TV is loud and flashes blue on her soft face. "Maybe just not very neighbourly. It's three women I think. A girl Kiah's age and her mom and grandma, looks like. I've seen them coming and going."

Ken hasn't seen them. He leaves too early and comes home so tired that all he can see is the front door and all he can think of is dinner.

"I do miss the Carters," he says, thinking of their neighbours who had to move out. Their landlord decided it was a good time to sell, and the family had to pack their home into a U-Haul and move farther north. It's an unstoppable thing, Ken thinks. The condos will keep going up, and the boutiques, and the rent. How long will we be able to hold onto this house?

He brings a mug of tea upstairs to his daughter. She'll be studying late into the night by the light of her desk lamp, highlighter in hand, dry eyes scanning her textbook.

IN KIAH'S FIRST YEAR OF university she almost dropped out. On the first day of school, she and two friends had walked into their history class a few minutes late.

"Excuse me, ladies, are you in this class?" the white prof stopped lecturing and directed the attention of the auditorium full of mostly white students to the three girls.

They nodded and sat down.

"You're enrolled here?" he persisted.

"Yeah, we are," her friend Carla retorted.

"Okay, okay," the professor said, raising his eyebrows and putting his hands up, mocking her in the offence she took to the question. Some of the other students giggled.

Kiah sat through the class between Carla and Denise, her friends a bulwark against the sea of unfamiliar faces. But she could barely listen. Fuck you, she kept saying to the professor, over and over in her head. Fuck you, you racist fuck. Why should she listen to this guy teach

Canadian history? She hadn't seen her family or their stories on the sylla-bus. She could tell his class was going to read like those commercials—a part of our heritage. Our proud Canadian heritage, where settlers had friendly conversations with Indigenous people in their villages. Where enslaved people escaped America through the Underground Railroad to an unprejudiced public. Where white and Black folks sang hymns together in the mines. Where we were peacekeepers and champions of free health care. All those shameful parts of our heritage left out.

When she went home that afternoon to her sick mom, lying in bed, she told her sullenly that she wasn't going back.

"Yeah girl, you are," Leona said. "Don't give him the satisfaction. Don't you think I got that too, twenty years ago?"

Kiah held her mother's hand and nodded.

"And I felt the same as you do now. It's bullshit, and you'll deal with it your whole life. But you can use it to make you stronger."

She smoothed the baby hairs framing her daughter's face.

"Anyway, you better stay in school, 'cause I'm staying alive just to go to your damn graduation."

Kiah laughed as tears filled her eyes. They both knew Leona wouldn't live that long.

KIAH BLOWS RIPPLES ACROSS the surface of her steaming drink, still too hot to sip.

"Thanks, Dad, good night," she says over her shoulder as Ken closes her bedroom door.

Her eyes itch from staring at the glossy pages of her textbook. She knows it's time to quit when she looks back across the page to see she's highlighted every other word. But she needs to finish this chapter before tomorrow. She arches slowly over the low back of her chair until she feels the satisfying crack of her spine, then grabs the rungs to twist herself around and feels all her vertebrae pop into place. She presses the pads of her fingers against her closed eyes until she sees stars, takes a sip of too-hot tea, and picks up her highlighter again.

This is not the kind of history that thrills her, and it's easy for her mind to drift. She maps out a timeline of her future:

Finish school. Apply to U of T for a Master's in sociology. Or maybe do a law degree at Dal. Or take a year off. Take a year off and get a job, make some money. Have some spare time to read the history books I want. Time to read some fiction even. Move out of this house and away from my loser brother. Maybe get a boyfriend. Be nice to have time for that. Maybe I'd meet him in my Master's class. We could edit each other's theses. Jesus. I mean we could make love. We could fuck, for fuck's sake. Then do our Ph.D.s, both get hired to teach at Dal...cause Dal just loves to hire Black professors. We could co-write a book. And we'd get married and have this beautiful kid. Grandma could watch her while we went to teach. We'd have family dinners at our big old house that we'd buy up on the hill by Fort Needham. I'd push my baby girl so high on the swings that she could see the ocean.

Kiah sees herself pushing her daughter on those swings, her tiny sneakers kicking the sky, her hair in twists like Leona did for Kiah when she was a child.

"Okay, Kiah, you want that?" she says groggily, tucking her plans away in a secret drawer in her brain. "Then finish this fucking chapter."

IN THE LIVING ROOM, BETTY is almost dozing off in front of the TV. Truth be told, these shows can barely hold her interest anymore. She's pretty much seen them all. She finds the remote, wedged between the cushions, clicks the television off, and heaves herself up from the couch.

She likes this part of the evening, when the house is quiet and the street lamps project squares of light onto the floor through the windows. When the cat comes down from his windowsill perch, which Betty fixed up for him with a square of fleece so he wouldn't get cold from the draft, and winds himself sultrily around her ankles. He nudges her with his cheeks.

"That's right, Norman," she says. "Bedtime."

She pads in her slippers across the kitchen floor to the sink to fill her water glass. The room is dim and she can see the glow coming from the kitchen window of the house next door. An old woman stands at the sink, pouring herself a glass of liquor from a tall green bottle. When the woman looks up and catches her staring, Betty feels embarrassed. She's not a nosy person. But the small, white-haired woman lifts her glass in cheers, and Betty raises her glass of water and smiles back. Maybe tomorrow she'll go introduce herself.

7

❧

January 11, 2007

When Ada was ten she used to light matches and let them extinguish in her mouth so she could blow out the smoke, feeling so cool. But in high school she had a math teacher who spent every lesson drinking coffee and eating rice cakes, and smoked on breaks. When she would bend her head down to inspect Ada's faulty numerical manipulations, Ada shrivelled from the smell.

So it's strange, remembering the disgust she felt when her teacher blew her coffee and nicotine breath in her face, when all her body wants to live on is the air Pan pushes out through her mouth, infused with the same substances.

She makes Ada high.

Ada feels Pan in her head—a cloudiness—in the middle of her chest—a tightness—and in her stomach—more than butterflies. Bees. So she decided she would have Pan pierce her there, in the centre of her body. A four-needled compass pointing north, south, east, and west. Her mother had been talking in directions—leaving the south end, moving north. It had been only two months since Pan had hooked her through the lip like a most willing trout, and Ada wanted more.

Ada wasn't sure if Pan would pierce her in four places at once, but she put her soft brown book in her soft brown bag along with her wallet and pen, and left the house. Walking down to the studio, she could smell rich coffee and bitter cigarettes mixed with the salt of the harbour, confirming that Pan was working that day. Ada's obsession created a magic that was rarely wrong, so she was surprised when she pushed through the door to see not Pan, but a long-haired, bespectacled man at the counter with nostrils stretched large. Ada didn't want to let on that she knew Pan's name, so she asked, "Is your piercer in?"

"She's just finishing up," he replied, flipping his hair in the direction of Pan's room, the door of which was shut. Ada could hear the muffled waves of Pan's voice vibrating through the wood.

The door swung inward with a jerk and Pan stepped out, rubbing her hands together to dust off the powder from the inside of her gloves. She was listing off tips for piercing care, something about sea salt soaks, and the pale punk kid slouching out of the room after her nodded his head. He shuffled past Ada, scuffing his Chucks on the hardwood floor with every step, his nostril glowing red around a thick ring.

Pan moved behind the desk and leaned over the shoulder of the man with the long hair. She thumbed through an appointment book and glanced up at Ada. The man said softly that he thought "this girl was looking to talk to you" and Ada smiled, trying to look cute.

Pan pressed her lips together, courteous and businesslike. The smile brought out her dimples, strong lines that rest deep in the centres of her cheeks. Ada began by saying that she'd been in a couple months before, and pointed to her lip.

"Oh, yeah!" Pan said, throwing her head back at remembering, this time with a real grin. "How's it doing?"

"Really good," Ada replied. "Do you have time to do something now?"

"Yep. Free till three."

Pan said she would pierce all four at once, if Ada thought she could handle it. It would be a lot for her body to heal, she said, but it could work.

"Have you had anything to eat today?" Pan asked.

She had. It was several hours earlier and had been only a banana and a mug of tea, but Ada nodded.

"Okay," Pan said.

Ada hopped up onto the loud paper again and Pan stretched another pair of gloves over her brown hands with their dark, calloused knuckles. After the first time she saw her, Ada wondered what kind of brown Pan was. She knew it wasn't really right to ask that, and possibly not right to even think it. She was pretty sure the proper thing was to pretend she had never noticed Pan was brown at all. She tried a few lines out loud to herself to see how they sounded: "Where are you from, originally?" "What are you? Like, what's your background?" "What's your background? I mean, your *ethnic* background?" She was pretty sure that "ethnic" was the appropriate word. Or was it? Wasn't it like the PC term for "not white"? Ada thought maybe she should just make an educated guess and do some strategic cultural name-dropping to let Pan know she was down with her ethnicity. She had Googled "Pan name origin" for a hint as to Pan's ancestral geography, but all she came up with was *Greek, a faun, a shepherd, (Peter) Pan, mischievous, ageless.*

But Pan didn't look Greek to Ada. Like, okay, she thought, brown skin, black hair, full lips, big eyes…Indian? Ada didn't wonder much further than that. She had read half of the Bhagavad Gita and had once taken a free belly dance class. She knew the Hindi words for potato, cauliflower, cheese, spinach, and chickpeas. She considered floating one of these facts to Pan and seeing how it landed. But as she sat on the crinkling paper trying not to fidget, glancing at Pan's focused face as she searched through small plastic drawers for the proper tools and jewels, she decided against it. For a split second, Ada envisioned what kind of look a line like that might garner.

Pan dropped the jewellery onto a steel tray and the pieces fell with clicks and rolled around like tiny marbles. She selected paper packets containing needles, cotton balls, and swabs, and asked Ada to stand back up.

The paper rustled as Ada slid off the table. This least sensual sound is now her quickest trigger. Christmas was a bit uncomfortable, as she ripped and crinkled tissue paper and giftwrap, opening presents from her mother and grandmother, swollen with heat.

Pan told her she needed to mark where the piercings would be, and instead of asking Ada to lift her shirt she knelt down in front of her and began to roll the fabric up with quick fingers that grazed Ada's belly. Pan dipped the tip of a wooden toothpick in a drop of ink. The ink had sat as a tiny dome on the tray and when she penetrated its liquid skin with the stick of wood, it released its hold on itself and spread.

Pan told her to relax, her voice steady and low, eyes level with Ada's stomach and looking up.

"Don't contract your abs," she said, "or the jewellery won't sit right."

Ada exhaled shakily and let her muscles unclench. Pan surveyed the terrain and marked south first then north, east, and then west.

"Check it out," she said, and took hold of Ada's hips, rotating her toward the mirror.

The first needle felt good—sharp, hot pain punching through the northern mark. Three drops of blood on the tissue Pan used to dab it. Like in the fairy tale with the talking horse, where the mother cut the tips of her fingers, let the blood fall on cloth, and gave it to her daughter to carry as a charm. Could Ada take the tissue with her? She thought she probably shouldn't ask.

The second, south, did not feel so wonderful. The skin of the north is thinner and made for piercing, but south is fleshier and the passage of the needle through it made Ada's whole body tense. She could feel cold sweat spreading up from her stomach and across her face. The ceiling tiles were obscured by grey islands that collided and filled her vision.

Ada could feel Pan touching her hand, and then her clammy forehead. Pan's fingertips on her cheeks, Pan's voice asking if she was okay. Ada heard her move across the room and unscrew the cap from a bottle of something, which turned out to be pomegranate juice when it hit her lips. It was tart and tingled in her cheeks.

The room and Pan's face reformed themselves. Pan asked if that had ever happened to her before. She asked what Ada had had to eat that day.

"A banana," Ada said, and Pan clicked her tongue and shook her head.

"Girl, not enough!" she said, as Ada sat up slowly, "I'm about to take a break before my next appointment. Come get something to eat. I want to keep an eye on you."

Ada swooned.

"You're not going to pierce the other two?" she asked, still dazed and feeling disappointed with herself.

"Yeah right," Pan laughed. "We'll make another date to finish it. Sound okay?"

It certainly did.

Ada bought Pan a coffee to pay her back for the pomegranate juice and her concern, and because really, she would have bought her anything then, and kept offering—date square? cookie? oatcake?—she was so overwhelmed by the fantastic reality of being with her.

Pan asked where she lived, and Ada said in a blue house in the south end with her mother and grandmother and her grandmother's ghost lover.

A few days before, Ada had been in her room after dinner, sketching Pan's face from memory. In the version of the story she told Pan, though, she was reading. She was leaning up against the wall, reading, and felt a thump that echoed in her chest. She waited to see if she would hear a moan.

The moan came a few seconds later, followed by, "Oh, Edith…" and Ada thought, Who?

The next fifteen minutes were marked by more low moans and more *Edith*s. Ada wondered if her mother could hear, but she was running water for dishes and listening to talk radio.

"I realized then," Ada told Pan, "that my Nan couldn't have been masturbating. She's arthritic. Painfully so. She can barely feed herself. So Edith must be real."

She told Pan the story partly because she thought it was an interesting way to break the ice and partly because she needed to say it out loud to someone in order to believe it herself. Ada wanted to believe her grandmother, and it honestly did seem more likely to her that Mattie was making love to a ghost than managing to move her fingers nimbly enough, for many minutes, several times a day, to get herself off.

Joan does not find this explanation likely. She thinks Mattie has a vibrator stashed in her room and does quick searches for it when Mattie gets up to go to the bathroom. Joan thinks that if she can confiscate this vibrator, her mother will stop having so many orgasms. They are a danger to her weak heart, her doctor says.

Mattie assured Ada one day, with a gentle pat on the hand, that she did not have a vibrator.

"Why would I need one?" she said coyly. "Edith is plenty."

8

September 1, 1948

The welts remained as ridged scars, a furrowed field across the skin of her backside. Almost a year later, Edith could still feel the thick tissue under her fingertips. She knew the nuns could make her disappear into the infirmary, never to be seen alive again, for the slightest misstep. So she swallowed her resistance. Kept it suspended halfway down her throat. Sometimes she hid it underneath her tongue, speaking Mi'kmaw in her head, careful not to let it escape past her lips. Silently insulting the nuns in the language they so hated and feared. They knew its power.

But the power of Edith's language was slipping away from her. Years of watching her friends' faces punched and slapped until they were bruised and swollen and bleeding, their bodies shaken and thrown across the room by furious nuns just for speaking their mother tongue, had beaten most words out of her. Too scared to speak her language out loud at school and barely able to recall the words she used to talk with her parents when she saw them in the summers, Edith still remembered enough Mi'kmaw to brand the nuns with names that reflected their cruelty.

But because the nuns could not detect her quiet rebellion, they thought her a changed girl. They believed they had convinced her with fists and straps that she should be grateful. And she did appear so, smiling demurely as she silently charged them for their crimes. So it was decided that Edith should go to public school in Shubie village. A fine representative of the nuns' diligent, civilizing work.

With her books under her arm, Edith walked along the road to the school. She was not to go into any of the stores in town, and especially not to buy a treat with the pennies Susan and Dorothy and her cousin Maureen had secretly saved and pooled together, hoping she would return one day with something so sweet it would make them forget, for a moment, where they were.

In class, Edith was snickered and stared at by the students and embarrassed by the teacher, who liked to make a public point of how little she knew. She was one of the brightest in her classes at the Resi, but years spent labouring in the laundry and kitchen when she should have been learning left her lagging behind the public school students. The nuns had prepared her well for the cutting words and mocking glances of the students and teacher, though, and she knew how to shut them out. She had become so accustomed to white stares that she didn't notice the focused eyes of a girl, two desks behind her, until the teacher's ruler came cracking down on the girl's knuckles.

Everyone turned to look at the girl, now clasping her red knuckles in her other hand, her face crunched up in pain, holding back tears. She opened her eyes long enough to catch Edith's before the teacher barked at everyone to face forward and keep their eyes on their own work.

"Why would you try to copy answers from an Indian, Martha?" the teacher asked the girl. "She can barely speak English."

She walked briskly back to her desk, smacking Edith in the back of the head with her firm open palm as she passed. Edith's face burned, but she swallowed the heat down. She was used to this.

Mntu'-maqe'k, she said in her head, naming the teacher's cruel arrogance.

She could feel the eyes of the girl, still glancing at the back of her head as the teacher read at her desk. When she'd caught a glimpse of them right after the ruler came down, she saw they weren't the eyes of most public school kids', staring at her like she was a dumb animal. The girl had looked at her as if to say, "Remember me?"

At the end of the school day, Edith worried the girl would try to talk to her.

Don't follow me, Sparrow, she thought.

She stacked her books and began to walk along the road uphill to the Resi, not daring to look back to see if the girl was behind her. She couldn't hear any footsteps. Edith missed going to school with her friends. There she was still shamed by nuns and hit for wrong answers or for no reason at all, but at least they were in it together. And it was almost over, only one more year. At the public school she was a spectacle. The other kids were waiting for her to say something foolish, she could feel it. Everyone seemed so sure she was stupid. Or almost everyone, anyway. Were they right? The sisters certainly thought so. They hadn't sent her to the public school because she was smart. Only obedient. Wasn't that true?

"*Pssst!*"

Edith turned to look before she could catch herself, but saw nothing. The school was up ahead and any of the windows could contain a watching nun. She kept walking.

"*Pssssst!*" it came again, from the shrubs along the road.

"Who's there?" Edith said without turning her head, still taking small, slow steps forward.

"Sparrow!" answered the voice.

Edith crouched down, slowly unlacing and lacing her shoe.

"You can't talk to me," she whispered hoarsely. "Go home!"

"But I have something for you."

Edith paused and weighed the consequences, and then, with a quick hand, knocked over her books, letting her pencil roll away. She followed it to the bushes and came face to face with Mattie, crouching behind sparse leaves.

"Hi." Mattie smiled.

"What is it?" Edith demanded, but couldn't help smiling back at her boldness. The girl held a Peppermint Pattie in her outstretched palm.

"Here," she said.

Edith reached for the candy and Mattie placed her other hand overtop of Edith's. The soft warmth shocked her and she snatched her hand back as if she'd singed it on a stove.

"Sorry," Mattie said, looking embarrassed. "I don't know why I did that."

"It's okay," Edith said, her touched hand still clenched in a fist against her chest. At the Resi, she couldn't hug her friends or even her own brothers without getting strapped or made to stand in a corner for hours. She uncurled her fingers and tentatively reached back out. Mattie placed the chocolate coin in its silver wrapper carefully into her palm.

"I've got to go," Edith whispered.

Mattie looked at Edith as if she were trying to tell her some secret in a silent language. "See you tomorrow!" she said then, and crawled away, crackling through the twigs.

Still facing away from the school, pretending to look for her pencil, Edith quickly opened the wrapper and popped the chocolate into her mouth. The foil fit neatly between the pages of one of her books and she stacked them back up. She held the cool mint and bittersweet chocolate puck on her tongue, letting it melt from the heat, not wanting to chew so it would last longer, and also so the nuns and their student spies wouldn't see her eating. She walked briskly up the road.

Her tongue darted around her mouth, cleaning the remnants of chocolate from between her teeth as she approached the school. What if the nuns could smell peppermint on her breath?

Edith stepped quietly through the school doors and darted into the closest washroom. She filled her cupped hand from the tap and drank, swishing and swallowing the cool sweetness down until all she could taste was musty, metallic water.

"Edith!" a nun barked as she left the washroom. "What were you doing out on the road?"

Her black-cloaked form stood menacingly large in front of the wiry sixteen-year-old, and her small blue eyes stared coldly, trying to detect any thread of a lie.

"My shoelace came undone, Sister," Edith replied, keeping her voice steady. "And while I was tying it, well, I was so clumsy that I knocked my books over and lost my pencil in the bushes. I was trying to find it. I'm sorry."

The nun stared down her nose at the girl.

"And did you find it?"

"Yes, Sister."

Edith kept her face clear and her breathing slow. She had become quite good at this, deceiving the sisters. It was almost like a game.

"Very well," the nun replied. "Go clean yourself up for supper."

And away she clicked down the hallway, rosary beads rattling in her pocket.

9

⚘

November 6, 2007

After *Ada quit her job as a grocery clerk she became a server at a Thai* restaurant, or Thigh restaurant, as the middle-aged American couple called it last night. They were her last table of the evening. They didn't stay long and got all of their leftovers wrapped up to go, including the puffed shrimp crackers that come free at the beginning of the meal.

On the cover of the menu below the name of the restaurant, stylized mock-Asian letters proclaim the authenticity of the place. The owners assume their customers won't notice the Japanese characters on the chopsticks, the Nepalese cook, or the Mandarin pop playing over the stereo system. Only a few people have remarked about this interesting combination, but Ada likes to point it out to customers, especially those who exclaim, "Well, I have never been to a *real* Thigh restaurant before!"

Ada began this job a few weeks after her first encounter with Edith, and before she had come up with a way to ask Pan out for coffee. She spent her first shift filling up water glasses, dropping baskets of fishy puffs onto tables, rolling fork and knife sets into cloth napkins, and tonguing her piercing.

The owners of this place desire hip customers and so seek out alternative-looking employees. Ada's favourite person to work the dinner shift with, James, has maps tattooed on his forearms and wears kids' plastic dollar-store sunglasses on his head. He has a Master's in sociology and likes to observe the customers. He feels like he's not wasting his degree if he can treat serving like fieldwork, but Ada can watch people fine with a high school diploma.

Nearly a year later, after several coffee dates and twice as many piercings, Ada's routine is much the same. Tonight, without fail, she is thinking of Pan. It's a combination of what she will get pierced next, how she will ask Pan out for coffee again, and what it would feel like to finally, actually, kiss her. As she travels between tables, to the kitchen, to the till, and sometimes downstairs for bottles of wine, her mind wanders through memories, picking up moments, lifting touches, borrowing words to form new scenes.

Pan is such a star of her imagination that sometimes it's a shock for Ada to be reminded that she's real. Like now, when Pan's ex-lover has just strolled through the door with their friend.

Elin is a fox. Ada knows Elin and Pan were lovers because she was told so by James. He had his tattoos done at the place where Pan works and knows the mildest version of Ada's infatuation.

With their friend in tow, Elin sidesteps around tables until they arrive in Ada's section.

A tendency Ada has, with the ex-lovers of her lovers and desperate crushes, is not to be jealous, but rather to fall for them too. It's like a crush. She idolizes them. Nothing they can say or do is ever awkward or wrong and in comparison, she is clumsy, with stuttering tongue and ill-timed smiles.

They set the dress code. If Ada passes them in the street, they in jeans and a hoodie, she in a dress (this is rare), they are casual and cool and she is frivolous and overdressed, prim and embarrassed. If they are in a dress and she is in jeans and a hoodie, they are carefree and beautiful, fabric loose around their perfect bodies, grazing them lightly and moving with the wind, and she is slouching and self-conscious, encased in heavy cotton. With makeup they are stylish but she is self-involved; without, they are confident and natural but she is homely. In silence they are dignified and mysterious while she is insecure and young. In talking they are vibrant and witty, but Ada is always saying too much, too loud.

Elin has a lean like Pan's and short hair like hers too. Their eyebrows are thick and black and make their shining teeth look so white. As Ada approaches the table, basket of shrimp crackers in hand, she is so conscious of her movements, trying hard to replicate the casualness that Pan and Elin both understand. But her concentration causes her body to respond with poorly oiled steps that escape out from under her centre of balance.

Ada doesn't fall and the puffs make it to the table, but now that she's standing between Elin and their friend, she is feeling, as always, deficient. Now up close and standing over them, looking down at their smooth face and red mouth, Ada sees that the one other lip Pan pierced like her own was Elin's.

Ada deposits the shrimp chips on the table and the friend announces that she and Elin are vegetarian and don't eat seafood.

"Actually we already know what we want," Elin says. They look at Ada's mouth. "Hey," they say with a smile, "I like your piercing."

Ada returns the smile, too big.

Elin's order is perfect. Of course the fresh spring rolls. And of course the green tofu curry. Ada has always had a sort of reverence for people who eat spicy food, the same way she admires people who love olives. As a result of this she will order the green tofu curry at the end of her shift and eat it like a martyr. Her lips will sting and swell. Her eyelids will sweat in the creases. Her cheeks will flush. Spicy food, like sex. Mattie can always tell when Ada's been at it because her cheeks bloom a deep red and don't cool for hours.

When Ada brings the food out, she tries so hard to be normal. Don't smile too much, she tells herself, and though it goes against her most primary instinct, try not to make eye contact.

During the day, Ada can't not think of Pan for more than four seconds, or for however long she keeps her eyes open between blinks.

She sees her every time she closes them. Like those abstracted images in black and white—you stare at them for as long as you can and then close your eyes, and they've impressed themselves into the light-sensing rods on the curved back walls of your retinas. The image is reversed and no longer abstracted. Imprinted inside your head. But it fades after a while.

Pan doesn't fade. It's the image of her, frozen in time, when she paused for a second, inches from Ada's face, with lips parted and needle in hand. Captured in the memories of tiny rods and cones. Since Pan was the right shades and shadows to begin with, it's the reverse Ada sees when she closes her eyes. Like a negative photograph. Pan's hair is light blue and her skin dark green. The edges of her teeth that show through her parted lips are indigo. The image has been there for a year and Ada is starting to feel like it won't ever leave.

When Elin and their friend finish their meal, Ada brings them the bill with warm glances and as reasonably sized and genuine a smile as her nervousness will allow. Together they leave her five dollars and Elin has scraped the grains of sticky rice they spilled on the table into a neat pile.

Her final customers of the night, two boys with matching haircuts, keep Ada an hour late, slowly draining their last bitter sips of red wine. When they finally finish, Ada clears their table, cashes out, and goes to change in the small bathroom. In the mirror, she finds that her lips have swollen from the green curry. They are fat and pink and covered with nearly invisible tiny bumps, which feel so interesting when she licks them and rubs them together. She seems to be allergic. The silver kiss skewering her top lip is not impressed.

When she gets home, she pours a glass of cold water from the jug in the fridge and drinks it down fast. Joan should be asleep, she thinks, and when she saunters down the hall, the dark space beneath her mother's ill-fitting door tells Ada that she probably is. Ada wedges her own warped, thick wooden door into its frame behind her, walks across her mattress on the floor to where the pillows are piled in the corner, and lies back.

She closes her eyes and licks her lips. Slides them over each other like fine grain, wet sandpaper, and sees Pan's face, a negative imprinted inside her eyelids. She wants to get up and have a shower, heating and releasing her muscles in a hot stream of water. Washing away food smells, the grease shining on her skin, the tiredness in her feet. But the abstract shapes of Pan's backward face are hypnotizing her to sleep.

Ada floats a little above her bed and Pan floats above her in turn, facing her and fitting the shape of her body perfectly, curving where she swells and swelling where she curves. There's an inch between them at all points and they don't touch. Ada feels heavy sleep settle over her as Pan descends the offending inch and together they sink into the mattress, now touching completely, filling each other's spaces.

A small knock from the other side of the wall lifts Ada's eyelids, and she lies still until it comes again quietly, *knock knock knock*, through layers of paint and plaster. Ada and Mattie share a wall in the new house too, and can tap codes through it like kids staying up past their bedtime. Ada knocks back softly—*knock knock knock*—and the small knock grows, replying, KNOCK KNOCK KNOCK. She lumbers on hands and knees across the sinking mattress, unwedges her door, and turns the handle of the door to her grandmother's room.

Mattie's little box of living space, identical to Ada's, is dim, lit by a small bulb plugged into a low outlet. The bulb is covered by a tiny green lampshade with glass beads dangling from its bottom edge. Joan bought it and Mattie finds it ridiculous, but not so ridiculous as to override her need for it in the presence of a lifelong fear of the dark. She lies flat in her bed, watching her granddaughter in the doorway with eyes wide open, not a bit sleepy. Ada walks over and sits down beside her, reaching for her hand.

"What's up?" Ada asks.

"What's up," Mattie replies. She doesn't like the kind of questions people ask that mean nothing at all. That they ask expecting a canned answer: not much. So she always responds by asking their question back to them.

Ada rephrases her question.

"How come you're still awake?"

Mattie smiles in thanks and says she missed Ada today, that Edith is out visiting an old friend and she was lonely. Joan worked all night on some story that Mattie doesn't give two hoots about and no one was here to talk to. Though she did wave through the kitchen window at the woman who lives in the house next door and who seems very nice.

"That is nice, Nan. Maybe you can be friends," Ada says as she crawls into bed with her grandmother and reaches up to rest her hand on the soft skin of her neck, like she did as a child. When Ada was little,

Mattie would come and crawl into bed with her after Ian had fallen asleep, and Ada would curl into her grandmother, her tiny fingers resting on Mattie's wrinkled neck all night.

"Can I tell you about someone I saw today?" Ada asks.

Her grandmother nods and squeezes her hand. Ada begins to tell her about Elin. Mattie already knows all about Pan.

Since Mattie started seeing Edith—or, according to Joan, since she started showing signs of Alzheimer's—she has been rather open about her sexuality.

"I never knew it before," she told Ada one day.

She calls it the tide. Says it feels like the tide coming in, rushing over the rocks. Every time the tide passes over Mattie's head she thinks she's been drowned, because she can't move and just lies there, completely still with her mouth open. It recedes more slowly than it comes in, making her body feel like her body again.

Mattie didn't know the tide with Ian. She had found the way to the water once before, she told Ada, horseback riding when she was young. The muscled heaving of the animal beneath her, the hard, polished leather between her warm thighs, bare in the summertime beneath a blue dress. It never released the tide, but it felt good, she said. So good. It frightened her. But the night she woke to find a gentle ghost pushing her to feel that again, she wasn't afraid. The first time it happened, she told Ada, Edith woke her up very late, slipping beneath the covers while she slept.

"Please tell me you've felt it," she said to Ada hopefully, and Ada smiled and said yes, she had. Mattie was glad to hear it. Sorry that she'd gone so many years, all of her youth and marriage, without, and now her joints wouldn't oblige her.

"That's why Edith came to you," Ada said.

"It's more than that," Mattie said. "We're in love."

10

November 14, 2007

"**W**hy're you baking cookies, Grandma?" Shawn asks, reaching his finger into the bowl to scoop out some of the dough.

Betty swats his hand away.

"Get out of there!" she scolds. "Every time I make something sweet you're in there with your hands, getting germs all over everything. Don't you know any better?"

"Nope," Shawn replies, grinning big at her.

"Well somebody ought to teach you some manners. Go on. I'll tell you when they're ready and you can have one."

"Just one?"

"Just one," his grandma says. "If you helped me in the kitchen more, it might earn you two."

Shawn opens the fridge to see if anything's new.

"Who're they for?"

Betty mixes the dough with a wooden spoon, squishing the powdery balls of flour in with the eggs, adding vanilla and chocolate chips. "The neighbours."

"The Youssefs?" Shawn asks, opening a carton of orange juice and taking a swig.

"Put that in a glass!" Betty admonishes. "Were you raised in a barn? Good Lord." She passes him a glass from the cupboard. "No, I mean the new neighbours."

"Why would you make them cookies?" Shawn asks. "They never even came over to say hi."

"I don't know," Betty says as she mixes. "Maybe they've been busy, or maybe they didn't want to bother us. I'm just trying to be nice."

"Huh," Shawn says, putting his glass down on the counter.

"In the dishwasher, Shawn!" Betty calls after him as he leaves the room.

He shuffles back in and does as he was told.

The cookies will be done in twelve minutes, so Betty goes to change. She isn't sure if the mother or daughter are home—maybe at school or work. But she saw the old woman walking through the kitchen this morning and thought she would go over and have a chat.

The woman seemed older than Betty, but it was hard to tell from that far away. Maybe it was the way she moved. She looked frail. At sixty-three, Betty still looks young. It's being part of something bigger than just yourself that slows your aging, she thinks. A community. Betty was baptized in the Basin, taught in the school, married in the church. She watched as her house was bulldozed and made a new home for her family in the Square. Sang in the church choir, raised her kids, including her aimless youngest son, and thanked the Lord when Leona came along.

Leona had been like a daughter. When Ken's father died, Leona refused to allow Betty to live alone. Betty had no need for a retirement home, but it was so lonely in her house with her kids and husband gone. So Leona and Ken sold their house and rented a bigger place on the same street with enough room for all of them. Not many children look after their parents in their old age these days, so Betty was glad to see three generations move in next door. She likes to see families stick together.

Betty runs her fingers along the sleeve of a soft, periwinkle blue sweater set, and lifts it off its wooden hanger. Chooses beige pants and vibrant pink lipstick—the same shade she's worn since the eighties. She has clear eyes framed by eyelashes that curl on their own, soft cheeks, and crowded teeth. She appraises herself in the mirror and nods. Looking good.

The cookies cool while she scrubs the bowls out and wipes down the counter. Ken's at work and Kiah's at school. Shawn's in the basement, playing video games far more violent than Betty's crime shows. It seems the world today encourages boys to be useless, she thinks. When Ken was young he had to think up ways to waste his time, but Shawn just needs to choose from a wide selection of pointless, expensive activities.

The cookies are in a Tupperware and Betty's out the door, crossing the small patch of grass between their houses. She knocks and waits, knowing it can take some extra time to get to the door as you age.

"Hello?" Mattie says in a thick voice as she opens the door, looking sleepy.

"Hi there," Betty says, reaching out her hand. "I'm Betty from next door. Just came by to say hello. Did I wake you from a nap?"

"Not at all, not at all! I was just resting my eyes. I'm Mattie," she says, shaking Betty's hand. "Please, come in and I'll make us some tea."

Betty enters and takes off her shoes, following Mattie into the kitchen.

"I brought you some cookies as a bit of a late welcome to the neighbourhood."

Mattie looks back with a smile.

"Well that's lovely, thank you, Betty. Let me put those on a plate and you make yourself comfortable in the living room. Would you like tea? Coffee? Juice?"

"Tea, thank you."

Betty sits down on the velvety green couch and looks around at the house where she used to visit her old neighbours. She tries to remember the way they had the room set up—an armchair in that corner, the television there by the wall, a bureau covered in framed family photos. The faded wallpaper has been painted over in beiges and taupes, the carpet torn up and hardwood-looking laminate laid down. Betty misses the lilac print of the old walls and the iron burn in the carpet from the Carters' absent-minded daughter. These folks have no pictures of their family up, Betty notices. Strange. She's always wondered about people who don't have family photos around. But maybe they haven't fully unpacked.

From the kitchen, she hears a cup smash.

"Is everything okay?" she calls.

"Oh yes," Mattie says. "I forget how rickety I can be. I have a touch of arthritis."

"Can I help you?" Betty is careful not to sound patronizing.

"Yes, thank you," Mattie says as Betty enters and bends down to pick up a ceramic shard. "Oh, leave that. I'll sweep this up if you can reach us some cups and a plate."

The electric kettle clicks off and Betty pours the water into a teapot.

"So nice of you to come by," Mattie says as she nudges the broken pieces of ceramic into the dustpan with the broom. "I've been meaning to come and introduce myself to you and the other families on the street, but I seem to always end up falling asleep. You were right—I was napping when you came," she says, looking up with a quick wink.

"No shame in that," Betty says. "Now is it your daughter and granddaughter you live with?"

"Yes, my daughter, Joanie, and her daughter, Ada."

Betty arranges the cookies on a plate and puts the plate, cups, saucers, and teapot on a tray.

"No men in the house?" she asks, hoping Mattie won't be offended by the question.

"No, no men. My husband died five years back."

"Oh I'm sorry," Betty says. "I lost mine only a few years ago as well. The men always seem to go first, don't they?"

"They do."

"And your daughter's husband? My son lost his wife to cancer. It's heartbreaking when they pass so young."

"Such a sin. I'm so sorry to hear." Mattie dumps the shards into the garbage can. "Everyone's getting cancer these days." She shakes her head. "But as far as we know, the donor's still alive."

Betty nods. "Did he run out on her?"

"Oh, no," Mattie says as she leads the way to the living room. "He really was just a donor. I guess when Joanie got older and still hadn't met someone, she decided she would become a mother on her own. Well, with my help, of course."

"Truly, what would they do without us?" Betty says. She pours the tea and hands a cup to Mattie.

"She's married to her job anyway, at the newspaper."

"Well I respect that," Betty says. "Sounds like your daughter's a strong woman."

They sip their tea and talk. About their grandkids, about the neighbourhood. Betty's eyes wander beyond Mattie's sleepy face to the rest of the room. Is that a lilac branch she sees, the soft purple of the wallpaper seeping determinedly through the boring beige paint?

"I myself didn't move to the city until '49," Mattie says. "It was quite a shock, coming here from such a small place. Did you grow up in Halifax, Betty?"

Betty brings her attention back to her new neighbour.

"Sorry?" she asks, trying to recall what she just heard. "Oh, no," she says, resting her cup in its saucer. "I didn't grow up here. I moved to the city in '66, when they tore down Africville."

Mattie nods.

"Yes, I do remember reading about that in the paper. Joanie covered the reunion last year. Did you go?"

"No, we didn't go. You know, it was too sad without my daughter-in-law," Betty says and sips her tea. "How are the cookies?"

"Very good." Mattie smiles. "Thank you again, Betty."

"Glad to. You know, I should be getting back home," she says. "See what that grandson of mine is up to. But thank you for the tea, Mattie, and welcome to the neighbourhood."

THE NEXT MORNING, ADA BRINGS Mattie's breakfast to her early.

"Soft-boiled egg, Nan," she says, pushing the door open with her shoulder, her left hand balancing an egg precariously in an egg cup on a plate and her right curled around a mug of tea.

"Who?" Mattie asks sleepily, sitting up in bed. She is so soft and small in her flannel nightgown. The entire room smells like her—sweet and stale, polyester and Tums and old lipstick.

"Breakfast."

Ada puts it down on the dresser beside her grandmother's bed in the small room. She sits next to Mattie, leaning up against her sleep-warm body, and asks if she had any dreams worth telling, which she always does.

That night she had lain in a bathtub full of plump apricots while a woman with short silver hair and warm brown eyes played to her on the oboe and sang about water.

"How did she sing and play at the same time?" Ada asks.

Mattie mumbles that the woman had two mouths and begins to fall back asleep. Ada asks what the woman's name was and Mattie sighs.

"Wouldn't you like to know?"

ADA'S GRANDFATHER DIED in his sleep, beside Mattie in their bed. He had spent the five years before living in a dream. They started to notice it one evening, when Joan placed a knife and cutting board in front of him as he sat at the kitchen table and dropped a freshly washed carrot onto the warped wood.

Mattie was cutting potatoes into clean cubes across from him and Ada was slicing beets beside her. The beets had originally been given to Mattie, but it disturbs her the way the juice stains her fingers purple; Ada loves stains on most things—ink on hands, coffee on paper, bike grease on jeans—so they switched.

Ian, looking lost, peered across the table at their hands and knives and pared vegetables and, with a nod, began to chop the carrot with deliberation. They were like children doing crafts at a birthday party—given felt and glue and dull scissors and popsicle sticks and dizzy cartoon eyes, not sure of the purpose or end result but absorbed in the task.

Then, like now, Mattie's favourite thing was to have Ada tell her about the people she saw around the city. She liked to have them described like characters in a book. Sometimes Ada would sketch her favourites while she watched them at school and bring the drawings home to her grandmother.

Ada was telling Mattie about a girl in her class. Her name was Noël. Her mother had named all of her children with words containing umlauts, though at the time Ada would have said, "those two dots, you know?" Ada told Mattie how Noël bit her nails so short. How pretty Ada thought she was and how no one else seemed to notice. How her pants all ended above her ankles and her shirt sleeves all ended past her knuckles and how Ada always noticed her smiling to herself—not little smiles, but split grins flashing teeth, like she was telling herself hilarious jokes in her head.

Mattie was asking questions about Noël's voice and height and the way she walked, trying to picture her, when Ian finished chopping the thick carrot into chunks and started to sweep the pieces off of the cutting board and into his large, flat palm. He heaved himself slowly up with a swishing release of breath and stepped heavy and dreamlike over to the corner of the kitchen, where he stopped at the potted palm and bent at the waist, very sweetly placing the pieces of carrot around its trunk.

Joan, noticing this, asked, "What are you doing, Dad?"

Standing up, Ian replied that he was all finished.

"Doesn't that look nice?" he asked the room.

Mattie chuckled and said quietly that he was losing his marbles, but that she did think it looked nice.

Joan, however, marched over to the palm and began picking the carrots out of the soil.

"Oh, Dad," she said, sounding sad and disappointed.

Ian looked so sad himself that Ada asked her mother to please leave the carrots. She said she would cut another one up for the soup. Joan relented after some convincing and dropped them back into the potted plant, returning tensely to the stove with words about making a doctor's appointment. Behind her back, Ian shuffled over to the palm and nudged the carrots back into place.

"I WOULD LIKE TO KNOW what her name was, actually," Ada says to Mattie, trying to keep her awake. "But you're always so coy."

Ada doesn't have to go in to work today, so she decides she will take her grandmother for tea after she finishes her breakfast. Joan has already left the house and there is no note. This is fine, because she is so many places in one day, and Ada's not really very interested in whatever story she's covering anyway. It is likely either meaningless small-town fluff or depressingly cruel, big-city crime. Because Halifax is in-between sized, the news shifts back and forth from local fisher catches blue lobster to stabbing outside downtown club.

Mattie dresses in peach-coloured slacks, a white blouse, and a cream sweater. Ada helps her with the buttons and the long, long zipper that zips all the way up, three inches past her bellybutton. She floats a flat paddle brush through Mattie's thin, permed hair, lifting the curls into a silver halo around her skull.

Ada hasn't brushed her own hair since she was fourteen. Joan used to brush it for her every morning until Ada was nine, while she sat eating cereal at the kitchen table. Ada took over after that because Joan's brushing was vicious—raking her waist-length, wavy hair against the wooden back of the chair, tugging relentlessly at her scalp, making her head jerk back and forth so she felt like she was trying to eat breakfast on a mechanical bull.

Ada brushed it herself for five years until she felt that, at fourteen, Joan would no longer hold true to her promise that if Ada didn't brush her own hair, she would. It hangs tangled at all lengths now. Parts of it are long and parts of it are short and parts of it are shaved to her scalp. It would never be satisfied being one thing.

As Ada brushes Mattie's hair, Mattie pushes oily, coral pigment into the edges of her thinned lips. Ada has seen old pictures and Mattie used to have lips just like hers, full and soft with sharp peaks. She tells her grandmother to smile and wipes a smear from where Mattie overshot her top lip, and a coral smudge from her front tooth.

"Beautiful," Ada tells her.

She calls a cab to pick them up at the house. Her coffee shop is only about a twenty-minute walk away, but the dampness of the grey day has seeped through Mattie's windbreaker, through her slacks and sweater, and has settled in her bones. They rub up against each other like grumpy strangers on a crowded bus, even though they aren't strangers, having lived in her body together for so many years. Maybe they're just getting tired of each other. After that much time, relationships get strained. People start to rub each other the wrong way. And so her bones jostle and bump up against one another. She can't walk far.

The cab driver is friendly and old-fashioned. Seeing Mattie, he opens his door and gets out to help. But with Ada at her side, Mattie is quick and nimble. Ada has her door open before he makes it around the jutting front of the old car. She gives him a cordial tip of her invisible hat.

When they step inside the café, Mattie looks around at the colours on the walls and Ada looks around for Pan, but none of the chairs hold her grey-clothed form. That's fine, Ada says to herself, but continues to wonder what Pan's doing and where she is as she follows her shuffling grandmother over to the table in the corner—Mattie's choice, and it's the one Ada has sat in since she started coming here a few years ago.

"What can I bring you, Nan?" Ada asks, helping Mattie into her chair.

"Tea, of course," Mattie says.

Ada doesn't know why—she likes tea far better, the sweet, milky taste, the bergamot smell—but Pan is stuck in her head, sitting as a memory ghost in her usual chair by the window, so she orders a cup of Italian dark roast, Pan's favourite. Because she adds milk while Pan takes her coffee black, Ada reasons that she is retaining some sense of self.

I will never lose myself, she thinks. Never let bits of my character slip away to be replaced by traits that mimic yours and allow me to feel closer to you. And then she reviews her monologue, noting the *you*s, sips her bitter coffee, and checks over her shoulder every time she hears the swing and snap of the door.

Mattie is a good distraction. She points out interesting characters and makes cheeky comments. She makes eyes at the old man behind the counter and then, behind her hand to Ada, makes fun of his eyebrows.

"Nan, I have to ask," Ada says over their steaming cups. "For all Edith does...I mean, for you...do you ever, you know, return the favour?"

Mattie's forehead crinkles into crepe paper in offence.

"What kind of lover do you think I am?" she asks her granddaughter.

"Uhhh," Ada monotones, caught off-guard by the question.

Mattie leans back, looking, Ada thinks, a bit smug.

"If you could hear the way she carries on you'd never get any sleep," Mattie brags. "I know I barely do. That's why all the naps."

Ada smiles.

"But what about your arthritis?"

"That's nothing!" Mattie scoffs. "Don't you know anything about pleasing a woman? Fingers aren't everything. The tip of the tongue, the teeth, the lips, as they say."

"Oh my god—Nan!" Ada shushes her grandmother. Her cheeks flush as she scans the room full of staring eyes.

But the gazes of all the bored patrons are broken when the door creaks open and snaps shut behind a group of old men, trundling in single file. They look around, slightly dazed and with mouths open. One of them is tall and lumbering and nods a lot, jiggling his slack jaw. Another is very small and squat with short arms. With his large glasses, tiny nose, and ears like two halves of a paper heart glued to the sides of his head, he looks like a mouse.

The greyest of the group buys a piece of biscotti. It's hard, the biscuit, and he's trying to eat it with a fork. He doesn't know what to do. He looks around, looks at his friends. He can't bite it because it would crack his teeth. He doesn't want to complain. He looks to the mousy man, who wraps the offending cookie in a paper napkin and drops it into a pocket inside the older man's coat, giving it a reassuring pat. They smile at each other.

Mattie says to Ada that the man should have just dipped it in his coffee and then it would be soft and he could eat it, and Ada thinks to herself that her grandmother's Alzheimer's is not nearly as bad as Joan imagines. Then Mattie sits up straighter and peers at the man with the biscotti in his pocket.

"Ian?" she asks loudly.

Ada tells her that no, that isn't Grandad, and Mattie looks at her granddaughter, frightened, like she doesn't know her face.

Ada says her own name and gets no response, no change of expression. Mattie looks over at the old man again.

"Ian?" she asks.

Ada tells her again. She reaches across the table to hold Mattie's hand and repeats her own name.

"It's me, Nan. Your granddaughter, Ada."

Nothing.

"Joan's daughter," she explains. "I'm Joan's daughter, your granddaughter."

Mattie lifts her head and her eyes begin to clear—she can see Ada, her face. She smiles and shakes her head.

"Silly," she says. "Silly."

Back at the house, Mattie lies down in bed as Ada arranges pillows around her, propping her up. She can still read through her thick glasses so Ada finds her book, tangled in the sheets near the bottom of the bed, and lays it on the covers by her hand. "I won't need it," Mattie says with crinkling eyes. "Edith will be home soon."

She rests her head back on the pillow and closes her eyes as Ada leans over to kiss her warm, papery cheek.

And now Ada is at a loss as to what to do. It's too soon to go see Pan for another piercing, but she craves it just the same. She doesn't want to go back to the café—she'll just stay there all day if she goes now, reading and writing and sketching, looking up every few minutes, just in case, and coating her mouth with coffee again after she's just brushed her teeth.

If only she could clear Pan out so easily. A quick scrub to start fresh, for someone who reciprocates her fascination. She's tried to cultivate other crushes, but none grow. Though the map of Ada's body holds the landmarks of Pan's touch—she even crafted the compass—she did it all with latex gloves and a professional air, leaving no fingerprints. Traces of her touch live only in the cracks and crevices, the hollows of her mind, and Ada can't reach in there with her clumsy fingers to remove them. After over a year's worth of daydreams and nightdreams, Ada's body fervently believes they've fucked, and she doesn't have the heart to convince it otherwise.

She gets it from her mother, her imagination. When Ada was younger, from the time she was four until she was eight or so, her mother used to tell her a particular version of the story of her birth. Having a child was good for Joan because she remembered how to imagine again. Journalism had dehydrated it out of her, shrinking her into a news-reporting, fact-seeking, formula-bound storyteller. Back then she told Ada fantastic tales. Joan said Ada was born in the ocean. The story goes like this:

One night, Joan went to a fancy dinner party in a blue dress covered in sequins. Ada has seen the dress in Joan's closet, but never on her. When she was small she used to stand underneath her mother's clothes on their hangers, reaching her little hands up to finger ruby-coloured buttons, rub her cheeks against the dangling sleeves of silk blouses, and stroke the blue dress, which looked to her like it was made of fish scales.

There were penguins at the party, walking around with silver trays of liver paté, scallops wrapped in bacon, and caviar on crackers. Joan is morally opposed to foie gras so she had the caviar. Took a cracker and put it in her mouth. The eggs felt cold and smooth, she told Ada, like tiny, soft marbles. They rolled over her tongue. She said she had a strange feeling about them, that they were alive. She swallowed them.

Later in the night while she was dancing, her stomach felt strange.

Like a fish was swimming around in her belly. She went to the kitchen and found the jars of caviar so she could inspect the labels.

They were mermaid eggs.

She guessed it was some combination of the mermaid eggs and the fish scale dress, because nobody else at the party that night got pregnant.

She told Ada that when her water broke, it gushed out of her like a waterfall and smelled of the sea. With her fishbowl belly empty she said she could feel Ada gasping. She didn't know what to do and didn't want to go to the hospital, so Mattie drove them to the beach. Joan couldn't just jump into the harbour. The water is vile. She drank eleven bottles of water on the car ride and licked table salt from her palm to keep Ada from suffocating.

Mattie carried them over the stones and over the sand and waded into the water with her daughter and granddaughter in her arms. It was night and the moon's light spread long and bright in a path from the edge of the beach to the horizon.

Joan swam along the moon path until the water was deep enough, and she treaded water while Ada swam out of her. They were still attached by the cord and Ada couldn't yet breathe air, so Joan held her breath and went under. They floated beneath the surface, face to face. Ada had liquid eyes and tiny gills, and she shimmered. They swam together back to shore, where Mattie cut the cord with a sharp rock and Ada learned to breathe air. And that's how she was born.

When Ada was nine, she learned that her mother had been artificially inseminated. But she likes the first story better.

11

November 18, 1948

Mattie *kept her eyes on her work or on the chalkboard, denying them* the rush of a glance at Edith's shining hair, the sweet back of her neck. And Edith sat stiff and nervous, not trusting the impulsive girl to keep herself, and Edith, from being punished.

"Take out your writing assignments, everyone," the teacher said.

They had been instructed to write a poem. Edith pulled hers from between the pages of her book and unfolded it with clammy hands, hoping not to be chosen.

"Frances, please stand and read your poem."

The pale blonde girl at the front of the class rose from her chair and cleared her throat.

"'Ode to Springtime,'" she began.

The teacher nodded.

> "Trees of green and bright blue skies
> Gentle wind and butterflies
> Springtime dresses new and fine
> Laundry hanging on the line
> Oh how I love to sing and rhyme
> For my favourite season, springtime!"

"Lovely, Frances," the teacher smiled. "Now," she scanned the room. "You, Edith. Why don't you read us *your* poem."

The students snickered.

"How can she rhyme if she can't even talk?" one whispered.

"Quiet," the teacher admonished. "Go on, Edith."

Edith stood, blood hammering in her ears and hot in her cheeks.

"'My Dress,'" she said, her small voice loose in her mouth like a baby tooth.

"Speak up, Edith," the teacher called.

Edith stood taller, lifting her chin.

"My dress floats in muddy water," she read. Paused. Swallowed.

> "The…the uniform of absent daughters
> To cover up the scars and wounds
> So no one will know what they do
> I seen a bird up in the trees
> Who tells me of the things she sees
> She wished that we could fly away
> My wings were broke, I had to stay
> But if I ever have a child
> She'll never wear a dress like mine."

The class was silent as Edith took her seat. She wished she had written something simpler, sweeter. What would the teacher say? Would she tell the sisters? If they read her poem she would be strapped for sure.

"Stand up, Edith," the teacher said.

Edith stood again, though she couldn't feel her legs. She pressed her fingertips into the wood of her desk, like bird feet gripping a branch.

"What an…interesting poem," the teacher said, rolling a piece of chalk between her fingers. "Now Edith, do you know that 'child' does not rhyme with 'mine'?"

"Yes, Miss."

"And that the assignment was to use *rhyming* words?"

"Yes, Miss."

"And do you also know that it is incorrect to say 'I *seen* a bird'? Do you know that, Edith? Frances, what is the correct *English* tense of 'to see,' in this sentence?"

"It would be 'I saw,' Miss, or 'I have seen'."

"That's correct. For some reason I can't comprehend, Indian children cannot seem to get it right."

The students chuckled.

"And finally, it's *broken*, not broke. Do you understand, Edith?"

"Yes, Miss," Edith replied, her ears burning. *Ketanuet*, she said silently. Pay her no mind, this spiteful woman.

"Perhaps you will try harder next time," the teacher said.

"Yes, Miss."

"You may sit."

The students rose in succession, reading poems about their cats, their fathers, Frank Sinatra, God. Mattie read a poem about her older brother who was killed in the war.

"That was very nice, Martha," the teacher said, sounding sympathetic.

Some of the girls wiped away tears. Edith wanted to tell Mattie that she liked her poem, but she dared not turn around.

As the students stacked their books at the end of the day and slid their arms into the sleeves of their coats, Edith felt a hand dip into her pocket. She whipped around to see whose it was and saw Mattie's brown braid swinging past. Something warm buzzed in her stomach. She looked to see if anyone else had noticed. The teacher was busy erasing the chalkboard and all of the other kids were packing up their things.

The ridges in the road were tricky, and tripped Edith when she wasn't paying attention to her feet. She fingered a small piece of paper in her pocket, trying to feel its message. She tripped again.

"Damn feet," she swore at them.

She remembered Mattie's face through the leaves, eyes bright. The girl's warm hand.

When Edith reached the Resi she rushed again to the washroom, darted into a stall, and latched the door, finally able to pull the note from her pocket.

Do you want to go for a walk with me?

Edith smiled. Her smile spread, humming down through her chest, tingling along her arms and filling her stomach. Maybe, she mouthed silently through her smile, and dropped the note in the toilet. *Flush.*

12

❧

November 30, 2007

It's *Friday night, but all that means for Kiah is that she has two uninterrupted* days of studying to look forward to before she has to leave her room to make an appearance in class again. Regardless of how uninspiring or infuriating she finds a course, she's never been able to operate at anything less than full throttle. It's just her brain, how it works, how it prioritizes.

It's not that she thinks only of school. Sometimes a pocket of memory or a gauzy dream of her future life will insist on her attention. *We interrupt your regularly scheduled programming with proof that you are a porous, yearning human with regrets and desires and untouched skin.*

But mostly she's memorizing rather than remembering. And because there's so much to memorize, there's not time for much else.

Once in a while she'll take a break to go with her grandma to church, but in the weeks leading up to exams, her tailbone sends roots down through the flat cushion tied to the rungs of her desk chair, and into the grain of the wood itself. Her elbows wear grooves into the desktop from the weight of her head leaning on them, so saturated with information. Her toenails become like Norman's claws when they catch and stick in the upholstery. Hers hook around the stiff carpet fibres. She's only able to untangle, uproot, and heave herself up for tea, snacks, and bathroom breaks. And family dinner, of course.

So tonight, after Shawn skips out early from the dinner table to steal virtual cars and shoot up rivals from his sunken seat on the basement couch, leaving Kiah to load the dishwasher and wipe the counter, she heads upstairs to fit her elbows into their grooves and send down roots for the evening. At least from up here Kiah can't hear the carnage. After a few discussions with Shawn about the virtues of a game that rewards you for killing sex workers turned into door-slamming fights, Kiah's mostly given up. At this point she's become a pro at self-imposed sensory deprivation, mostly to avoid combusting from fury. She can do a trick she can never quite explain where she closes off her nose from the inside, which is good for when she has to walk past the organic bakery that was once a convenience store where her cousin worked. A well-rehearsed ocular choreography allows her to avert her eyes down certain streets, avoiding sleek condos and pricey boutiques when she needs to conserve energy rather than expend it on angry internal monologues. And she can usually sing verses in her head on repeat to block out bullshit if needed, but Shawn's video games are so consistently loud that it's best to just avoid the basement.

An explosion crackles from downstairs, loud enough to make Kiah twitch in her chair.

"Fucking Shawn," she growls through gritted teeth.

She looks online for a chill playlist and turns the volume up. Fits her head into the gentle vise of her hands and trains her gaze on the pages on her desk. But the lyrics are messing with her, sliding between the printed words and infusing them with longing. Why is every god-damn song about love? She hits skip to escape the sentiment. There are other things to think about, you know. Kiah tells herself this as she closes her eyes and feels the vast space around her. Who is she tied to? She tries to think: Dad, Grandma, Shawn. And her mom, who had been the softest place to land. One-sided conversations and prayers can't replicate that comfort. All her close friends have fallen away because her drive to excel means she has no time to hang out anymore. And her one cousin who always got her, at every age and in every way, moved to Toronto a few years ago.

So that's what's up. Her closest relationships are with her textbooks and computer. And with artifacts that remind her of people who aren't around anymore. Photos of her mother, old handwritten and craftily folded notes from her friends in the time before cellphones, witchy paraphernalia from her cousin. Kiah's not sure what caused more upset in the family—when her aunt found Marcus's tarot cards and crystals or when she found texts from his boyfriend, both in the course of the same snoop. Both were considered un-Christian, weird, and worrisome. Leona had her sister over after dinner one night, when she thought Kiah and Shawn would be in bed. Of course Kiah wasn't, and listened as best she could to her mother counselling Marcus's mom about how to overcome her shock and support her son. How nothing was more important than this. But ultimately, between neighbourhood gossip and quiet stares, and the Halifax scene of mostly white guys who either only dated each other or shouted in his ear at the bar that they'd always fantasized about being with a Black guy, Marcus moved away.

Kiah didn't argue with him about it, and she didn't cry in front of him either. Marcus had enough to worry about without carrying her heartbreak. He was always her first choice to sit beside at family get-togethers, the best person to complain to about her brother, and the only guy she knew who called himself a feminist. And when she felt lost, he could tell her future.

She was nervous the first time Marcus read her cards. What if they told her something she didn't want to know? Something awful. The Death card. The Devil. The Tower. But he tailored his reading to her nervousness, sifting through potential meanings and offering her only the gentlest interpretations. That's the thing she likes about the cards. There are so many possibilities to fit to your circumstance. You can let them tell you what, deep down, you already know. Uncannily though, when she read them for herself before her mother got sick, they told her things were going to get tough. That she would lose something beloved. This was not something she already knew. She assumed it meant she was going to fail a test, and studied harder.

The singer of the song emanating from her shitty speakers howls about love. Why are we so obsessed with it, all of us? I mean, love for our family, friends, community, yes, Kiah thinks. That kind of love can stoke revolution. It's the romantic part that irks her, and it's everywhere. Every song, movie, book, and ad seems to feature it. Marcus used to tease her when he read her cards. "Ah," he'd say, pulling the Hierophant or Hermit. "Looks like you'll be a professor after all. A celibate academic for life."

It's not that she would say no if it came her way. It just hasn't, at least not in a way that feels right. She has this idea of how her love will look, what he'll care about, how he'll hold her name in his mouth. But if that ever came together in one person, would it last? That's the worst part, she thinks. It never seems to. Most of her friends' parents have split up. Her own parents seemed to be this glowing exception, and then look what happened. No one gets to keep their love. If two people don't tear themselves apart, circumstance will do it for them. Truthfully, though she's never said it out loud, love scares the shit out of her.

A high note sounds outside, the yelp of an old window heaved open. Kiah looks out her own window to the house next door, where a head of messy hair emerges from a rectangle of light on the ground floor and into the sharp night air. Just watching makes Kiah cold. The girl's face turns up to the dark sky and Kiah follows her gaze. A half moon hangs behind thick clouds, glinting like an eye through the holes of a crocheted blanket. This is what love makes you do, Kiah thinks. Lean out your window in November to gaze at the moon. It's so cliché.

Though, she must admit there's a magic to the moon. It makes her think of Marcus, timing tarot readings with its phases. She smiles. Opens her desk drawer and pushes aside pens and highlighters, excavating his deck in its worn box.

"Just one card," she says. "Since you're not doing any work anyway."

She pulls the cards from their box and spreads them out on the desk, sifting through, wondering what to ask. She gathers them up and splits them three times, three times, three times as she concentrates and says softly, "What can I expect? What's coming next?"

She draws the top card and flips it over.

"Give me a break," she sighs, thinking of what a kick Marcus would get out of this. The Lovers.

This has got to have another meaning, she thinks, and takes to the internet. She starts to read.

"The Lovers, okay," she mutters as she skims the page. "The Lovers do not always signify romantic love. Umm…building connection, cooperating to accomplish joint purposes…that sounds more like it. Not lovers, but accomplices. That's what's coming."

13

❧

November 30, 2007

A *week ago Joan told Ada that a girlfriend of hers in university* (platonic, she insists) bought her a sex toy.

"A dildo?" Ada asked, and Joan knitted her eyebrows at her daughter and shook her head no.

"Was it penis-shaped?"

"I don't know," Joan said and turned away, meaning to end the conversation.

"Sorry," said Ada. "What I meant to say is, was it *vagina*-shaped?"

"I'm sorry I said anything."

"Why did you then?"

"I don't know, Ada," Joan said with her back still turned, busying herself at the kitchen counter. And then out of the silence she said that she wanted Ada to know she didn't think all sex toys were bad. Just bad for Mattie.

"She could give herself a heart attack, for Christ's sake."

"I really don't think she has a vibrator," Ada told her mother.

Joan told her not to be ridiculous.

"She can't do it by herself," Joan said. "She can barely put on lipstick anymore."

"Exactly," Ada said. "Has she told you about Edith?"

Joan said that Mattie would not *stop* talking about Edith, of course she'd heard of her.

"And you are aware," she said to her daughter, "that Edith is not a real person?"

"I mean, I suppose she's no longer a *corporeal* person," Ada said.

She caught her mother's unblinking stare, eyes narrowed and lips pursed. Then Joan whipped back around, her short hair swinging like panelled drapes shut fast.

"Beat it," she said.

Ada wondered if her mother still had that dildo. She went to her room and wrote herself a note as a reminder to ask her more about it later. Sex had been a pretty loaded issue in the house for a while—who's having it and when and with whom—and Ada thinks the biggest issues are that Joan is having it never and with no one, not even herself, and Mattie is having it every day with her ghost lover.

Fine, Joan thought, still standing at the counter. They won't listen to reason? I can play their game. If they think there's a ghost in the house, I'll call someone to find it.

That someone turned out to be Robert Rainsong, a self-proclaimed shaman. His Kijiji ad for Party Psychic and Mystical Healer described him as adept at chakra balancing, soul fragment retrieval, and aura cleansing. But his true specialty was detecting spiritual presences and convincing them to move on to a higher plane.

Joan decided Robert was the man for the job. If nothing else, she thought, it would make a good piece for the Sunday edition. Halifax loves a good ghost story.

ROBERT ARRIVES AS SCHEDULED THE following week, wearing a leather-fringed coat and matching headband. He requests the presence of all the ladies in the house so their energies can be assessed and they can be smudged.

Mattie, Ada, and Joan sit at the kitchen table as he drifts through the house, visiting each room and wafting sage smoke from a shining shell with an eagle feather, its spine bejewelled with the colours of the chakras.

"Who's the hippie?" Mattie whispers to Ada.

"Robert Rainsong," Ada replies. "He's here to chat with Edith and tell her to move on."

"She'll do what she pleases," Mattie says.

"Robert, would you like some water? Orange juice? Tea?" Joan calls to him.

"Green tea would be lovely," he replies from the living room. "Thank you so much, Joanie."

"Gross, Mum," Ada says, wrinkling her nose. "I think he's flirting with you."

Robert enters the kitchen and Joan hands him his tea.

"Now, where did you get that beautiful feather?" Joan asks, flipping open the small notebook that lives in her back pocket and pulling a pen from behind her ear.

"Ah, a very special vendor on Amazon." He smiles. "They sell them in a set with the abalone shell and sage too. Every household should have one—I can send you the link."

Joan looks at him over her glasses and smiles back.

"How interesting," she says.

"Now ladies," says Robert. "If you would care to follow me, I will take you on a journey through your home, revealing to you the spirits who reside here and communing with them in order to determine how to help them move on from the physical realm."

"All right." Joan claps her hands together. "Let's find some ghosts!"

"Where's Edith?" Ada whispers.

"Napping," Mattie replies.

Robert Rainsong leads them around the house, down the hall and through their bedrooms, stopping every now and then to close his eyes and take a deep breath, fingers outstretched, head cocked to one side. They follow him into the basement where they store their carrots and potatoes.

"Chilly down here," Mattie says.

"I'll go get you a sweater, Mum," says Joan and runs upstairs.

Robert begins to hum and breathe deeply, rolling his head around and stretching his arms out as he travels the basement on the balls of his feet. Joan returns with a sweater and Ada helps her grandmother do up the buttons.

"What did I miss?" Joan whispers.

"Please tell me you're not paying this man, Joanie," Mattie says.

"I was trying to make a point," Joan replies. "But I'm beginning to regret it."

Robert draws a tiny djembe from his leather-fringed coat and begins to beat it while he hums and sings with his eyes closed. Suddenly, he stops. The women stand silently, huddled by the stairs, peering at him and wondering what he'll do next.

"Greetings, princess," he says.

"Who?" Mattie asks.

"I sense the presence of a Native princess, long dead," Robert Rainsong explains.

"Joanie, what did you tell this man?" Mattie says quietly, annoyed.

"She was a chief's daughter," Robert continues. "Princess, tell me your spirit name." And he begins to hum and beat his drum again.

"Give me a break," Mattie mutters. "Joanie, send him home."

Robert beats his drum faster and faster in the cold basement beside the crate of carrots until finally, he stops again.

"Wind Dancer. That was her name."

"Well, thank you very much, Robert," Joan says. "My mother just reminded me that I need to take her to a doctor's appointment. Why don't we go upstairs and I'll settle up with you."

After he leaves, Mattie says she needs some early afternoon whisky. Ada gets her favourite green glass and pours her two fingers.

"It's a good thing Edith was napping," Mattie says. "'Cause she would've scared the shit out of him."

14

December 14, 2007

Even though this class is much smaller than Kiah's first-year lecture-hall courses, the professor still talks to the back of the room, giving a grand performance without looking at his students' faces. The course sounded good on paper, but now, at the end of the semester, Kiah can confirm it's a waste of time.

Because this guy just can't get past that old us versus them bullshit. Maybe if he looked his students in the eye when he talked, he would recognize that the "we" he's always spouting off about doesn't encompass all the people seated in front of him. He certainly doesn't speak for Kiah. The way he talks about brown women in other countries waiting to be saved by Canadian soldiers. He's all for the invasion of Iraq and Afghanistan. A liberation, he calls it. A rescue mission.

"But what do Afghan women think of North American armed forces in their country, bombing their homes?" Kiah asked once.

"Those women are oppressed by Islamic fundamentalism and aren't permitted to engage in politics, so it's difficult for them to think beyond their traditional gender roles," he replied, aiming his pen at her like a dart. "But they are thankful, I'm sure, to the troops fighting for their freedom."

Of course, his lectures fail to touch on the oppression of women in Western society. It's just "other" cultures. No problems here.

Kiah can barely bring herself to study for his exam. She knows the answers he wants. As she sits at her desk, writing her last test in her last class of the semester, she debates whether to give them to him, or whether to tear him apart eloquently and concisely along the blue lines of the thin exam booklet. In the end, she grudgingly delivers the responses she knows will earn her an A, even though it hurts her to do so. It had been too much for Kiah's friends in first year. Both Carla and Denise dropped out by second semester.

Kiah hadn't known then about the school's centre for Black students, or she would've reported that first-year prof. It feels too long ago to dredge up, but she's grateful to know about the centre now. A place she can go where she won't feel like an anomaly on campus. Where she can drop in to chat or rant as needed with the advisor and whomever else happens to be hanging out. Where she can hear stories about her mom. If it weren't for her mom and the centre, Kiah might have dropped out too.

She would head there now to unwind after this fucking exam, but it matters to her dad to have the family together for dinner, and she gets that. Because of her mom's long shifts at Camp Hill it didn't often happen that they all got together at the dinner table. But then she got sick and priorities changed. Ken started coming home from work an hour earlier than usual to spend time with Leona and help Betty make the meal. Kiah would leave her books and Shawn would pause his video game and they would all sit around the table, talking about their days, teasing each other, keeping it light, not mentioning the cancer.

Leona brought it up sometimes. She wanted to tell them things. She seemed to know she wouldn't survive it, and a few times told Ken that she didn't really want the chemo. That she would rather just let it take its course than slow down the process and make it more painful.

As a nurse, she knew how painful it would get. Burning in the muscles, soreness in the mouth, sharp needles of pain shooting through hands and feet. Deep, dull aching in the core of her bones. The beams of the house of her body getting brittle, breaking down.

Sometimes during family dinners, Kiah could barely make herself eat, looking at her mother across the table, thinking about the cancer cells multiplying and marching steadily through her bones. Before she died, one of the things she asked them to do was keep eating their evening meal together.

"This is so nice, guys," she said. "Keep this up when I'm gone, all right?"

And everyone said no, no, stop it, don't be ridiculous, I don't want to hear it, you're not going anywhere. Leona smiled and grabbed their hands and squeezed them tight.

So they kept it up. It's the one thing Shawn can manage to be on time for. Tonight it's a pot roast Betty has been basting all day, accompanied by Ken's classic Caesar salad with the peppery dressing. The house smells amazing when Kiah walks in from the cold.

"So did you ace your test, Brainiac, or what?" Shawn says as he comes up the stairs from the basement.

"Of course she did," Betty says from the kitchen, carving the roast and serving up slices. Ken heaps piles of romaine onto his kids' plates, filling all the remaining space. Even though Shawn and Kiah are eighteen and twenty, he still feels the need to monitor their vegetable consumption, at least for one meal of the day.

"I see the first signs of scurvy," Betty will tease Shawn when he complains about his mandated serving. "Your eyes are all sunken back in your head."

Caesar salad's the only thing he won't complain about. Ken's dressing is so creamy and garlicky and peppery that you can barely taste the lettuce. Shawn always asks for more, drenching the leaves until it's more like dressing soup with romaine garnish on his plate. It's a mystery to everyone how he's so thin.

He'd pack on more pounds if he could. In his room at night before he goes to sleep, Shawn does his routine of crunches, push-ups, and bicep curls with his dad's old set of neon orange dumbbells. But when he looks at himself in the mirror, he never sees what he wants. Pathetic, he tells himself. Weak. One of his friends told him he could hook him up with some juice, just for a boost to build some muscle, gain some weight. But Shawn doesn't know. His mother told him too many times about street drugs and how sick you can get if you shoot them. He seems to remember her turning health PSAs into skipping rhymes and clapping games when they were kids. He can't feign ignorance on this one. Every time he starts to consider it again a singsong warning echoes in the back of his mind.

"The roast is great, Grandma," Kiah says.

"Who wants more?" asks Betty, offering the plate around.

But everyone's stuffed.

"Gimme a minute," Shawn says. "I'll have some more in a minute."

Ken wipes his mouth with his napkin and leans back in his chair.

"So, Kee, what are you going to do now that you're finished classes for the semester?" he asks. "You hanging out with some friends tonight? Celebrating? Mom, we should've made her a cake or something."

"Mhm," Betty agrees. "I forgot this was your last day before Christmas holidays."

The fact that she has free time coming up hadn't fully registered with Kiah, either. She's so used to her routine—getting up early, working all day at school or studying at home, maybe dropping by the centre, and then reading in her room until late late at night—that when she's presented with many empty days in a row, she isn't sure what to do. It's intimidating. She feels useless.

"Oh, I dunno, nothing tonight. Some of my friends still have exams. Maybe we'll do something when everyone's finished," she says, as if she can still think of a friend she would call.

Shawn takes another helping of beef, cutting it into chunks and sopping up the juice.

"Now that you have some free time you can go shopping for my Christmas presents," he says with his mouth full. "New games. That's all I want."

"Man, I told you I'm not buying you that garbage," Kiah says.

"Come on!" Shawn cries. "Why not?"

"Because it's disgusting. Who are you supposed to kill in those games, huh? Yeah, Black migrants and prostitutes."

"Kiah, that's not appropriate dinner table talk," Ken says.

"But it's true, Dad," she says. "Shawn's sitting downstairs all day, shooting up Black folks and raping sex workers."

"Kiah!" Betty admonishes.

"It's just a game!" Shawn exclaims, incredulous. "And I don't do that, Kiah. Jesus."

"Okay so it's *just a game*, but you're what, an Italian dude? Starting gang wars between Black folks?"

"So?" Shawn challenges his sister, jutting out his chin.

"And from what I've read about it, you can hire a sex worker and then kill her to get your money back, am I wrong? Tell me I'm wrong."

"All right stop it," Betty says, smacking the tabletop. "I've had enough of this. Can't we just have some nice conversation around the dinner table?"

"Yeah, Kiah. Stop it." Shawn says. "It's just a game. It's not real life."

Kiah glares at her brother.

"What do you think Mom would have thought about you playing those games, Shawn? Huh? Do you think she'd have thought it was cool?"

Shawn leans over the table into his sister's face, his eyes welling up. He shoves his chair back and stomps to his room.

"Shawn!" Betty calls after him.

Kiah sits at the table, anger burning in her cheeks.

"Kiah, that was uncalled for," Ken says, looking hurt himself at the mention of Leona.

"I'm sorry, Dad. But you should really take those games away from him."

"I don't know, Kee," Ken says. "He's old enough to make his own choices, and they're just games. He's a good kid."

But he does wonder what Leona would say.

Upstairs, Kiah sits at her desk, fuming over her open textbook. Her heartbeat fast and insistent. She chomps on the end of a highlighter, imagining she's a witch chewing the bones of her stupid brother. It's how she used to torment him when they were little, when she would boss him and chase him around the house while he screamed for their parents to save him from his bone-crunching witch sister. Now he's too damn cool. Too cool to joke around with, too cool to listen to anything she says.

Kiah remembers Shawn back in his first year of junior high. Chasing after her and her friends in a hoodie down to his knees, squirting his juice box at them, chanting rhymes about how Kiah Kiah has diarrhea and laughing his dumb little head off. He was a brat, but he idolized her. It was just his twelve-year-old-boy way of showing it. By the time he was in his first year of high school, though, he barely gave her a nod when he passed her in the hall. Kiah never thought that one day she'd miss her brother's relentless quest for her attention with disgusting rhymes and fruit juice stains, but she does.

Okay Kiah, enough with the nostalgia, she tells herself. She wipes the spitty end of the chewed-up highlighter off on her jeans and lets out a slow breath with eyes closed. You've got to stop chewing your pens, she thinks, running her tongue along her teeth, feeling where she's worn them down. She opens her eyes and retrains them on the rows upon rows of words she plans to pack into her brain before classes start up again in January. She reads aloud to herself to help "facilitate information absorption," a study tip she was taught in high school.

"Critical studies must be linked to new theories," she begins, the words dry and bland in her mouth like stale bread, "must be connected with critiques of identity and subjectivity," she continues, trying to chew, trying to swallow, "and most pertinently, to the technoscientific means by which...."

But the words just won't fit. It seems Kiah's up-till-now infallible brain is finally protesting, is declaring maximum saturation and demanding a break.

"Fine, quitter," she says disdainfully. "It's not like you have anything better to do."

Her finger and thumb pull apart her knitted brows, trying to smooth the crease that has been deepening between them. She leans back in her chair, cracking her spine and surveying the room. Exam schedules, class syllabi, and study notes are tacked up on the walls, lifting gently with the hot air rising from the baseboard. They block out the Pepto Bismol paint she meant to cover up after they moved in. She'd like to paint her room a deep, deep red. Warm and embracing, like a womb. Like the inside of her eyelids when she shuts them and turns her face to the sun.

Beyond the field of papers, on the bureau with the oval mirror, is a photo of Leona on her graduation day. Kiah put the photo in a little oval frame too, so that when she looks at herself in the mirror and holds up the photograph, it's like an antique picture-in-picture. She can't wait to hold the photo of Leona up to the mirror on her own graduation day. She would've been so proud. Kiah turns back to her desk, lifts the screen of her ancient laptop, and waits for it to start up. The fan whirs, lights flash, and speakers crackle as the digital orchestra signals the computer's triumphant awakening. She opens the browser, types in "Nat King Cole" and the internet delivers her a fifty-three-song playlist. Should be long enough to fall asleep to.

15

✗

December 14, 2007

Ada waits in the kitchen for a pork satay, which is being prepared for a man who is deathly allergic to peanuts. Coming into a Thai restaurant was maybe not the best idea then, Ada had suggested. He puffed up and went red in the face, telling her with a tight mouth that it was really none of her business, and that he wanted a pork satay and to make sure there were no peanuts, or traces of peanuts, or peanut sauce or peanut oil on or near his food.

It's my business if he wants me to make sure his food won't kill him, Ada thinks. And he isn't doing a good job of ensuring his own health by being so chest-swellingly rude to the girl into whose hands he has placed his life. Ada doesn't want the responsibility, certainly, and now in the kitchen, recalling his tone of voice, she thinks of a joke: the joke is that she hides a peanut in his pork cubes and the punchline is that he dies. She shakes off a grim smile as James tramps into the kitchen.

"You have a table of two by the window," he says, reaching past her to lift a soupy dish of fish pieces swimming in sweet and sour sauce and a deep bowl of sticky rice.

"They just keep coming tonight, don't they? I already have my hands full with this peanut asshole."

As he sails back out into the restaurant, James sings over his shoulder that, lucky for her, the deuce is Ada's "little crush and her ex."

No, Ada thinks. No no no. Too awkward. Way too awkward. I'll trip over myself for sure. Faced with two beautiful people who make her feel so self-conscious and homely, young and insecure, faced with two fixations, one minor and one overwhelming, something is going to get broken. She moves to the door to call James back with a hoarse whisper but he is across the room and can't hear her.

"Make sure those don't touch the peanut sauce," Ada reminds the cook, who looks at her reproachfully.

"I know," he says in a hard monotone. She apologizes for being obnoxious. She just doesn't want the guy to go into anaphylactic shock, because that would make things even more awkward.

James returns to the hot kitchen to give the cook an order slip. Ada clutches his arm, her fingers contorting the tattooed map.

"Take them," she pleads.

James raises his eyebrows and gives her a snotty look.

"I already have five tables, thank you very much," he says.

"It's only a two. Please, James. Take it, please? I'll get the next one and help you with the tables you have now. Is that a drink order? I'll make it."

James smirks.

"You baby. Can't handle your little crush, can you?" But he rolls his eyes and sighs. "Fine."

Ada squeezes his arm in thanks. She takes the slip of paper he's scrawled drinks on and heads to the bar. As she passes Pan's table, Ada doesn't look over at her. Can people sense when someone is pretending to not see them? When someone stares at them without looking? Ada thinks so.

She measures shots of vodka that slip over the edges of the thick glass and seep into the parts of her finger that she sliced clumsily along with the lemons. She rattles ice into narrow glasses and tips the shots in. Unscrews the plastic cap of a jug and fills the glasses the rest of the way up with thick red juice. Shakes in Worcestershire sauce, pepper, and salt. Wedges lemons onto rims—more juice in her cuts. All the while she watches Pan's table, but the bamboo wall obscures most of it so she stares only at Pan's shoulder and upper arm and is thrilled just the same.

Last night Ada dreamt about her. Maybe it was the snack she ate before bed or maybe it was that she jerked off right before she fell asleep. Maybe it was both.

It was three in the morning and she was lying frozen, like Mattie does, with her mouth open and eyes heavily shut. Ada's tide comes flowing in over her feet first. She can feel it, rolling in, filling her up. She's learned that if she stalls it, holds off being submerged for long enough, she will be that much more overcome when she finally submits. Like when she was young, running from waves on the beach, the water lapping at her toes. The next wave washes over the tops of her feet. The next licks at her ankles. When she finally runs in far enough and gets hit full in the body by a heavy wave, it feels so much more exhilarating having played a teasing game with the water.

And this time the wave knocked her back into many long minutes of pulsing stillness. She began to sink into that nonsense stage between sleep and wakefulness, where your dreaming mind starts to take over but your waking mind is still awake enough to know how absurd your dreams are.

I am lying in my bed and my sheets are layers and layers of tissue paper, dry and rustling as I shift my weight. And now you're here, sitting on the end of my bed, paper crinkling beneath you. I tell you that I want something pierced and I don't know what, but you say you know how to tell.

You begin to pull the tissue paper off of my body. You scrunch each sheet into a tight ball and throw it across the room until you have balled up the last layer and I am naked and shining, laid out on my bed. You touch a finger to the centre of me, the compass, and it begins to spin. The four points of it are lit up bright and as it slows, all of your metal fingerprints begin to glow. Lip. Septum. Nostrils. Nipples. Then all of the landmarks fade and only the compass is glowing.

First west goes out—dims like a burnt out flashlight. Then east, followed by north. Now it's only south, glowing, shining bright.

South? I say out loud to you, and you stretch a latex glove over your right hand and slide it up the inside of my thigh.

You start to tell me a story about how you travelled south with your lover and it was so hot you could barely move. You lay in bed together all day, sleeping and drinking gallons of water and sucking on ice cubes, your sweating bodies sliding over each other so smoothly that every movement was erotic and you couldn't be satiated.

South, you tell me. The compass pointed south. South is where I want you to pierce me and so you will prepare the area. You drag a gloved finger now north, now south.

You are going to determine the perfect placement, you say. You tell me to breathe deeply, in and out. In and out. You draw on my body in circles with the rubber tip of your finger. I can feel your moist breath being sucked up by my pores. You put your mouth on me and I fall back into a glowing night sky of x-ray constellations.

Ada blushes as she passes Pan again, dropping off Bloody Marys at one of James's tables. But Ada doesn't look over. She decides that the next time she passes, she'll look.

First she has to stop in the kitchen to check herself out. Her work shirt, with its crocheted gold buttons and stiff mandarin collar, is dirtier than she realized. Peanut sauce dried to a crusty film, grease seeped into the fabric where she rests the plates against her ribs when she picks up more than she can handle.

And what is Pan wearing? Loose, dark grey shirt, faded jeans. It's her chosen uniform and she wears it so well. Elin is wearing black.

Ada examines herself in the unflattering back of a spoon. She bares her teeth to check for remnants of her dinner, something she probably should have done before she left for work. Her teeth aren't gleaming like Elin's, from their years of being dipped in and out of red wine and Earl Grey, plus now one year in and out of coffee. Her teeth, like most of the cups at the café—years of holding coffee and tea and no amount of scrubbing or hot water or soap can restore them. But teeth are too white these days anyway, Ada tries to reassure herself. She's sure Pan wouldn't find teeth bleaching very punk.

"New table for you," one of her coworkers says as she swings around the kitchen doorframe and snatches the spoon from between Ada's fingers. She drops it into a bowl of yellow curry and swings, more slowly, back out and around the corner into the dining room.

Ada plunges her hand into the hot tray of shrimp puffs, coating her fingers in shining grease. She strides over to her new table and trips a little on her feet as she looks over at Pan, a smile ready on her lips.

But Pan is deep in conversation and Ada feels like an idiot. She tries a few more times before Pan leaves but she can't catch her eyes as they glance around the room from time to time, unpredictable. Ada can't imagine not noticing Pan the way Pan is not noticing her. But that's the thing about this—it's not mutual.

James tells Ada near the end of their shift that he and some of the kids who work lunch are going out tonight to get trashed and dance and yes, Ada says, she does want to come.

First she goes home and pushes her hair around on her head in front of one of the three mirrors she has up in her room—one that's full-length and leans against the wall, one that is like a large portrait of whoever looks into it and one that is the size of her hand with the fingers spread out. The small mirror hangs on a nail on the wall she faces when she sleeps so that the first thing she sees when she wakes up is herself. Only she keeps turning over in the middle of the night, so the first thing she sees when she wakes is a print of Pan's that she bought, tacked up on the opposite wall.

Ada drinks a tall glass of vodka and orange juice in large gulps as she digs through piles of clothes on her bedroom floor. She dances better drunk. The orange juice is thick and syrupy sweet and masks the burn of the alcohol until the end of the gulp, when her body realizes what she's making it swallow and sends jerky little shudders down her spine. She's been drinking vodka since she was fourteen, her drink of choice, and she still can't shake these tiny convulsions.

Joan is still up—Ada can hear her tapping out a stream of staccato beats on her keyboard into the quiet of the house. Mattie murmurs from the other side of the wall, sleeping. Or something. Ada pulls a black dress from beneath a pile of musty clothes in the corner of the room where it's been packed in tight. A dress? She never wears a dress. She can't even remember when this one got stuffed into the corner. But the vodka is starting to numb her limbs, flowing out to her fingertips, and the idea of dancing in a black dress makes her feel good.

This one's tight and when she zips it up in the front, it's like encasing her chest in a second ribcage. The dress presses her breasts up into little crescent moons, resting on the black fabric. Ada downs the rest of the juice and sways her hips down the hall to the bathroom. She snatches a tube of deep fuchsia lipstick from the cabinet, which Joan bought by accident and never wears because it's ludicrous, she says. Ada presses it into her lips, moving the colour around in a circle and edging the tip into the points of her upper lip, careful to trace around the pretty metal and not smudge any lipstick on it that would dull its shine. She flips the tube over to read its name: *Lewd-i-crass*, it's called. Huh. She grabs a black elastic from the countertop, already tangled with strands of her strawberry hair, and wraps it around her locks.

She takes a last swig of vodka on her way out and wedges two twenties between her tits. Slides her feet into old skate shoes, zips up the smallest of her winter coats, and walks downtown toward the bar through falling snow. In front of her on the sidewalk, all the way down the hill curving around the Citadel, walks a bouncy girl in a short leather jacket, her flouncy ponytail skewed to the left. Right, thinks Ada. Side ponytails are the thing. She grabs her own ponytail in two hands and yanks it into place.

Ada can already feel the bass beating in her chest like a second heart as she waits in line at the door. It outbeats her own heart in both speed and strength. Her bare legs are so numb from the walk that they're not even cold anymore. The thick bouncer pats his hands gently down her sides, barely touching her, and nods her in.

It's dark inside and smells like sweat and spilt liquor and so many kinds of cologne. As Ada steps through the people surrounding the bar, trying to get to the dance floor and find her familiars, a surge in the crowd forces her toward the wet counter. It is a wave peopled by pretty fags drinking expensive beer in shirts the colour of decadent food— salmon, mango, olive—and with hair so perfectly windswept and rigid they're like walking pictures of themselves at the beach.

Ada goes with the flow.

In a few minutes the butch bartender with beautiful shoulders and octopus tentacles tattooed down her arm is nodding at Ada. She leans forward and Ada shouts double screwdriver please into her ear, grazing her salty cheek with her lips. She smiles at Ada and slams a shot glass down, splashes vodka up to the rim, and tosses it twice into a cloudy glass with watery juice from the gun.

Ada pulls a twenty from her dress and the woman returns her

change with a wink. She drinks the harsh mix in one go, sucking it through the ice cubes, and forces her way upstream. Now she's drunk enough to dance with strangers.

With eyes closed she begins to move. She doesn't even have to try—the music moves her. Smiling at the feeling of her body in the midst of so many other bodies, she starts to get lost in the sound when a hand around her fast-moving arm opens her eyes, and she's spun around to come face to face with James. He kisses her drunk and happy on the mouth and his stubble pokes into her skin like a bed of baby anemones. Ada dances up on him wild and shameless like they're in some cheesy music video, covered in dirt and oil and wearing assless chaps.

And then over his shoulder she catches the stare and smirk of a tall dyke—messy blonde hair, long, slender neck. Crooked teeth. Ada loves crooked teeth. She lowers herself from up around James's hips, keeping eye contact with the woman. James gets a peck on the cheek and Ada moves around him until she and the woman are eye to nose, and she's still smirking. She presses her hand into Ada's lower back and Ada feels her pulse, the way she moves. Ada arches her head back and bites her lip, smiling, and the woman's hand tilts Ada's face toward her, taking over the bite with her own teeth, melting into tongue and lips. A few beats later the woman has her by the hand, leading her to the bathroom. Ada follows because it's the only thing she can do, and holy Jesus Christ, she wants sex and it seems like the universe is about to deliver.

The woman doesn't try to make it inconspicuous. She squeezes in front of the lineup of sweating people full of piss and liquor, and when a stall opens up she pushes by the stumbling girl fumbling with her zipper and kicks the door open. Snaps Ada in after her like the tail end of a whip and slams her up against the flimsy metal wall, shoving the door tight into its frame and jamming the bolt lock into its sheath with a twist of her wrist.

They collide with a moan and clumsy drunken hands, but the woman's hands know what they're doing. Ada's dress can unzip from the bottom up and the woman figures this out fast. With one hand she lifts Ada's thigh to rest on her black-jeaned hip while the other hand slides up, her palm sticking to Ada's skin in the humid, close air, their bodies glowing with the condensation of other people's sweat.

The kids in the bathroom talk so loud, layers of drunken raspy shouts. So Ada figures she can be as loud as her body wants. Slip of the woman's fingers and Ada almost collapses in on herself. She forgets where she is when she closes her eyes—for a few long, drunken seconds, she is back on her tissue paper-covered bed with Pan, Pan's mouth, Pan's touch, and Ada hears with clouded ears her own voice, fuck, fuck, fuck, fuck—until an impatient kick to the stall door reminds her. The blurry-featured face between her knees, soft lit like in a soap opera, shouts "Fuck off!" into her cunt, laughing, and then sucks her until she comes.

Ada's legs are so weak, she feels like the muscles are going to drop off and fall to the floor. The woman comes up smiling and zips Ada's dress back down. Ada kisses her wet mouth and the woman slips out ahead of her, weaving through the lineup and back into the tight, thrumming crowd.

16

December 17, 1948

Yes but not now, *Edith scratched onto the papery inside of the foil* wrapper with her pencil. She folded it into a tiny square, creasing the edges with her fingernail.

On the way to school that morning Edith turned the square over and over in her pocket. How could she give it to Mattie? She didn't trust herself to get it into her coat pocket without being caught. But how else? She couldn't walk past the girl's desk because it was behind her. Could she throw it? Drop it as she walked and hope Mattie and no one else picked it up? Surely passing notes would be punished severely. But then, anything Edith did was punished severely. She had been slapped for being stared at. That being the case, she felt the game was worth it. Not much to lose, and only six months left until she was finally free.

As they worked silently at their desks near the end of the day, puzzling over arithmetic problems, Edith decided she would pretend to drop her pencil. It had worked before. Why not now?

She glanced up at the teacher, who was reading at her desk. She looked back at her math problem and began to chew on the pencil's end. The eraser came out easily between her teeth. The teacher appeared to be absorbed in her book as Edith reached into her pocket for the note. The tiny square became a tiny tube and she fit it into the now empty metal cylinder. She scanned the room to see if anyone had noticed. They hadn't. So with a flick of her fingers, Edith knocked the pencil to the floor, back toward Mattie's desk. She turned to look and saw it come to a stop near her feet. The girl looked up into Edith's eyes and down at the pencil.

"What's going on back there?" the teacher snapped from her desk.

"Edith dropped her pencil, Miss," Mattie said.

"Well then give it back to her, Martha," the teacher replied, annoyed.

Mattie reached down and, seeing the silver paper stuck in the end, pulled it out before returning the pencil to Edith, careful not to hold her gaze too long. Mattie dropped the wrapper down the cuff of her blouse. This girl with shining hair and a poet's mouth—Mattie wanted so badly to be her friend. Forbidden friends, even better. They could form a secret society, like in a book. Create their own language and write letters in code. The note in her sleeve tickled her impatient skin.

In her room at home, after her little sister had fallen asleep, Mattie unfolded the foil. She could smell it—peppermint.

Yes but not now, she read. It was good enough for her. Whenever. She could wait.

17

❧

January 10, 2008

On their second coffee date Ada told Pan that she only wanted to kiss people who would want to kiss themselves. Pan looked skeptically amused, a small grin curving her lips, but Ada could tell she was thinking about it.

This time Ada had come to her for east and west. She said she hadn't eaten yet that day, which was true though strategic, and asked Pan if she would like to come and have a date square with her or something. Pan said she could use a cup of coffee.

"So would you do it?" Ada asked.

"What, kiss myself?" Pan looked at Ada like she was a tireless child, and then satisfied her with, "Sure."

Ada nodded her head in approval. She offered Pan a bite of her square. Broke through the sweet crust with the tines of her fork and slid it down through the sticky filling, lifting a perfect triangle up to the middle of the table.

"No thanks." Pan shook her head. "I have soup at home that I'll go eat once I'm finished with you." Pan has soup for dinner every night, she told Ada once. The same kind of soup, even. She says she never gets tired of it.

Ada had hoped so hard on that second coffee date that Pan would accept her offer of a bite of date square. Pan's ridged teeth scraping along the steely fork, her tongue licking sugar from the tines. Ada would have put it back into her own mouth when Pan was done and sucked her spit from its surface. Would have licked all the silver plating off until she was left with the bloody tasting metal beneath.

I love you, she thought to Pan then. Although she knew she couldn't love her, not really. She didn't know Pan well enough to love her. Ada loves the idea of Pan—she knows this. Though, somehow, she can't quite convince herself that's all it is. Ada is like two selves: the rational self, and the self who curses the rational self under her breath and then hangs out her bedroom window to look for Pan's face in the moon.

Almost a year later and, since having the dream about the compass and what it decided she should pierce, Ada has decided it was right. But Jesus Christ, if she could barely look at Pan, blood burning in her cheeks as she remembered her dream, how is she going to manage to ask her in a professional sort of way to thread a thick needle through the hood of her clit?

What if I get wet? Ada thinks to herself.

She will, she's almost sure. And what then? She can't disguise her lust if biology sells her out.

Another coffee date is in order, she thinks. Coffee, the perfect nonchalant excuse. Everyone needs their cup of coffee. You can dress it up any way you like, tailor a cup to suit each individual taste. And it's a universal code—the perfect way to say that you would like to spend time with someone, but it's not really a big deal. I mean, may as well. May as well sit with you while I drink my requisite cup of coffee. Why don't you just ask someone to join you beside the sink in the morning while you brush your teeth?

But the code has been established so Ada will make use of it. She's exploited it pretty well so far, especially for someone who doesn't even like the stuff. Over coffee she can introduce the idea to Pan casually, but not just as a customer. Barely not just.

She calls the shop.

"Hello?" Pan picks up. Normally at a business people don't just answer the phone like they're at home. The long-haired, bespectacled man who works there doesn't. He has a whole line about good afternoon and you've reached and this is so and so speaking. When you just say hello, people don't know what time of day it is or where they are or who they're talking to. They stutter and get awkward. But Ada knows Pan's voice so she says hey, and asks her how she is.

"I'm good," Pan says. "What can I do for ya?"

And now Ada does stutter, but manages to get her name out. Strange that this nervousness still hasn't worn off. Ada wants so desperately to hear care in Pan's voice that as they speak her body is trying to shrink so it can climb into the tiny holes in the phone, zip down the line, and emerge inside Pan's mouth.

Ada spits it out fast because otherwise she won't be able to ask at all.

"I was wondering if you'd like to have coffee with me."

Pan laughs.

"You don't want a piercing or anything?"

Ada's only ever asked under the pretense of needing nourishment before being pierced. Just coffee is pretty suspicious. She sticks with it though, despite her protesting body, which feels like one fast pulse pumping blood to nowhere.

"Well maybe I do." Ada smiles. "But for now I just kind of want some coffee."

Pan hesitates.

"I thought you didn't like coffee?"

"I'm learning," Ada says. "Remember?"

"Sure," Pan says, and though she resists tacking "kid" on the end, Ada can still hear it. "Meet me at three?"

Ada nods yes, and then realizing Pan can't see that spits out, "Yes, yes."

Pan laughs, a short exhalation of air, and hangs up.

Ada gets dressed. Puts her foot through the frayed hole in the knee of her jeans, pulls it back up, slips it through the hole once more, and finally uses her hand to help her foot reach the bottom. She goes to the kitchen and drinks a glass of water very slowly to kill time.

It's 2:07 now. It takes Ada twenty minutes to walk to the shop or maybe twenty-two, if she has to stop at crosswalks. But wait—no. She's not going to the shop. The café is closer—eighteen minutes if she walks fast, nineteen with the crosswalk. So she should leave at 2:41.

But she doesn't want to get there exactly on time—that's weird. There was this guy who pursued her once, very diligently. He kept calling for her at the house and she kept getting Mattie to answer and say she wasn't home. Mattie would tell her, "He says he'll call back at six." And then he would call at six on the dot, saying he'd call back at eight. And he would, at eight exactly. It was creepy, thinking of him watching the clock, his twitching hand reaching for the phone at 7:59 and him saying no, no. One more minute. Just one. More. Minute.

So Ada tries to relax. But she doesn't want to get so mellow that she winds up late, or too late. What's too late? Ten minutes is too late. Ada wants Pan to know that she cares enough to be on time, to know that she wouldn't want to keep her waiting. She couldn't possibly lose track of time, though. When Pan said three into the phone Ada could feel her body synch up with all of the clocks in the house and start to count down.

"Five minutes is too late," Ada says to herself. "Three minutes is the perfect amount of lateness. 3:03 is a good time. Not late enough to be rude, just casual."

But it's not casual. She will be exactly on time to the minute she's planned. And that's maybe more pathetic, because then she won't just be obsessively punctual but will have planned her lateness.

"It's 2:13 now," she says to herself. "I should leave at 2:44 if I want to get there three minutes late. Plus my shoes take a while to tie if I want to wear my lace-ups, which I do, and I'd like to brush my teeth and look at myself in the mirror, so I'll start to get ready at 2:35. And now it's 2:14, so I have twenty-one minutes."

To do what?

"Listen to music, maybe," she thinks out loud. "Twenty-one minutes is like, what, four or five songs, depending on the band?"

"Oh, god," Ada says. "Stop it. Stop. In and out. Breathe."

In her rubber-soled slippers, she steps outside into the soggy yard and walks toward the tree by the back fence, her footprints turning into small ponds of cold water behind her. The brown January slush soaks into the faux suede of the slippers and she reaches up to grasp the wet, dark bark of the lowest branch. She hauls herself up. The branches offer themselves to her as ladder rungs and she climbs easily until she is fifteen feet up, where she rests, sitting on a thick branch, feeling the cold seep through her jeans and into her skin. She leans against the swaying trunk and stares out through the tree's bare limbs.

When she climbs down and comes inside it's 2:40, so she brushes her teeth, peels off her damp jeans for a dry pair, and stuffs her feet into her skate shoes, kicking her lace-ups out of the hallway and into the closet on her way out the door. She checks her watch outside the café. It's 3:06.

Inside, she scans the shop and doesn't see Pan. Has she come and left? Has she adapted her camouflage so she can hide in here too? She scans again more slowly, her eyes resting on each person inside and declaring them not Pan. She orders a coffee and sits down.

Pan strolls in at 3:08. She's so much better at this than Ada.

"How are you?" Pan smiles down at her.

"I had a weird dream," Ada says.

"Let me get something to drink first," Pan says, holding a finger up to hush her and turning toward the counter.

Ada starts talking as soon as Pan sits down.

"I was lying flat out on my bed and all my piercings started to glow."

Pan sips from her mug, the ceramic cylinder covering half her face, her eyebrows raised very slightly. Ada notices and stops speaking. Pan lowers the mug.

"Go on," she smiles, just on the left side.

"Sorry," Ada blushes. "I can't believe I just started telling you my dream. I should have segued from small talk."

"Nah." Pan grins. "It's not weird. I actually just started a new linocut based on this crazy dream I had the other night."

"Yeah?" Ada says, grateful that Pan's calm nature is settling over the table, smoothing out the kinks of their conversation and lubricating the workings of her brain.

"The dream took place inside a whale," Pan says. "Two lovers lie together in the whale's mouth, on its tongue. They reach out and touch its huge teeth, polished and cool and smooth, like beach glass."

Ada lets Pan's smooth, sand-polished words fall on her like pebbles. When she's trying to be reasonable, she tells herself she's idealized Pan, made her more amazing in her mind than she really is, and that if she ever needed to escape her infatuation, she could dismantle her imagined Pan the same way she has built her up. But then Pan says something like this that needs no doting to make it incredible. There's nothing not amazing about creating art from erotic whale dreams.

"So I've told you mine," Pan says. "Go on, finish yours."

Ada lets the rest of her dream fall out of her mouth, and she's afraid she hasn't done much to veil the want that fuels it, or hide what she's really asking when she says, "Will you?"

Her stomach turns cold and she smiles awkwardly with eyes that plead for gentle judgment, because Pan's looking uncertain. She keeps the mug up by her face. Ada can just see her eyes and they squint a little, as if Pan's trying to bring her into focus, to see some telling detail she's missed.

Pan rolls the mug back and forth in her hands and presses her dry lips together. Looking at Ada, in a low and quiet voice, she says, "Okay," like she thinks she'll be sorry. And then, after a pause, "Do you want to do it now?"

They walk to the shop without saying much more and Pan's a step ahead of Ada all the way there. She unlocks the door and leaves her handwritten note (*gone for coffee, back soon*) taped to the glass. The tattoo artists don't work Mondays, so they're alone.

Ada gets up on the table without prompting and Pan shoves the sticking door into its tight frame. She looks through drawers for the right needles and jewellery.

"You're sure you want this?" she asks, looking over her shoulder.

Ada nods very certainly.

Pan sounds less casual than Ada's used to and it makes her nervous. She feels like she's in a dream.

Pan comes to her with bare hands. No words, but they look at each other and with finger and thumb Pan reaches over and unbuttons Ada's jeans. Pulls at the top of the fabric and the zipper undoes itself. Slowly, slowly, Ada inches out, lifting her hips left and right, dry paper scratching her buzzing flesh. The brush of Pan's ungloved fingers on her body fills her with a swarm of bees that fly zipping just under her skin. If sips of Pan's scent before were like the drops of wine her mother used to feed her from her finger as a baby, then this is like swimming in a bathtub of homemade red. Fruit and sugar and acid staining her lips and fingers and clothes. Pan smells like sweet warm bread, bitter nicotine, iodine. Ada drinks her in, breathes her scent so deep she can taste it. Pan looks up at her through the loose curls that fall against her forehead. Her lips crook in a grin.

And finally Ada knows what it's like to slip her tongue past Pan's serrated teeth. Pan slides her palm smooth and firm up Ada's side, fingers climbing her ribcage, one rung at a time. Ada breathes out shaky, like when the doctor has her cold stethoscope pressed into her chest. Pan kisses her full and hard—their teeth knock and it rattles through Ada. With every kiss and touch Pan presses into her, sharp and wanting, and then pulls back the slightest bit, Ada can feel it. Her lips hurt already from Pan's bite. They sting and swell as if she had pepper in her spit.

Ada's hands twist tissue paper on the table. She unlocks her stiff fingers from around the pieces she's torn and lifts them up around the clothed form of Pan's body. She doesn't touch. And then, as they kiss with sharp teeth and shining lips, Ada places her hands soft on the sides of Pan's neck—and Pan grabs her hips and slides her across the table, tissue paper tearing, and slams her against the wall. She grabs Ada's legs, one in each hand, and lifts them to rest on her shoulders so she can pull off her jeans.

They look each other full in the face, Pan grinning her half grin and looking at Ada like, what the hell are we doing?

And now Pan's mouth, warm between Ada's legs. She's so hard she moans like she hurts she wants her inside filling her up in every place she could fit. Pan fucks her thick and smooth, fingers curve and press deep and strong.

Strange to be seeing with open eyes what she always sees behind closed lids when her spine arches and body flushes as she tips over the edge by the skill of her own hand. Pan draws circles on her like in her dream and bites Ada's still-angry nipples, teeth clicking on metal. Ada breathes quick and hot and she is submerged by a tide that doesn't come in growing swells but as a rogue wave that drags her under before she has a chance to take one last gulping breath. Her lungs fill with salt water and she thinks she will drown until she realizes she can breathe it now. She would swim around in a daze like a lazy fish if the snap of gloves and flash of metal didn't catch her attention. Curved hook punctures and slides through tender skin and Pan pulls her to the surface, spluttering.

18

January 10, 2008

"**I** wouldn't be surprised if they tore down the Square next."

Betty has barely touched her dinner, she's so angry.

"Aw Grandma, they wouldn't do that," Shawn says, shaking his head. "Yuppies don't want to live in the Square."

"Haven't you been listening to your father?" Betty counters. "They don't want to live there, but they'd tear it down. Probably set up another dog park. Bet you didn't think they'd want to live on Gottingen either, and now look at all the condos."

Late last week the owner of a rat hotel with a sunken-in roof on Gottingen Street started making plans to sell his property to a developer, and Ken will likely be part of the crew to tear it down. Better a rat-infested eyesore than a sterile new condo, some folks in the neighbourhood said. Stores and people have already been evicted from buildings with affordable rent on the street. And the lots are being snapped up to be converted into eco-chic urban lofts so tall you can gaze out your window right past the subsidized housing to the glimmering blue of the harbour.

"It's true," Ken says to Shawn. "Half a dozen condos are going up around there. They've got me tearing down buildings, other folks building them up or converting them. They're moving in, that's for sure."

Kiah hadn't really been listening to the dinner conversation up until now. She started her second semester of classes earlier that week and has been trying her best to keep up with the impossible amount of reading assigned by all her profs. But her grandmother's words have managed to creep in through her concentration.

"So does that mean all the people in our neighbourhood go the way of the Carters?" she asks, closing her book. "Does rent just get so expensive that we can't live here anymore?"

Ken chews his stew for a while before he speaks.

"Renters could get forced out, I guess. Our rent could be raised and it might make sense to move somewhere more affordable. The owners could make a killing selling now that the area's getting popular. A small killing, anyway."

"But I don't want to move," Kiah says.

"Yeah, but would you want to live here if all the people on the street were like our new neighbours?" asks Shawn. "Who don't come over to say hi and don't look at you when they pass you on the street? Not me."

"Not me either," Betty says. "The grandmother's nice enough, but they're not real neighbours. And you know the people in those condos don't even know each other's names."

As if one eviction wasn't enough, Betty thinks. Now they're pushing us out of the part of the city they stuck us in in the first place. A bit more subtly this time, but still. After so many years she finally felt like she'd made herself a home, and now this.

"You don't really think they'd tear down the Square do you, Grandma?" Kiah asks.

"Don't you?" Betty asks, pointing her fork at her granddaughter. "You think they care about us? They won't even build our church back up. Don't wait for anything from the City. You'll wait forever."

No one talks for the rest of the meal. Kiah doesn't open her book and sits in silence, letting her father's and grandmother's words sink in, turning them over in her mind and thinking of what's to come. If her mom were alive, Kiah's sure she'd be spearheading some campaign, sitting on the phone all evening, calling friends and relatives.

She'll never understand how her mom found time between nursing shifts to be so involved. Kiah can barely keep up with school on its own, with all the readings and assignments. Leona's reputation is quite the thing to live up to and she's doing her best. But some people are superhuman. They literally do it all. It's almost annoying. Her mother was one of those women. Raising her kids with plenty of care, keeping things good with her husband, even if it meant staying up late on a work night to talk out an argument. And she was always being commended for her work as a nurse. She had a healing touch and a soothing voice, her patients said. Just having her in the room made them feel better. When she died, the whole community grieved. There were people over at the house every night for weeks, sharing stories, cooking food, looking at photos, and crying.

Kiah admires her mom. She really does. But a quiet part of her wishes Leona had done just a little less. Partly because then, maybe, her body would have been strong enough to survive. Did she work herself to death? Long hours at Camp Hill and in organizing meetings like a constant, low-grade storm, weathering her, wearing her down. And also, though she'd never say it out loud, if Leona had done less, Kiah could give herself a break now and then. How can you ever feel accomplished when your mom set the bar so high above your head you can't even touch it if you jump, like a little kid on a jungle gym? Some of Kiah's friends were the first in their families to even go to university. As soon as they got in they were success stories. But Kiah is like a little plant trying to grow at the shady feet of the glorious statue of Leona which, though the City would never fund such a thing, stands nevertheless in the minds of pretty much everyone she knows. *Honey*, she can hear her mother saying, *you're not a plant at my feet, you're a strong young woman standing on my shoulders, just like I stood on the shoulders of my ancestors and they on the shoulders of*—. Kiah gets it. But still she feels like a little plant.

IN THE BASEMENT, SHAWN'S THUMBS twitch and click over plastic buttons as he sits slumped on the couch. Fuck Kiah, he thinks. Nothing wrong with playing a game. It's a fucking game. Now that she's in school she thinks she knows every goddamn thing. And it's all "problematic." TV is problematic. Ads are problematic. Music is problematic. Video games are problematic. Kiah's got no idea how to relax and just enjoy life anymore.

Shawn jumps from rooftop to rooftop in his beat-up, stolen car. His sister's crazy. He knows this isn't real. But as he drives by the pixellated ladies on the strip, he thinks a bit about what she said.

"I'll do anything for you!" a Black girl calls to him. His friend Kyle, a white kid Shawn's age with his own apartment off Quinpool Road, showed him once how to get your health levels up without wasting any money. It's Kyle's favourite trick in this game, he said.

Last time they hung out, Shawn sat on Kyle's duct-taped couch, feeling sick. It's the weed, he told himself. I'm just hungry and took too big of a toke, went to my head too fast. But he couldn't shake the feeling as he watched the screen—the car rocking, the girl leaving, and Kyle clicking the controls, chasing her down, beating her with a bat so spurts of blood sprung from her head, throwing petrol bombs at her until she was screaming, rolling on the ground in flames, and finally, pulling out the Uzi and filling her with bullets. And then collecting the dough.

Shawn pauses the game and sits on the couch, frozen in the cold glow of the TV.

"Fuck," he says out loud.

A FEW YEARS AGO LEONA sat down to talk to him about the music he'd been listening to. He'd been playing it in his room, sitting on the floor, nodding his head, and rapping along to the chorus when he looked up and saw his mother in the doorway, arms crossed. He reached over and turned the volume down.

"Sorry Mom, too loud?"

"No baby, the volume's okay." She stepped over a pile of clothes on the floor and sat down on the edge of his bed. "I want to talk to you about the lyrics."

Shawn was fourteen and had saved enough money to start buying his own CDs. The bestsellers at HMV that he would bring to school and show his friends. They knew all the lyrics, would walk around town together rapping songs in synch.

"Do you know what you're saying when you're rapping these songs?" his mother asked.

"Yeah," Shawn said, not sure where she was going.

"Okay, let me put it this way. How would you feel if someone called your sister a ho?"

Shawn laughed in surprise at the question.

"I dunno. She's not."

"Okay, well what would you think if someone called me a ho, or a bitch? How would that make you feel?"

"Angry," Shawn said.

"So what about the women these rappers are talking about? The women in their videos? Don't you think some of them are sisters, or mothers?"

"I guess," Shawn said, looking up at her.

"And besides that, that they have hearts and brains and deserve respect, just like Kiah and I do?"

"Yeah, I guess."

"They do, baby. Don't you think we should stick together and not disrespect one another?"

Shawn nodded his head.

"Plus these rappers," she picked up a CD case lying on the floor. "I bet they don't even write their own rhymes. Just doing what their labels tell them to so they can sell more records. There's better, smarter music you can listen to."

Shawn took the CD from his mother.

"That's not true, Mom. You don't know that. Just because you listened to different stuff way back when doesn't mean I have to listen to it too. Music changes, you know."

Leona gave Shawn a soft punch in the shoulder.

"Way back when, huh? Are you calling your mama old? Huh?"

Shawn laughed.

"Look, I'm not saying you have to listen to Grand Master Flash tapes all day, but there's good music out there by men who respect women, you know? Who write rhymes about politics and history. You could even listen to women rap about themselves. There's some good stuff out there. I don't want you to miss out."

On the frozen TV screen floats a little box, a list of what Shawn
can say to the girl:

I'd say you're worth $20.
I'm with my buddy, how 'bout a 2-for-1 deal?
Get lost ugly bitch.
Men who respect women.

19

June 2, 1949

For the rest of the school year Mattie waited for a sign from Edith. Whenever they were able to lock eyes undetected, she would raise her eyebrows as if to say, "Soon?" and Edith would shake her head no, ever so slightly. Mattie didn't want to get Edith in trouble, but she so badly wanted to talk to her again. To hear more about the dress, the school. About Edith's family and home. Mattie didn't bother with the boring girls in class. They wrote childish poems and were too concerned with their hair and would never have drowned their dresses in the river. But she was sure that she and Edith could be such great friends. Like Anne and Diana, even. Except that white and Indian kids did not mix. Her teacher had made sure everyone understood this on the first day of school: no one was to talk to or even look at the Mi'kmaw girl. But a secret friendship was all the more exciting.

It was not until the last month of school that Mattie asked Edith again with her eyes and got a tiny smile in return. She could hear her heart beating while she sat as still as she could at her desk.

Shhh, she thought to the excitable muscle. Don't give me away.

As the students filed out the door at the end of the day, Mattie walked close behind Edith, looking for a sign. In Edith's dangling hand she spied a small piece of paper slotted between two fingers. Her hand darted forward to snatch it. In front of her, Edith suppressed a grin.

Mattie glanced into her palm.

Follow me Sparrow.

Fifty paces behind, so no one would guess their plan, Mattie followed Edith along the road. As the road to the Resi came parallel to the Shubenacadie River, Edith stepped off the path and began to follow the water instead. Then she started to run. She ran downhill through the brush until she came to the bank of the muddy red river where it bowed out furthest from the road. She turned around breathless and hid behind a bush, waiting.

Mattie came stumbling along shortly after.

"Boo!" Edith shouted as Mattie neared her hiding spot.

In her surprise Mattie tripped, slipping down the muddy bank.

"Oh, shoot!" Edith called, laughing, running out from behind the bush. "Are you hurt?"

Mattie beamed up at her.

"Just a little muddy."

Her yellow socks were soaked with mud and it clung thickly to her shoes, her legs like birthday candles pulled from a cake.

"I'm clumsy."

"No," Edith said. "I shouldn't have scared you."

She grabbed Mattie by the arm and pulled her to her feet. A strand of hair stuck to Edith's lip where she'd licked it. Mattie was close enough to see. She swallowed and smiled as if the hair meant nothing. What conversations had she imagined between them since that day the dress was drowned? Mattie had never had trouble talking to the other girls at school, though she didn't really care what they thought of her. But what would she normally say? What do people say to one another?

Words, any words. Mattie scanned the landscape for help. Water, grass, mud, sky. Come on, she begged her tongue, but it lay on the floor of her mouth like a mussel.

"I wanted to tell you I liked your poem," Edith finally said.

"Thanks," Mattie replied. "And I liked yours, too."

Anything else? she implored her brain. Please.

"They found my dress, you know. I was strapped."

Mattie's mouth filled with spit. She'd never been strapped. Her father strapped her brother once for back talk and she had been horrified by the marks.

"I swear I never told a soul," she said.

"I know you didn't."

"How?" Mattie asked.

"The birds would've told me if you had," Edith replied with a wink.

Mattie smiled and glanced at Edith's lip, but the loose hair had been tucked behind an ear. Their feet ambled as if with their own plan, narrowing the space between them at what could pass for random intervals so their elbows could brush.

Reach for her hand, something inside Mattie suggested. But she couldn't make her own hand move.

Then it became a challenge. Was she chicken? What was Mattie afraid of?

All right, she told herself in the tone she used to boss her sister. By the time we've passed that tree, you'd better have done it.

"So your brother was in the war?" Edith asked.

"Yeah, he was a soldier."

"And he was killed?"

"He was."

You should feel sad for him, Mattie thought to herself, and promised she would later, as an addendum to her nightly prayers. Right then all she could think about was taking Edith's hand. Do it, she told herself, and reached out.

Edith felt Mattie's warm hand slide into her own. But it wasn't a hand—it was a snare, and Edith's hand a caught rabbit. This is very bad, a voice rattled deep in her ear. You cannot touch. Her rabbit hand made to struggle loose. But Edith didn't want to hear the nun's voice anymore. She hadn't held hands with a friend since she was small, before she was pushed through the doors of the poisonous school. She shook her head to quiet the sound. Mattie's hand is not a snare, she told herself. It's gentle. Heat bloomed across her chest.

"What will you do when school's finished?" Mattie asked, her tongue finally a tongue again. Careful, she told her eyes, keeping them trained ahead. A nervous laugh hung in her throat.

"I don't know," Edith said. "Go back to my family I suppose." She felt Mattie's thumb trace a circle around her knuckle and her head filled with fireflies.

"Will you get married?" Now why would you ask that? Be normal, Mattie implored herself.

Edith hadn't thought about it.

"I don't know. Will you?"

"Someday I suppose," Mattie said, glancing at Edith. "My mother's always asking me about boys at school. She and my dad got married real young."

"Won't that mean that your husband's in charge of everything?"

"Some things I guess. Isn't it that way for you?"

"No," Edith said. "Or at least, it didn't use to be. No one bosses my mother. And she never asks me about boys. Though I don't see her much."

The early summer sun began to dip below the trees as they walked along the riverbank with hands clasped, the mud caking new soles onto their shoes, making them taller for a few steps before it fell off again. Like they were older, and somewhere else.

"I have to go back," Edith said. "It's getting late. I'm sure I'm in trouble by now."

She felt nervous, but not the way she had for all those years before. Her time at the Resi was nearly through. Instead of the cold stones she'd grown used to housing in her stomach, this anxiousness lived in her hands and feet. They weren't so much scared, but restless. Like horses kept on a lead at the edge of a field, waiting for the knot to be undone.

"Maybe when we're out of school we can be friends," Mattie said, like it was possible. "We live so close. Maybe I can see you this summer."

Edith smiled at the unlikeliness of it. "Maybe," she said.

Mattie let her eyes stray from the path ahead to Edith's, which caught and held them. They already had a secret language. A silent speech that could only be understood when standing very close to another speaker. Without having to coax herself Mattie reached for Edith's other hand and stepped closer. Such little distance between them meant they had to choose which of each other's eyes to look into, pupils shifting back and forth as if reading pages of coded meaning behind their few words. Mattie tilted her face up to Edith as a question and Edith answered her with a kiss like a glowing gift.

"There you are, you little heathen!"

The nun's angry shout ripped the girls apart.

"What in God's name are you doing?" she bellowed. Two young students trailed behind her, running clumsily through the brush.

"Run, Sparrow," Edith whispered.

Mattie couldn't move. Edith pulled her hands away and gave her a shove, but she wouldn't leave.

The nun continued to blunder down the hill to the bank, holding her pointed black cap down with one hand, her robes flapping behind her. Edith could see anger boiling up in her mottled face. She wouldn't allow herself to cower, and clenched her teeth.

As the nun ran closer she drew back her hand and struck Edith hard across the cheek.

"Girls, take Edith back to school. I will deal with her later," the nun instructed.

"And you," she turned to Mattie. "I will escort you home."

The two younger girls attached themselves to Edith's arms and turned to walk her toward the Resi. The nun directed Mattie back down the school road toward town, and then west on the road to her house.

"What she was doing to you, I can't imagine," the nun fussed. "They are untameable. Just when you think there's an ounce of hope for them, that they've seen the light, they show their true nature."

Mattie couldn't speak. She cringed at the nun's touch. In the distance, the sun glowed red.

"LET ME GO," EDITH ORDERED THE GIRLS. One was Susan's younger sister, the little creep. Edith tugged the arm she held, testing her grip. "Shirley, I mean it."

They shook their heads.

"Sister said for us to take you back," Shirley said solemnly.

Edith sighed.

"I want to wipe my mouth, for crying out loud. It's bleeding."

The other girl let go and Edith pulled her arm free from Shirley's hands and pushed her to the ground.

"Don't follow me," she shouted as she ran off, around the lake and through the trees, toward the reserve.

The sun was sinking. The girls had no desire to run after Edith into the darkening woods. Her feet cracked through the floor of the forest, snapping twigs and crunching leaves as she ran. When she came to her parents' house, the sky was dark. She could see her father through the window, sitting at the kitchen table. Edith staggered through the door and into the light.

"*Tu's!*" her father cried, jumping up from his chair.

Her mother ran into the room and wrapped herself around her daughter.

"What did they do to you?" she demanded, holding Edith's face in her hands and wiping the blood from her lips. "My God," she said, looking at her husband.

"The Mounties will be here soon to take her back," he said, worried.

"Then she has to leave," her mother replied. "We'll give her money for the train."

Edith wished she could stay in her parents' home. It smelled so good, like it always had. Her mother's arms around her, after all of those years at school where any touching was forbidden, made her cry.

"But the train won't leave tonight, *oqoti*. They'll find her."

"What do you want to do, Edith?" her mother asked, her hands smoothing hair and salty tears from her daughter's face.

Stay with you, Edith thought. But she knew that was impossible. "I don't want to go back," she said. "I can't."

Before she left, Edith ate a bowl of hot stew. Her mother gave her bread to take and wrapped money in a piece of cloth that she pinned inside the hem of Edith's skirt. She gave her daughter her own coat and shoes, as they now had the same size feet, and Edith left behind the ill-fitting school shoes she had been wearing all year.

Her mother and father each held her close before they let her go, and Edith walked out into the quiet night, out to the road, in search of a car that would take her away.

WHEN MATTIE AND THE NUN reached her house the sun had still not set, but she could barely feel its heat on her face. She was numb with worry. What would happen to Edith?

The nun rapped on the door and Mattie's father answered immediately, as if he had been waiting with his fingers on the handle. He looked startled to see the sister in her black robes and hood beside his muddy daughter, surprise chasing anger from his face.

"Martha, where on earth have you been?" he demanded, not sure whether to be furious or concerned. "Grace," he called tensely toward the kitchen. "Your daughter's home."

Mattie's mother rushed to the door with Mattie's sister, Linda, close behind, small fists gripping her mother's dress.

"Thank you, Sister," he said to the nun, taking over her hold on Mattie's wrist and drawing her inside. "Please come in and sit down," he offered, taking a seat himself at the kitchen table. "Martha, sit."

The nun introduced herself.

"Perhaps we can speak alone," she suggested, her mouth tight. "I fear your daughter has been badly influenced by a student at my school."

"At the Residential School? An Indian boy?" Mattie's father stood up from his chair, fists clenched and face reddening.

"Perhaps we can speak alone," the nun repeated.

"All right," he agreed, breathing heavily through his nostrils. "Grace, put the girls to bed. Now."

Mattie's mother did not speak as she ushered the girls into their shared room, too flustered to tell Mattie to wash up or to give Linda a goodnight kiss. She closed the door behind her. The kitchen light shone through the crack beneath it, but the adults spoke in low voices and Mattie couldn't make out what they were saying. She padded across the linoleum in her mud-caked socks and put her ear to the gap.

"Mattie!"

"Shut up, Linda," Mattie whispered.

The nun's stern voice vibrated through the thick wood.

"The girl will be punished, I assure you. It's no wonder they're prone to such sin. They're born into heathen households. They know no morality."

"Thank you for bringing her home, Sister," her father said.

Mattie crept back across the room, peeled off her damp clothes, and slid into bed as her father showed the nun out. Her parents went to their bedroom, where she could no longer listen, and closed the door. Mattie lay on her back, staring up at the ceiling. If anything, she thought, she had been a bad influence on Edith. It was she who had pursued her so determinedly. After she had seen Edith in the woods by the river, she wondered about her often. Looked for her every time she caught a glint of sun on a wing.

I shouldn't have followed her, Mattie thought. She saw how the nun had struck her. How hard would she hit Edith once she had her inside the school walls?

Mattie brought her hands to her lips, kissed the palm that had been pressed into Edith's, and prayed.

"What are you doing?" her sister asked from across the room. "Are you crying?"

"Go to sleep, Linda," Mattie ordered, her voice cracking and muffled behind her hand.

But Linda climbed out of her own bed and into Mattie's, cuddled up to her, and clumsily stroked her hair.

"Your feet are freezing," Mattie said, glad for her sister's company in the dark.

IN THE MORNING, MATTIE SAT nervously at the kitchen table, waiting for her father's verdict to drop. She couldn't stop thinking about Edith. What had happened to her? Had she been strapped? Would they let her come back to school? Would Mattie see her again? Chairs squeaked and forks scraped and mouths chewed loudly into the silence as her father sipped his coffee, not looking up at anyone. Just before Mattie could get up to gather her books for school, he spoke.

"You won't be going to school today, Martha."

She sat still in her chair, watching as he continued to sip his coffee and pretend to read the paper.

"You will help your mother around the house today."

That's all? she thought.

"Can I stay home too?" her sister asked.

"No, Linda. Only Martha."

"Phooey," Linda said, kicking her little legs under the table.

"Linda," her mother warned, and took her firmly by the hand over to the front door to put on her jacket. Her hands shook as she wrestled with the sticking zipper on her daughter's knitted cardigan.

"But why does Mattie get to stay home and I have to go to school?"

"That's enough, Linda," her mother muttered, and as she yanked, the zipper unstuck and zipped all the way up to Linda's chin, nipping her skin with its metal teeth. Shocked by the pain, Linda began to wail and her mother gave her a quick pat on the back and pushed her out the door.

At home all day, Mattie swept and mopped and dusted the house. But when Grace brought out a ham and told her to start cutting apples for a pie, Mattie began to wonder. This didn't seem like punishment.

"Are we having guests for dinner?"

"The Campbells," her mother replied.

The Campbells had lived down the road from them all Mattie's life. Their eldest son had also not returned from the war, and it had brought their mothers very close. When she was young, Mattie would often play with their younger son, but as they grew older and Mattie became bolder, he became quieter and more subdued. He was gentle and soft-spoken and was picked on at school for it. It wasn't that he was small or weak, he just didn't like confrontation. As the students filed out through the school doors at the end of the day, boys would trip him up or push him down, kicking his books out of reach and jeering. Mattie would holler at them and they would move on, but the boy was too ashamed to thank her, gathering his books, eyes on the ground. He had once turned around to give her a quick nod, but that was all.

"What's the occasion?" Mattie asked.

"You know their son, Ian," her mother said, shredding lettuce for a salad. "Your father and I thought the two of you should be reacquainted." Mattie studied her mother as she slowly peeled the apples. Grace stood rigid, working briskly at the cutting board, her hands tense as she sliced the leaves.

"I see him every day at school."

"Well, Martha," her mother said as she chopped. "Your father and I thought, now that you're seventeen, almost finished school and— dammit!" she popped her bleeding finger into her mouth.

"Mother!"

It was not often that Mattie heard her mother curse.

"I'll get you a Band-Aid," she said, and went to the bathroom to find the tin.

What are they trying to pull? Mattie wondered. If they think they can set me up on a date with Ian, they have another thing coming. She liked Ian as a friend and felt protective of him like he was family, but they hadn't had a good conversation in years. He was so meek and boring.

Mattie took the Band-Aid out of its wrapper and began to wind it around the tip of her mother's finger.

"I'll do it," her mother snapped when Mattie touched her, taking the bandage from her daughter. "Just see to the apples, Martha. They're turning brown. Put them in a salt bath."

Mattie's mother told her to wear her new pleated skirt and blouse. She gave her daughter a pair of her own silk stockings and helped her curl her hair with the hot iron.

"Don't you look nice," she said to Mattie in the mirror, though it didn't sound like a compliment. "Why don't you put on some lipstick?" she offered.

"No, thank you," Mattie replied.

"This one would go well with your complexion, Martha." She rolled up the tube and applied it to her daughter's lips. "Now come help me set the table."

Linda had come home from school and was hopping around the kitchen asking questions.

"What smells good? Why's Mattie dressed up? Who's coming over? Can I wear some lipstick? What happened to your finger?"

But she was shushed and sent to wash up.

The Campbells arrived at six, dressed smartly. Ian's hair was slicked back and his mother could barely help herself from continually smoothing pieces of it down. Every time she reached toward her son's head, her husband cleared his throat.

"Hi Ian, Mr. and Mrs. Campbell," Mattie said flatly.

"Hi Mattie," Ian said, as if in apology.

Mattie felt sorry for him. He too was probably forced to dress nicely and put on a show for their parents. He looked miserable.

During the meal the children were silent. The fathers talked politics and summer fishing plans and the mothers talked about new folks in town, dresses to be bought, recipes to share. Everyone complimented the ham, and Grace diverted the compliments to Mattie.

"What a wonderful cook you are, Martha," Mrs. Campbell smiled, patting her hand.

After they had eaten the apple pie, Mattie's father cleared his throat for the speech he had been rehearsing all day.

"And now for our special announcement. Faye, Jim, you have been wonderful friends to Grace and I over the years. It was a very sad time for both of our families to share the loss of our sons. I'm happy this evening for us to come together over a far more joyous event. In response to Ian's request for Martha's hand in marriage, I am proud to give my permission and celebrate with you as our families join together."

"What?" Mattie demanded, shocked, as the parents clapped and clinked their wine glasses together. "What?" It was all she could say. Her mother and father wouldn't look at her. Ian studied his plate. It didn't seem as if he'd had much say in this decision either. In her confusion, Linda started to cry.

"Oh dear," said her mother. "It seems our Linda is getting tired. Off to bed!" She pulled Linda's chair back and took her hand as Linda cried into her sleeve.

"We are so happy to welcome you into the family, Martha," Mrs. Campbell said, raising her glass.

Mattie felt like she was going to be sick.

Mr. Campbell elbowed his son.

"Ian's a lucky man," he grinned. "I'm sure you'll make a wonderful wife."

Ian could barely bring himself to look Mattie in the eye. Was this a dream? Like the one where you're on fire in the middle of town and no one notices? Why wouldn't her parents look at her? Mattie got up from the table with her cheeks burning and her head spinning slanted like a wheel out of true. She could hear her father calling her name as she made for the bathroom. She closed the door behind her and slid down the wall onto the cold floor. "What?" she whispered again. She had not seen this coming.

She heard the Campbells leaving and her father's footsteps. The bathroom door opened with a jerk and he stood in the doorframe looking like a stranger.

"What is wrong with you?" he said. His voice was quiet so Linda wouldn't wake but it vibrated with ire. "Get up off the floor."

Mattie felt like she was made of water and couldn't move.

"Listen to me," her father said, grabbing her by the wrist and hauling her to her feet. "You will act as a good, Christian daughter and do as I say, or I will report the Indian girl to the Mounties and you will be sent to the hospital in Dartmouth for treatment. Do you understand?"

Mattie tried to talk but her throat was thick. Tears slid into her mouth.

"She's just my f-friend, we're friends," she stuttered.

Her father jerked her toward him, his mouth close to her face and fingers tightening.

"Your mother and I won't endure embarrassment for the sake of your unnatural friendship. You will go with the Campbells' son to Halifax as his wife or you will go to the hospital across the harbour until you are yourself again."

He released her arm and Mattie fell back to the floor, made of water and leaking everywhere.

20

January 10, 2008

Body-drunk again, but a thousand times more stumbling than the blue-haired boy ever made her. Ada sees Pan's black curls and the sharp lines of her jaw fitting into the V of her split thighs. Did that happen? She presses her fingers against the front of her jeans and the sharp pain of the new metal suggests insistently that it did.

Her cheeks burn so red they pulse. Ada catches the toes of her sex-drunk feet on every salty sidewalk crack, but catches herself just before she trips over a soft grey something in her path. A bird. Pigeon. Did it drop out of the sky, frozen in the frigid air? Ada doesn't really want to look closer, but then again she does. Red something. Red neck. Have the crows got to it already?

No, it's something else, because crows wouldn't do this. She can see now from this angle—its head has been pulled off. It's still attached, lying a few inches from its body, connected by thick sinewy muscle. So red, under all those silver-blue feathers.

She wishes she could put the head back in. There's a perfect dip, right where the red rope comes out of the bird body, where the head would rest if the pigeon were sleeping. It reminds her of talking toys she had when she was small. She was so eager to have them speak to her that she would yank their cords hard and break them. The cords would dangle from the backs of bears and dolls and not retract, rendering the toys speechless. So who did this? Not someone eager to hear life come from something lifeless, but to make life less.

Does Ada's eagerness break things? She wonders if Pan will still talk to her after today. Can she call again? Will Pan touch her again? Or did she pull too hard, pull too close, break the flimsy string that connects them with her wanting?

The pigeon head on a string lies on its side, glazed eye open and staring at the sky. Ada wants to move it but she can't bring herself to touch it. She's shaking. Her cheeks are cold. She takes a last look and walks sober down the sidewalk.

Ada left Pan with only a thank you, but they locked eyes and she was sure Pan could see how dismembered she felt. Maybe the pulled-apart pigeon is not what Ada did to Pan but what Pan did to her. Ada feels cut apart, cut apart and put hastily back together. The way Pan cleverly, skillfully, removed her clothes—a dissection. She pinned her down to the table, pierced her through the centre after pulling apart the folds, then let go and breathed out a quiet, unbelieving laugh.

"I won't charge you for that one," she joked, as she turned her back and started to clean up. Ada pulled herself together, stitched herself up, buttons mismatched with buttonholes, fly undone. Seeping through sutures, wet through her jeans.

I can't go home yet, she thought. She was too shaken, is still shaking. So she walks down to the water along the damp harbour planks, past the docks and along the gravel path to the cold rocks. She sits down and lets the chill travel up through her body.

"Jesus," she says into the sharp wind. "Jesus Christ."

If she smoked she would want a cigarette. She does, maybe only because it's one of the flavours that make up Pan's taste. But there's something about a cigarette between numb fingers while sitting on dark oceanside rocks that feels right.

How did that even happen? It won't happen again. Will it happen again? Ada wants it to happen again and again. She wants it to happen now. She wants to go back to the shop, shove the sticking door out of its frame, stride into Pan's room, and show her that she can split her too. That her fingers and tongue can learn the codes of Pan's body and make her come.

Fuck, she thinks. I want a cigarette.

She would jump into the ocean if there wasn't a washed up tampon a few rocks over. And if it wasn't so bitterly cold.

The dusk steals a few more degrees from the winter air and her body's desire for survival kicks in, but Ada can't go home yet. What lights glow and where can she go? Back up on one of the main streets, only a pizza shop and a convenience store are still open. She chooses the latter.

At the counter she asks for the blue pack on the bottom shelf because she likes the design. And because they aren't what Pan smokes. Pan uses a lighter so Ada opts for matches. Plus she's cheap and matches are free.

Outside, her hands don't know how to do this. Hold smoke between lips and somehow light and shield match from the wind at once. Two, three matches drop dead on the sidewalk. Finally one blazes long enough to singe the tip and Ada inhales, her lungs burning as if in some kind of flaming-heart religious fervour. The nicotine numbs her and she feels strange.

She wanders home lightheaded, peering into the lit windows along the street like a creepy moth. You're not supposed to stare, but wouldn't her neighbours just close their curtains if they really cared? She knows this is bad reasoning but continues to look. Televisions bathe living rooms in blue, a small window fogs with shower steam. A cat sits sentry on a sill. In the house next to hers on the top floor, her neighbour is reading at her desk by lamplight as usual, her shoulders hunched and head propped on hand. And in Ada's house, a dim glow comes from the kitchen. She walks in to see a wispy old woman in a nightgown, teetering on a wooden chair to reach the whisky Joan keeps on top of the cupboard.

"E...Edith?"

It takes Ada a second to realize the ghostly woman is Mattie and she rushes over to steady her. Mattie grabs her hand tight and keeps reaching up.

"Nan, what are you doing?" Ada asks.

"Just want a little nip before bed," she says. "My bedroom's so cold."

"I can get that for you. Do you want to come down?"

"No Joanie. I'm fine," she says. "I can reach it."

Joan is away for a few days, doing interviews in Digby for a story on fisheries. Ada had forgotten her mother had already left. I should've been home, she thinks. Nan could have broken her hip, or worse.

"It's Ada, Nan. You sure you don't want me to reach that?"

Mattie looks down at her granddaughter and smiles.

"Hello, sweet girl," she says, and touches Ada's cheek with the hand that had been reaching. Her eyes unfocus and she sways as the blood rushes back to her arm from her head. Ada steadies her, placing her other hand on her grandmother's waist. Mattie steps down from the chair.

"Did you want the Glenfiddich?" Ada asks.

"Yep," she says. "The good stuff."

Ada takes the bottle down and looks in the cupboard for Mattie's favourite whisky glass.

"The green one, if you please," she says, and Ada nods as she finds it near the back.

"One for yourself, child," Mattie scolds as Ada sets the glass on the table.

Mattie pours the whisky, her hands shaking. Ada's not a fan of it. It burns her throat and gives her liquor shivers, but Mattie sips it like liquid candy and Ada can almost see her getting warmer, a glow that spreads out from her belly.

"So," Mattie says. "Tell me more about the fisherman."

"Fisherman, Nan?"

"The one who keeps hooking you, my girl."

"Oh," Ada says. "Well, she's a woman."

"I know that. Man, woman, they're all fishermen to me."

"Right," Ada smiles. "Well...I don't know. What do you want to know?"

"For starters," Mattie says, taking a long sip with her eyes closed. "How's she for a kisser?"

"Ah…" Ada laughs bashfully. "Well, she's good." She stares into her glass, grinning. "Really good."

"That metal doesn't get in the way, does it?" Mattie asks. "She doesn't chomp on it?"

"Nope." Ada shakes her head.

"Well good. I don't understand why you're so keen on those things but so long as you aren't biting down on them and chipping your teeth or swallowing them in your sleep, no harm."

Mattie raises her glass and Ada meets it with her own. They swig what's left in their cups and Mattie pours them each another finger.

"And how's Edith, for a kisser?" Ada asks.

Mattie pauses and stares beyond her granddaughter, tapping the pads of her fingers on her glass. "She was better when she was alive, but she's still not ba—ouch!" she shouts and looks behind her.

"You rascal!" she hollers, swatting at something as it moves past.

"I didn't hear her come in," Mattie explains. "She's better than not bad. She's very good."

She rubs her arm.

"Wait—Nan," Ada says, incredulous. "You knew Edith when she was alive?"

"Of course I did. When I was a girl."

"In Shubenacadie?"

"Yes, in Shubenacadie. Just before I married your grandad."

21

✦

January 11, 2008

Shawn sits on the couch in the basement, swigging a pop. He turns on the console and basks in the familiar glow. He took some time off from it. Just needed a bit of a break, he told himself.

But when his saved game loads onto the screen and he's back on the strip, where the girls are begging him to take them into his car, he starts to feel sick again. The drink bubbles in his empty stomach and he can feel the acid rising in his throat.

"Stop it, you pussy," he says out loud and slumps down into position.

But he can't do it. He can barely drive down the road straight. All he can think of is his mother and what she would say if she saw this game. She would ream him out worse than his sister did, he knows it. His stomach gurgles as the neon soda threatens to climb farther up.

He flicks the machine off and trudges up the stairs.

"Hey Grandma," he says to Betty, who sits at the kitchen table working on a crossword.

"Hey my boy," she says. "Weren't you supposed to get out of the house and look for a job today?"

"Tomorrow," he says.

"Why not today? Just go drop off a few resumés."

"Like where? McDonald's? No one wants to hire me so I'm not gonna bother. It's embarrassing."

"Don't be embarrassed, sweet thing," Betty says. "It's not you who should be. Anyone who doesn't hire you is missing out on a very special young man."

"Grandma," Shawn groans.

"Okay a cool young man, is that better? And smart, and dedicated."

Shawn slouches toward the basement.

"I mean just look what you can do when you put your mind to it," Betty jokes. "Winning all the rounds of your games."

Shawn smiles.

"Beating all the levels you mean."

"Yes dear, that's what I mean."

Betty picks up her pen and cradles her chin toward the chequered page in front of her. Shawn lets out a slow breath and ambles over to his grandmother.

"What are you up to?"

Betty's shocked to be asked the question.

"Just the crossword," she says.

"Can I help?" Shawn asks, leaning on the table and looking over her shoulder.

Surprised by this quick change, Betty wants to prolong it as much as possible.

"Of course, sweet thing," she says. "Why don't you take a look while I get us some snacks. You want a ham and cheese?"

"I got it, Grandma," Shawn says. "I'm already up."

Betty stares at Shawn as he takes the ingredients out from the fridge.

"Well, I wasn't even aware you knew how to make a sandwich," she teases. "Now that I know I'll be putting in my orders daily."

Shawn laughs, laying out the bread on the cutting board and spreading the mustard.

"So what were you doing downstairs? Playing your games?"

Shawn pulls pieces of cold cut ham apart and layers them on the bread.

"Naw," he says. "Just sittin'."

"Just sittin', huh?"

He slices the sandwiches and brings them to the table on one big plate. Sits down beside his grandmother and looks over at the chequered newsprint, her carefully written letters in the little boxes.

"What's left?" he asks.

"All right," Betty scans the crossword. "Maybe you'll know this one—Jurassic preservative?"

"Um," Shawn thinks as he chews his sandwich. "Amber, from tree sap. Does that fit?"

"A-M-B-E-R," Betty spells out loud as she fills in the letters. "Sure does."

"Grandma, how can you not know that but you got the word for ablutionary vessel?"

"You don't know that?" Betty asks. "Well, I wasn't baptized in a font, but I still know the word. I was baptized right in the ocean."

"Must've been cold," Shawn says, taking a bite of his sandwich.

"You know it. But when you come out of the water you feel brand new."

Shawn swigs his pop. His stomach feels better now with some food in it.

"Why don't you drink some milk? Don't you remember your mother always saying how that stuff'll weaken your bones?"

"I like it," Shawn says. "You want a sip?"

"No way," Betty says, waving it away. "It'll give me diabetes."

Shawn looks at the clock. Almost five.

"Are you gonna start dinner soon, Grandma?"

"Why?" Betty asks. "You hungry again already?"

Shawn drops the last bite of sandwich into his mouth.

"Nope," he says with his mouth full. "But I could help you."

"Help me?" she looks him over. "Is your dad paying you to do this? Did you lose a bet with your friends?"

Shawn shakes his head.

"Naw," he says. "I just wanna help. Maybe learn somethin' about cooking and stuff."

For the next hour until Kiah and Ken come home, Betty and Shawn work in the kitchen. She decides to teach him something special, something he can use to impress a girl someday. She helps him fry the mushrooms and leeks, simmer the carrots with soup stock and a bay leaf, thicken the stock, and cook the chicken. He can't quite get the hang of rolling out the pastry, but Betty's patient and reforms the dough when he rolls it too thin so he can try again. They pour the chicken and veggies into a dish and lay the pastry lid on top. Betty shows Shawn how to crimp the edges, and he does it well. She glazes it with a beaten egg and they put it in the oven. While it cooks they clean up the kitchen, wiping flour off the counter and scooping carrot peels into the compost. When Ken gets home they're sitting at the table, working on the crossword again.

"Well hello, family," he says, surprised. "Nice to see you above ground, son."

"Dinner'll be done in twenty minutes," Betty says.

"Smells amazing, Mom," Ken says as he creaks open the oven door.

"Don't let the heat out, Kenneth," she says. "Your son pretty much made it all by himself, you know."

Ken turns around and stares at Shawn, who's embarrassed by the attention and keeps his eyes on the crossword.

"This kid?" Ken rubs his son's head. "Who knew he could cook?"

22

June 1949–May 1951

Her last ride dropped her off in downtown Toronto at Jarvis and Gerrard at five in the morning, with two dollars left and no place to stay. Edith was glad to be out of the truck. The driver had stopped to pick her up just outside Kingston and though she didn't like his face, it had started to rain. He looked like a man who would slip his hand under your skirt as soon as you fell asleep, and Edith's body wanted to give in and rest. She'd been travelling since the night before but wouldn't let herself close her eyes. She bit the insides of her cheeks and pinched the skin on the underside of her arms to keep from dozing. And she kept the driver talking about his kids and little grandkids. "You must have a boyfriend, pretty girl like you," he'd say. And she'd ask, "What was your granddaughter's name again? Is she named after someone special?"

And now she was on a sidewalk corner being stared at by shining street lamps, bright and harsh to her bleary eyes. She looked around, reading signs, searching for a soft patch of green to lie down. Why were there so many women out at this hour? Shouldn't they be home in bed? Heels tick tocked toward her.

"Hey kid," said the woman, voice soft with cigarette smoke and red hair vibrant in the lamplight. Edith had never seen hair so red. "This is our corner."

"I'm sorry," Edith said, unaware a corner was something you could claim. "I just got here. I'm looking for somewhere to sleep."

The woman tilted her head, taking in Edith's long brown skirt and worn coat, her unbrushed hair.

"Just got here, huh?" she asked. "Where from?"

"Nova Scotia," Edith said, not wanting to be too specific.

The woman smiled.

"An ocean girl, hey? Same here. But I'm from St. John's, even farther."

"I've got cousins in Newfoundland," Edith said, for a moment wanting connection more than she cared to be careful.

"That so?" the woman asked. "What part? Maybe I know 'em."

"I don't think you would," Edith said, trying to think of the English name for the place but too tired to remember. "*Miawpukek,* I'm not sure you'd know it."

The woman knitted her eyebrows and Edith worried she'd said too much.

"Please don't report me to the Mounties," she murmured.

The woman laughed.

"The Mounties!" she scoffed and looked back at her friends, sharing a smoke under a street lamp. "The cops ain't friends of ours. Don't fret." She pulled a thin, silver case from the pocket of her coat and opened it. "You want a cigarette honey? You look beat."

"I'm okay, thanks," Edith said.

"You hungry?" the woman asked, lighting one for herself.

Edith nodded quickly.

"We're almost through. Why dontcha come with us? There's a diner up the street we always finish up at. How's eggs and toast sound?"

Edith's mouth welled up.

"Amazing," she said, eyes wide.

"Amazing, huh?" the woman repeated in amusement. "I'm Iris. Come with me, I'll introduce you to the girls."

IRIS AND HER GIRLS TREATED Edith to breakfast. It had been a good night. Did Edith want to come out with them the next night, they asked? It's easy money, and after the first couple times it ain't so bad. Take a shower, have a smoke, crawl into bed with your butch lover, and forget about it. Butch? Edith had a cousin by that name but hadn't heard the word used in such a way. The women laughed. They said they'd fill her in.

A few days later they took her to their haunt, the women's bar at the corner where she was first dropped. Edith's eyes and ears adjusted to the dim and din as she took in the scene. Everyone was shouting or laughing, posturing and pushing each other or gazing morosely into their drinks. The girls introduced her around. Such a sweet face, some said. But not all the women were so kind.

"What d'you think this is, a goddamn pow wow?" said an old butch as she swaggered over to Edith's table where the girls sat huddled, still damp from working in the rain. She stood in front of Edith, cold eyes peering down her narrow nose, arms crossed above a silver belt buckle and legs spread, looking like a Mountie, a nun, a priest, a schoolteacher. Iris slung a cool arm around Edith's slim shoulders.

"Why dontcha get back to your seat, Vic? We already told ya we ain't gonna date ya, so quit bothering us."

The femmes cackled and smirked up at the now slightly deflated Vic. But the momentary embarrassment only made her more determined to stake her place.

"You broads think you're gonna turn this skinny kid into a butch of your own, huh?" she said, leaning down into Edith's face. "Best of luck to ya. If you want the real thing, you know where to find me."

"Passed out in the bathroom—am I right, Vic?" called Iris as Vic moseyed back to her beer, reminding them all with her snappy comeback why she was the queen of their girl gang.

"Don't mind her," she said to Edith. "We ain't all so ignorant."

They weren't all, but Vic wasn't the only one in the bar to take issue with Edith. If it wasn't some drunk white femme greeting her with a "HOW!" it was a crew of bored butches made nervous by the scarcity of femmes on the scene and Edith's reluctance to pick a side.

Her friends eventually managed to convince their territorial lovers that Edith wasn't trying to steal them away. "Like dogs with a piece of prime cut meat," Iris said to her at the table one night. "I'm training mine to share." Apparently it didn't matter if you were a white man or a white butch—women were something you thought you owned. Though woven through their tattoos and trucker tales and thick fists gripping bottles of beer were warm thumps on the back, knowing nods, and rounds for the table on a good night. They were charmed by Edith's polite requests for juice rather than beer, and once for a virgin Old Fashioned. "Old-fashioned virgin, sounds about right! Can I get an old-fashioned virgin for this one over here?" Iris's lover Mitch hollered at the bartender across the crowd, and the lot of them busted their guts laughing, clapping Edith on the back to let her know she was in.

When she asked the boss to let her do some work around the bar he wasn't so sure. But after a week of mopping he graduated her to bussing tables, and a month after that to serving drinks. This is how she met Ruth. Iris teased her at first about having a taste for older women, as Ruth was twice Edith's age. But it wasn't lust that drew them together. It was language. Ruth was always reading. Poetry, in particular. She noticed Edith peering across the bar at the pages laid out before her and beckoned her to come closer so she could recite a line into her ear over the many layered voices of the crowd. Her clear cadence cut through the sound, recounting a butterfly's death in a dark squall. *It clung between the ribs of the storm, wavering / and flung against the battering bone-wind.* The words were stunning. Edith had never heard English words put together in such a way: *a spruce-green sky, bound in iron…the larger irridescence of unstrung dark.* Edith's awe prompted Ruth to read the poem through. *The meaning of the moth, even the smashed moth, the meaning of the moth*—she spoke, the *m*s humming into Edith's ear. What was the meaning of the moth? Edith asked. She thought she knew but couldn't find the words to say. Ruth smiled. She would be teaching the poem to her students next week, she said. If Edith would promise not to tell anyone she'd seen Ruth anywhere near this bar, she could come.

Edith's heart hammered so hard as she walked up to the enormous stone school that she felt faint. It was too familiar. But the meaning of the moth, she had to hear. And once she had, she wanted more.

Ruth loaned her the paperback book. Folded inside was a form, already signed by Ruth, waiting for Edith's name and a fee. It wasn't a small sum. But after a month, Edith had enough money saved up from work and the pooled coins that Iris, Helen, and Doris took to calling her scholarship fund. Her application to audit the class was granted.

Some of the students were shocked to share a classroom with her. One dropped out in disgust. Was she so contemptible? Despite Ruth's encouragement, Edith found herself getting smaller. Eyes cast down and chin resting in the dip of her collarbone like an egg in a nest, back curled over like a fiddlehead. Trying to be somehow less conspicuous. It made her body ache. Once she showed up at the bar after class but before she'd unfurled. "Straighten up!" Mitch laughed as Edith shuffled over to their table. "Not really, E, but you catch my drift. Gals want to see some confidence." So that's who Edith held in her mind—her friends who'd likewise been told they were contemptible but swaggered nonetheless. She lifted her chin from its nest. She spoke soothing words silently to herself until her blood coursed calmly like a slow river. She read a poem in class with a steady voice. She thought of mailing it to Mattie.

Where are you, Sparrow? What are you doing now?

Edith imagined Mattie must be married with children, though she hoped not. She wished she could go back to Shubie to find her, but leaving had been such a relief she couldn't yet bring herself to return. In a letter to her mother, she asked if she could find an address for a Miss Martha MacLeod. A cousin of Edith's had married a white man from Truro the year before, and she thought he might be able to track her down.

It would be so good to have her here. Since Edith had found a home at the divey bar at Jarvis and Gerrard, where women could go without escorts, dance with their hips pressed close, hold hands and neck at the sticky tables, she knew she could be with Mattie how she wanted—at least after dark. She wished they could have run away together. Hitched out of Shubie that night, before they'd been caught. Edith wanted to dance with her.

But it wasn't always safe. She'd been in the bar during the raids and watched the most indignant of her butch friends beaten and carried away in cop cars, to be thrown in jail or left bleeding down on Cherry Beach. It was too much like the Resi. Edith had heard stories of the demands priests and brothers made of boys in the name of God. And if the boys refused, they were beaten in God's name too. She and the other girls, humiliated by sisters who would inspect their underwear and bed sheets, shame them if they weren't clean, and strap them for a spot of blood. Edith had always been waiting, expecting a blow from a passing nun, not daring to raise a hand to shield her face. No one who had the power to do anything about it would have listened to her about how horribly wrong everything was. And this felt much the same. Sitting in the bar, waiting for the police to come and do with them what they liked. Who could they report it to? The best they could hope for was that the cops were in a good mood and would take a bribe. Second best was one of the femmes taking a cop out back and offering herself in place of her lover. Same violence but less blood.

After a while, Edith could barely stand it. Could barely bring herself to go to work and see her friends. She was so afraid of the raids. Steps from the door to the bar her body would slow to a stop, her limbs mired in mud and unable to move, her heart battering the bones of her ribcage. She was a kid again, standing small in front of the looming school, her stomach full of stones. And as the school once had, the bar held her friends. They were like a family of squirrels forced to make their home in a hawk's nest. Edith would stand frozen at the threshold until the glow of laughter and jukebox twang was finally able to melt her. Some combo of Iris, Mitch, Helen, Doris, Pat, and Lil would be sitting at the table, ready to make room for her when she came through the door. And she'd start her shift like she always did, by going to the jukebox and playing her favourite song, "I Can Dream, Can't I?," even though Pat said it was sappy.

Plus, Edith loved to dance and this was the best place for it. The ritual was beautiful. She would sit with her friends, sipping a soda, and catch the eye of a woman across the room. Depending on whether Edith was more butch or more femme than the woman, she would send a drink or receive one. She still didn't really understand that split, butch and femme. Didn't feel that she was fully one thing and not the other. She was herself—tall and lanky, short hair, handsome face, long fingers on delicate hands. She was the only one who could get away with not picking a side. And she always had a dance partner.

But still she felt lonely. It was fun dancing sweaty and necking in the dark corners of the bar before last call, but the hands and lips of these women didn't make her swoon like Mattie's had. She wouldn't take any of them home with her. "I have to get up early for class," she would say, even when it wasn't true. At the end of each night Edith would walk home alone through lamplit streets, one foot in front of the other, hands in her pockets, thinking of Mattie—muddy skirt, dancing in a puddle, crawling through the bushes, falling down the riverbank, holding her hand and kissing her like a revelation.

Eventually, her cousin's husband tracked Mattie down. She was now Mrs. Ian Campbell, living in Halifax.

How do you know this woman? Edith's mother wrote to her. *Why do you want her address?*

Though she thought her mother might understand, she chose to ignore the question. For now, anyway.

The letter stayed in Edith's pocket for a week before she finally got the guts to send it, along with a soft-focus glamour shot taken in a musty studio, where she had been dragged by Doris, Iris, and Helen. They wanted photos to give to their sweethearts and had done themselves up like movie stars. Wasn't there someone Edith would like to give a photograph to? Someone from the bar maybe, they asked? How about Ruth? Edith rolled her eyes, but allowed herself to be brought along. She second-guessed herself the moment she dropped the photo in the mailbox, though. Would Mattie find it ridiculous? And what if her husband read the letter? What if he knew what had happened between them? Would he beat her? Edith fiercely hoped not and sent out protective thoughts like an artillery of birds, flying determinedly east. She had given up praying years ago.

23

꙰

January 19, 2008

It's the Saturday lunch buffet shift and everyone's hands are full of dirty plates and heads full of drink orders. Ada weaves through her coworkers and grabs her crusty shirt off its jangling metal hanger. She feels lucky to have this job, even on buffet days. It's tough to find work in this town.

She figures they keep her around mostly because she's one of the only servers brave enough to do the flambés. James singed his eyelashes once setting a dish on fire at a customer's table and told the boss he loved his eyelashes more than his job and wouldn't do flambés ever again. The cook has to come out of the kitchen to do them for him now, or Ada does them if she's not too busy with her own tables.

In the clammy bathroom she pulls her shirt over her head and fastens the little gold buttons. Her fingers already feel greasy. No matter how many times she washes her hands after a shift, they still feel like she soaked them in cooking oil.

Despite the stress and rush and constant cleanup, buffets are kind of nice to work because all the servers watch all the tables so you don't have to worry as much about forgetting anyone, and if you do, at least the blame gets dispersed. As Ada walks around collecting empty glasses and sauce-smeared plates, James catches her eye, his face lit up with a smile like a dam about to burst. He tips his head toward the kitchen and they walk back and dump their plates in the dish pit.

"You!" he says, pulling her into his cologney chest for a tight squeeze. "I have something to tell you."

"So tell me."

"Not now," he teases. "I'm saving it for later."

Ada pokes him in the side and he gives her another squeeze before they go back out to clear up. They stack plates and reset tables until the last customer shuffles out and they can fill their own plates with sticky rice and curry and greasy spring rolls. Ada uses chopsticks to scoop the spicy, creamy lumps of warm food into her mouth. James is on a diet and sips lemonade.

They talk about customers with the other servers on shift—who left good tips, who was snarky, whose food they'd have liked to spit in—and compare encounters with the giant rat who runs around the restaurant. James says it's as big as a cat. There's a huge rat trap in a corner of the kitchen and every day when Ada comes in to work, she hopes the rat's not there, finally caught with its neck snapped beneath the spring-loaded steel bar.

After they clean up and cash out, James leans his head in to Ada.

"Okay. So. Did you know your crush came in to ask about you?" he asks in a scandalously low voice.

Ada grins as she pushes through the restaurant door and into the grey light of the slowly snowing sky.

"She came in like five times this week," he says, following her.

"Really, James?"

"Okay, twice," he corrects, fishing a half-smoked joint from his pocket. "But that's still a lot. And she asked me if I knew when you'd be working." James nudges her for an explanation. "So…?" He lights the roach and passes it to Ada. "Why all the visits, hmm?"

Ada tries to sound casual, but the story of sex on the piercing table is so huge that it can only get out of her mouth through a grin-shaped doorway.

James can't believe it.

"No fucking way," he keeps saying. "No fucking way."

"So what now?" he asks. "Are you just going to keep getting piercings from her forever? I mean, what else is there?" he asks, eyeing her crotch.

Ada pushes him off the sidewalk.

"I don't know," she says.

Because it's Saturday, Joan is home when Ada gets in, so she kicks off her shoes a bit quieter than usual. The radio plays in the kitchen, talking to Joan as she pushes something around in a frying pan with a wooden spoon.

"Hey Mum," Ada says.

"Hi chicken," her mother replies. "There's a message on the phone for you. A woman."

Ada's heart climbs up through her chest. She swallows it down and goes to check the machine. Skips one, two messages left for her mother who screens every call.

"Hi," the machine says to her, the almost-real sound flowing out through the tiny holes of the speaker and into the pores of her skin. "I'm looking for Ada—not sure if this is the right number. Call me back at the shop."

Ada grins wide like she did while telling James her story. Really it's the shape of Pan in her mouth. Full. Overflowing. But on Saturdays the shop's closed at four. She plays the message again. Her name in Pan's digitized voice, on those lips that Ada so badly wants to kiss again.

Ada eats dinner with Joan and the soft food rolling around in her mouth makes her wish for the hard click of Pan's tongue ring against her teeth.

"Who was on the machine?" Joan asks.

"The piercer I go to."

"So what, you haven't been by in a few days and now she's calling you?"

"Yeah," Ada says. "I'm her best customer."

The next morning Ada wants to call the shop, but so many places are closed Sundays in this town, aside from restaurants and newspaper offices and grocery stores. Joan's already at work today and Ada will be too in a few hours—time she never really gets to enjoy because she's always clock watching and calculating minutes. The time it takes to fry an egg. The time it takes to shower. The time it takes to find socks. The time it takes to gulp tea. To jerk off, if she wakes up early enough. To read a bit. She usually tries to combine them to get more out of her morning. Look for socks while the egg cooks, jerk off in the shower and read while she drinks her tea. Or sometimes she combines them in ways that make less sense, with a spatula in one hand and the other down her shorts, or a mug of tea in the shower, catching water from the spray.

She cracks an egg into the hot oil, trying to pick out a bit of shell while running the faucet, filling up the kettle with her other hand.

"Fucking shell."

Ada digs through the now opaque egg and picks it out, searing her fingertip on the cast iron. The phone rings and she answers it with her throbbing finger in her mouth.

"Lello?"

"Hi," Pan says. "Are you eating or something?"

"No, sucking on my finger."

"Burn it?"

"I did."

They pause and Ada's heart beats hard.

"What are you doing today?" Pan asks.

"Working."

"When are you done?"

"At four."

"Do you think you'll be hungry?"

"I often am."

"Then you should come over and make dinner with me," Pan says.

Ada feels like she's going to puke, in a good way.

"Okay," she says, smiling. "Do you want me to bring food? Wine, or something?"

"Well what do you like on your pizza?"

"Um, artichokes."

"That's pretty fancy. You got any?"

"I do actually. I'll bring some."

"Great."

Another pause. Thump thump thump.

"Come over at seven?"

"Okay."

"See you then."

"Wait!" Ada half shouts. "Where do you live?"

Pan describes the walk, using a red mailbox and a playground and large trees as landmarks instead of street names. Not that streets are very complicated in a small city. She lives above an all-night pizza place, about a twenty-minute walk away. Around the back, the place with a skull and crossbones painted on the mailbox with whiteout, above the words NO FLYERS.

When Ada gets there after what felt like the longest shift, she realizes she left the artichokes on the bathroom counter. She was so concerned about her hair that she completely forgot them, beside her mother's perfume and her extra-strong-hold hairspray. She hopes she didn't make her hair too crunchy.

She pushes the doorbell and waits.

"One marshmallow, two marshmallow, three marshmallow, four marshmallow, five marshmallow...."

Before she rings again, she sees under the doorbell, in pencil: BELL OUT OF ORDER. PLEASE KNOCK.

She raps and Pan thumps down the stairs.

"Hi," Pan greets her with a fast grin, then turns and runs back up the steps before they can stumble over whether or not to hug hello.

"Come!" she calls.

Ada starts to run up the stairs too and almost trips, emerging in the kitchen where Pan is busy moving her work off the table, gathering up delicate knives, and sweeping slivers of linoleum into her palm.

"Got the artichokes?"

"I forgot," Ada says. "But maybe they have some at the place downstairs?"

"Oh no," Pan says. "We're not ordering in. We're making our own. Or kind of. I bought the dough frozen."

The pie comes out of the freezer rock hard and hits the counter, rolling on its edge like a dropped coin.

"Yum," Ada says, sarcastic.

"It'll be good," Pan assures her. "It just has to thaw. And in the meantime I'll show you my place."

Usually this part comes at the end of the date, after you eat and talk and ease into flirting, walk home and stand on the steps, kicking at each other's feet. So Ada's not sure what to do. Showing off your place at the end of the night is the excuse to show off the bedroom. Everything's easier once you're in the bedroom. It's like you're in a movie and you know your lines and the perfect timing, so when your date puts their hands around your waist you help them by throwing yourself on the bed.

But Pan keeps her distance as she shows Ada around the small space. Here's the kitchen, the table Pan works at, eats at. Doubles as a living room. Who needs both?

"No one," Ada agrees.

"This is where shoes go," Pan says as she nudges Ada's haphazard lace-ups into place against the wall with her foot.

Here's the bathroom, freshly cleaned. And Pan's room. The bed's made and Ada's impressed. Pan has some of her own prints up on the walls and a large, wide window onto the back parking lot. Ada expects to see a cat sleeping somewhere but there's no cat to be found. It just seems like that kind of place. Ada would want a cat if she lived alone.

"Do you have a cat?"

"I don't. Why do you ask?"

"It just seems like that kind of place," Ada says.

Pan squeezes her hand around the doorknob, twisting it left and right.

"I have a dog," she says. "She's being taken good care of in Vancouver."

"By your parents?" Ada asks.

Pan lets out a quiet laugh like a wince. "No, not by my parents. We're still working on cordial phone calls. It'll be a while before they agree to look after my gayby."

"Gayby?" Ada says, confused.

"My dog is my baby," Pan explains.

"And…your dog is gay?" Ada asks casually, as if she knows lots of gay dogs.

"No genius, I'm gay. My dog is just tainted by my unnatural lifestyle. It's still a crime in India. But anyway, let's check out this pizza situation," says Pan, backing out of the room.

Ada's guess about India was right then, but she hadn't thought about this—a crime. It's hard to imagine. Her coming out had been such a non-issue she barely remembers it. It was something like her asking her mother for money to see a movie with her girlfriend back in grade nine and Joan confirming "girlfriend?" as she looked for her wallet, and Ada saying "yeah" and that being it. Then again, James has yet to come out to his Evangelical parents and he's pushing thirty, so maybe it's not so hard to imagine. Conviction versus damnation. Disownment. Caught in her thoughts and on Pan's turf Ada feels unbalanced, like a cat with its whiskers cut off. On her way out of the bedroom she slams her shoulder into the doorframe.

"Ouch," she whispers, rubbing it.

"You okay?" Pan looks back.

"I walked into your wall."

"That was dumb."

Ada smiles and pushes Pan, a little shove toward the kitchen, and Pan pops her on the shoulder. Same shoulder.

"Ow!" Ada cries.

Okay, she thinks to herself. Play fighting as flirting. I know this game.

Pan walks over to the counter and pokes her finger into the dough. Not quite ready.

"Wanna cut up some veggies?" she asks.

"Yeah," Ada says. "Whaddya got?"

Pan opens the fridge and digs through the vegetable drawer.

"Peppers," she says, tossing them at Ada without looking up.

Ada has terrible hand-eye coordination and is relieved to catch all three.

"Onion, purple. Mushrooms, brown. Asparagus, slimy," Pan continues. "Actually, throw those out. Compost's under the sink."

Ada empties the bag of rotten asparagus into the bin.

"How do you feel about vegan cheese?" Pan asks.

"Bad. Gross. Not worth it. That shit doesn't even melt."

"This kind does. It's good, I promise."

"No way," Ada says. "I'd rather have it with just oil."

"You're picky," Pan says with a grin, giving Ada a poke in the stomach. "I don't remember you being this particular when I was putting holes in your body."

"Yeah but you're a piercer, so I trust you with that. If you worked at the pizza place downstairs, I might trust you about the cheese. But as it is, I don't know. I've never met a vegan cheese I liked."

"Well," Pan says. "Let me introduce you to mine. Vegan cheese, this is Ada. Ada, the cheese."

God, Ada thinks. My name in your mouth.

But she won't be won over.

"No cheese," she says. "For real. We might as well pour that candle over the pizza." A beeswax candle flickers on the table. It smells so good. "Actually the candle would probably be healthier."

"Fine," Pan says, throwing up her hands. "No cheese. But you know, just because I don't work in a pizza place doesn't mean I can't make pizza. Do you think only professionals are good at what they do?"

She looks up at Ada as she sifts through a drawer for sharp knives.

"No," Ada says, as Pan hands her a paring knife and a pepper. "I'm sure you're good at all the things you do."

"Are you now?" Pan asks as she strolls over to the cutting board behind Ada, knife in hand.

Ada doesn't move, and when their eyes align they both know what's going on. Now that they're finally face to face, the food doesn't seem so interesting. Pan lets the knife fall from her hand onto the cutting board with a clatter. Her fingers press into Ada's stomach and with her other hand she brings Ada's face closer. Ada can feel Pan's breath and she likes it like this, slow. So slow she has time to lick her lips while Pan's linger an inch away. She almost grazes them with her tongue before Pan rushes to her mouth, pressing against it with a moan. Like this hurts.

Pan grips the edge of the counter and presses into her. Ada can feel the heat through Pan's jeans. Can taste the lonely want in her spit. She clenches her hands around Pan's hips and her fingers sink into her skin so deliciously.

Down her stomach, down her thigh, Pan's hand slides, pushing Ada's knees apart, making room for herself between her legs. Nimble fingers pop the button on her jeans.

But Ada wants to be the one to push and undo. She grabs Pan's hands and turns the tables—Pan against the counter, Ada pushing into her. She holds Pan's hands together with one of hers and fumbles with her pants. It's kind of a joke. She could never hold Pan down, but Pan keeps still and lets her try, patient as Ada scrambles to find the tab of her zipper. She inches it down, metal tooth by tooth, as she runs her tongue up Pan's soft neck, kissing the short hairs at the nape. Her hand finds its way to the band of Pan's briefs and her fingers curl around the elastic, searching for skin. Pan slaps them away.

Ada is stunned and pulls back to look at her. With an elusive smile, Pan slides Ada's hand between her legs but over fabric, moving Ada's fingers against her, stopping to let her try on her own. Ada loses her place, feeling stupid, clumsy, as Pan says lower, no, slower.

Finally, Pan pushes her down onto one of the wooden kitchen chairs and picks up where she left off, inching Ada's undone jeans down and spreading her bare legs, fingers wandering along her thighs, up high where she waits. Her fingers slip in slow as Ada curls over her hunched back, hands sliding and grasping, breathing hot on the back of Pan's neck. She kisses her there, and when Pan moans she sucks, bites, bringing her blood to the surface where she can taste it better.

Hours later the dough is soft and gummy. The oven warm and waiting. But it's late, Pan says.

"I'm hungry though!" Ada laughs as she does herself up again.

"Well, this will take half an hour to cook and then another half an hour to eat."

"But that's just an hour," Ada says. "And it's only eleven. Do you have a strict bedtime or something?"

"I have to get up early."

"Okay…" Ada says, slow and unsure.

"I have some peanut butter if you want. Maybe a spoonful, to fuel you up for your walk home? It's high in protein," Pan offers with a too-charming grin.

"Yeah," Ada says. "I know it is. I'm okay, though."

She walks over to where Pan lined her shoes up against the wall and slips her feet in, crouching down to tie them. When she stands up and turns back around Pan's in front of her, spoonful of peanut butter in hand.

"Open up," she coaxes, like a mother giving medicine.

"I'm all right," Ada says. "Really."

Pan tilts her head, grinning that grin out of the side of her beautiful mouth.

"Come on," she says. "I can't let you leave with an empty stomach."

"Then don't," Ada says. "Let's make the pizza and you can forfeit an hour of sleep. It'll be worth it."

"Open up," Pan tries again, sweeter this time, running her fingers along Ada's jaw.

Ada parts her lips and Pan pops the spoon into her mouth. She pulls it back out and kisses her.

"Good night," she says.

"Nungnigh," says Ada.

Confused and sucking peanut butter from between her teeth, Ada walks home, shaking her head, knitting her eyebrows.

"Wasn't that good, though? Did I say something wrong, or weird? Did I say something weird? Fuck. Does she think I'm too weird? Maybe she thinks I'm too young."

She covers her face with her hands and rakes her fingers back through her hair.

"Okay, shut up," she tells herself. "You're not helping."

"But why couldn't I stay?" she starts again, not caring who hears her mutter. "No, listen. It doesn't matter. It was a good time. She likes you. Clearly," she says, feeling the dull ache between her legs and grinning.

At home, all the lights are on but it's so quiet that Joan and Mattie must be in bed. When she glances down the hallway though, Ada sees that both their bedroom doors are wide open and her stomach goes cold. She looks around for a note, checking the fridge, pawing through envelopes on the counter, and finally sees on the cutting board in her mother's rushed handwriting:

CALL THE HOSPITAL.

She flips through the phone book, finds the number, and dials.

"Is there a Martha Campbell checked in with you?" she asks the calm receptionist.

"Let me just check," she's told, and the woman puts her on hold.

Ada tries to breathe slowly. She sits down but she can't keep her legs still. They dance on the floor while she sits in her chair at the kitchen table.

"God, could you be any slower?" she shouts into the empty kitchen.

The woman comes back on the line.

"Are you a friend or a family member?" she asks.

"Family. Her granddaughter. Can you just tell me what room she's in?"

"Three-nineteen, but we don't have visiting hours again until tomorrow."

"Can you put me through to her room?" Ada asks.

"Well, dear, I think she's probably sleeping."

"Is my mother there? Can you just put me through to her room so I can talk to my mother?"

"I'm sorry," the woman says. "We don't put through calls this late. Don't want to wake the patients."

"Fine," Ada says. "Thanks for all your help."

She hangs up and dials a cab. The hospital's not very far, but it feels like it now.

The waiting room is cold and tense. People sit, together, alone, staring silently at the clock, flipping finger-worn magazine pages. At the desk, Ada asks if she can go up to room 319.

"You just called," the woman says, recognizing her voice. "Remember, I told you that visiting hours are over for today?"

Ada's eyes start to sting like she opened them under water. Her throat feels like it's wrapped in dulse.

"Can't you just, just let me go up and see her?" she asks, on the verge of tears.

"I'm sorry, dear, I can't do that."

Ada lets out a noisy breath. Her hands are shaking.

"Can you please just let my mother know I'm here?" she asks, her tears spilling over. "Please?"

The nurse sighs.

"Let me call someone in that ward. Maybe they can let your mother know."

Ada sits down beside a father and his young daughter. Probably nine, she thinks, remembering herself at that age. The girl wears her right arm in a makeshift sling, reading an Archie comic with the good one. Her dad helps her turn the pages.

"What'd you do to your arm?" Ada asks, wiping her tears away with the sleeve of her coat.

The girl looks up at her with the wariness kids often have for adults. Or maybe it could have something to do with all those piercings.

"Fell out of my bunk bed," she says.

"Crummy," Ada says, the tightness in her throat starting to soften. "What's happening in your comic?"

"Um," the girl looks down at the bright pages. "Betty and Veronica are fighting over Archie."

Ada nods.

"Pretty sure I've read that one."

The father chuckles.

"Me too," he says.

Ada sees a figure walking toward her out of the corner of her eye and turns her head to see her mother. She's so grateful. It makes her feel so young. Her mother, here to make things all right and hold her and take her home.

"What happened?" Ada asks into Joan's neck.

"She had a heart attack."

"Oh no," Ada says, still holding tight.

"They think she'll be okay. She has to stay here tonight and maybe a bit longer. They just want to make sure she takes it really easy."

"Is she okay? Is she sleeping?"

"She's sleeping," Joan says, taking Ada by the hand. "Let's go home."

24

January 21, 2008

*K*iah *opens the front door with a piece of buttered toast between her* teeth and a travel mug of chai in her mittened hand.

"Bye, Grandma!" she calls through the door before she shuts it. Shawn won't be awake for hours.

The neighbourhood kids are already outside in their monochromatic snowsuits. Climbing and falling over each other, tumbling rainbow starfish in the strips of soft snow between identical concrete staircases, leading up to identical homes lining the block across the street. Kiah stomps through unshovelled snow layering the sidewalk in front of her house. It's her brother's job to clear it, dammit.

"Keeyah! KEE-YAH!" the kids across the street chant as they jump up and down and wave their well-padded arms, surrounded by lopsided snowballs that make up the walls of a fort, where they each have their own room and there's a toilet in the kitchen.

"Hi, you guys!" Kiah waves. "I'm heading to school but I'll check out your new place on my way home. Looks good!"

The smallest starfish, whom Kiah has babysat several times, reading for class while he napped beside her, continues to chant her name as she turns the corner down Buddy Daye. She walks alongside the bright blue houses and crosses the street, sidestepping folks hanging out on the corner as she turns onto Gottingen. The empty parking lot spanning half a block is full of snowdrifts, but across the street, the courtyard in front of the library has been cleared. The sculpture in the middle of the cobblestones stands rigid and monolithic, the copper figures climbing atop it laden with gentle flakes.

Kiah walks under a billboard advertising condo units for sale and shakes her head, thinking of her grandmother. She trudges past the legal-aid office and the gay bathhouse and the hostel, the architecture firm and the needle exchange and the Mi'kmaw community centre, all somehow coexisting on the same street, sleek and shining, worn and peeling, rainbows and condos and people always waiting, smoking, standing around talking. She takes a quick turn down a side street, picking up her lunch—a spicy warm patty that makes the detour worthwhile, even in this snow.

Around the corner up Cornwallis Street, a small man in a hoodie holds a megaphone, pointed up at the sky. Kiah rubs her sleepy morning eyes with her mitten. A few steps closer, she can tell for certain that it's not a man but a painting of a man, shellacked against the powder blue siding of a house. Close up she can see his perfectly sliced silhouette and beside it, posters for a show he seems to be announcing with his megaphone, a rapper from NYC performing downtown next week.

"Huh," Kiah says, smoothing her mitten along the man's paper arm, sealed against the wall.

At the end of Cornwallis she crosses North Park Street and follows a footpath through the Commons, the biggest stretch of grass in the city, now a temporary tundra where the wind is free to whip. She pulls her scarf up over her mouth, where it gets quickly wet from the heat of her breath, and leans forward, shuffling so as not to slip on the frozen footprints. Back on pavement, she turns to walk south down Robie Street, past the hotel, the hospital, and the Starbucks, into the realm of students and rich south-enders.

When she gets to campus and before she heads to class, Kiah climbs the six flights of stairs in the student union building and turns the corner into the Black students' centre, thighs burning and blood pumping. Curled up in the far corner of the couch with an open book in her lap and a forkful of arugula suspended mid-air, apparently forgotten, is Nadine. She transferred here from Toronto in her second year, when her aunt got sick and her mother plied her with poetry of the ocean and invocations of family loyalty. She's a fourth-year English major and a killer wordsmith with a thing for giant earrings and salad. Kiah sees her here often, chewing lettuce, moving her head gently as she reads to herself, the chandeliers hanging from her lobes clicking and tinging like little wind chimes.

"Hey Nadine," Kiah says, sitting down beside her. "Whatcha reading?"

Nadine taps the spine of the book as she finishes her mouthful.

"George Elliott Clarke, for my final paper," she says as she runs her tongue between her lips and teeth, checking for shreds of the peppery leaves. "You ever read this poem? It's pretty sexy."

Kiah cranes her neck and drinks in a few lines.

"Wish that's what I was reading. I've been wading through the least sexy text maybe ever written. Listen to this," she says, unzipping her backpack and hauling out her course pack, flipping to a dog-eared page. She reads, in her best impression of her mumbling professor, about the utility of things and exchange value and quantitative relations and—

"Whoa, whoa," Nadine stops her. "Slow it down and speak up. You'll put me to sleep with that voice. What is that? *Das Kapital*?"

"This shit *does* put me to sleep. You've read it?"

"Of course I have. Read it in first year. It's sexy in its own way I guess. You've gotta get through those equations and all, but there's good in it."

Kiah slides her reader into her backpack and checks her watch.

"Maybe, but I don't have *time* to try to find the good in everything. Read this, learn it, understand it, read critiques of it, critique it, and one day, maybe, find something that connects it to me. I got, like, three hours of sleep last night."

"Well I got four. But listen, I can help you with Marx if you want. I know it's dry but I can talk you through it. And here's my big tip, if you want to get through your last year and a half of school without sleeping through all your lectures or ripping your hair out."

"Okay, tell me," Kiah says, zipping up her backpack and slipping on her mittens.

"You've got to supplement these readings with something. If you don't, your brain is going to start to resent books. I'll make you a reading list. Gimme a pen."

"Nadine, you know I'd love that but I don't have the time. Besides, I'm gonna be late for class."

"Are you on a diet?"

"Uh, no? Should I be?" Kiah says, taken aback.

"Of course you shouldn't be," Nadine says, stabbing the last soggy leaves of lettuce in the plastic container in her lap. "I am—and don't give me grief, Kiah," she says to Kiah's reproachful look. "Even though I force myself to eat salads and carrot sticks and rice crackers, I always eat one good, warm, sweet thing every day to fill me up. That's how I can keep eating salad, day in, day out. 'Cause I know I have one delicious thing to look forward to tasting. I'm gonna make you a list. Every day, after you finish deciphering this theory, read a page of something just for yourself. I swear it'll save you."

When Kiah gets out of her last class, the sun is already setting. It'll be completely dark in an hour. Fucking winter. But she goes to find Nadine, sitting at a small round table in front of the campus Tim Hortons, halfway through a honey cruller.

"Best thing I could find in a three-floor radius," she says holding it up, offering Kiah a bite.

Kiah takes it, sinking her teeth into the stale, airy dough, her stomach already groaning for dinner.

"Tastes old. I hope they gave it to you half price."

"Oh no, I like 'em like this," Nadine says, snatching the donut back. "When they get a little crunchy, you know?"

Kiah laughs and sits down.

"So you're gonna let me in on the esoteric laws of the economy?"

"You know it," says Nadine, putting her donut down and dusting the flaky sugar frosting from her fingertips. "But first, I made you a list."

"That's sweet of you, but I told you I've just got no time," Kiah says as Nadine pulls a small square of paper from the middle of her poetry book.

"You'll make time," she says, passing Kiah the note. "You need this. Baldwin, hooks, Jordan, Shange—and Clarke, for some local flavour. I wrote down the best essays. And this one's like a poem play—you could read it in a night. I promise you'll thank me. Go to the library. Start with hooks. You know that cute dude who works the circulation desk? Ask him. He'll help you out."

Nadine jostles Kiah's arm, shaking a smile out of her.

"Okay okay," Kiah says. "I'll do my best. I'll *try*, all right?"

"Girl, you gotta take some time for yourself," Nadine says, taking another bite of her donut. "You going to that show next week?"

Kiah slips Nadine's list into her pocket.

"What show?"

"That MC from New York. I can text my boyfriend for the place—I'm blanking on it. He said it'd be good."

When was the last time Kiah went out with her friends? Who were her friends anymore, anyway? Was Nadine inviting her to go? She stopped saying yes to friends' requests back in first year, and eventually they stopped asking. She can't even remember the last time she had a drink, but remembers the stiff, shellacked arm of the paper man on the side of the powder blue house.

"Oh yeah!" she says. "There's a poster for that show up Cornwallis from the Greek place on Gottingen. You see it? Glued onto the wall or something."

"Yeah yeah!" Nadine says, looking up from her phone. "It's pasted on there good. I'd never touch that sticky shit. It's impossible to scrape off."

"That right?" asks Kiah.

"You'll see it around the city if you look—posters and art and stuff, wheatpasted onto walls. There was that big goldfish on the bus stop by the south-end Sobeys one time? I guess this MC's got people doing it in different cities to promote his shows. And you know what else it's called? It'll bring this full circle for you: Marxist glue. The glue of the people. Flour and water. Cheap as shit, and a bitch to remove."

"Huh," says Kiah, as she pulls her course pack from her bag and opens it up between them on the table. "Well, long live the proletariat."

25

January 26, 2008

They kept Mattie in the hospital for a week. Joan called the restaurant to tell the manager Ada couldn't come in. It was so nice to have her mother make the call, the ultimate authority on whether you have to suck it up and go or you don't because you've earned the day off with your suffering. Ada used to love staying home sick when she was little. She loved the ceremony of taking temperatures and would will the numbers to keep climbing, trying to find the hottest spot underneath her tongue. She loved the measuring of medicine, pretending she didn't like the taste. The feeling of her mother's cool dry hand on her hot clammy forehead. Getting to drink noodle soup through a straw and watching *The Wizard of Oz* over and over all day.

But when she was dry heaving over the toilet, she would think very seriously and resignedly that she would rather die right then than feel so awful. And this is much the same. She often longs for an extra day off work but when she has a good reason to not go in, like now, it's far from worth it.

It was strange to sit with Mattie and watch her, so small, breathing slowly under the bedsheets. Hard for Ada to comprehend the failure of her Nan's body. And she was afraid, now that Mattie had been confirmed mortal, that her heart would give out again. Old age seemed like a trivial thing for Mattie to succumb to, like she should be above it somehow. Ada wondered what her grandmother was dreaming about.

On Saturday Ada calls a cab to take them home. They drive through cold winter rain, the windshield wipers keeping time with Mattie's breathing. Wrapped in a blanket, Mattie sleeps beside Ada in the back seat on the short ride to their house, and Joan meets them at the curb with an umbrella and helps get her mother into bed. She needs to rest for a few weeks to let her heart heal, the nurse told them, and Mattie follows her directions diligently. Not that she could have done otherwise. She's so tired. It's such an effort for her to open her eyes and sit up, makes her blood pound fast in her ears. When she lies down, she can feel Ada's hand on her forehead, stroking her hair, and Edith's warm body curled around her, whispering for her to sleep, sleep. Whispering the ingredients for beautiful dreams in her ear. So she sleeps.

Ada wakes her every now and then to knock back a handful of pills—aspirin and beta blockers and nitroglycerin. The pills make her dizzy and cause her heart to beat so slow that she wonders from time to time if it has stopped. But she's not worried. Having a ghost lover for over a year now has made death seem not so bad.

Joan took a few days off from work too and the distance made her miss it. But after her first day back she comes home looking like she's going to be sick, lips tight lest she throw up—either food or words. Ada knows her mother doesn't want to talk about it, so she'll just have to wait until the paper comes out tomorrow morning to see why she's upset. She makes tea, pouring it into Joan's favourite mug, blue with shimmering patina dripping down around the rim like a cup of liquid mercury that overflowed. Joan smiles at the mug and holds her hands around it, warming them, and they sit quietly together at the kitchen table, listening to Mattie snore.

The next day, Ada walks down the street to a newspaper box and pays the fee to open the door. She rarely reads the news so still has some sensitivity to the horrible things reported daily, and usually cries at least once after flipping through a paper or sitting through an evening report. If something Joan reported on was bad enough to upset her, she who has been doing this for thirty-odd years, it must be bad.

And there it is on the front page in thick letters: LOCAL MAN CHARGED WITH SEXUAL EXPLOITATION. Ada squeezes her eyes shut and sucks in her breath sharp, like she does when she imagines tripping over a curb and cracking all her teeth in. She scans the story. The girls are fourteen, and friends. He went to their church. Jesus fucking Christ.

She imagines her mother reading the police report, calling in for quotes. Joan's words transform into a horrible movie in Ada's brain. She can't stop it. It replays, replays, replays again until she has to step in the moment just before he touches them and sink a dull, heavy axe into his stomach. She just steps into the nightmare and gives him what he deserves before he can do what makes him so deserving. Every time it replays Ada cuts him down, sinks the axe again and again into his stomach or cleaves deep into the space between his shoulder and neck. Once she almost cuts his head clean off, or as clean as you can with a dull axe, but she decides against it because he needs to have a head so he can fully comprehend the pain he needs to suffer.

She feels sick and shaky. She's not violent and is rarely angry but she can't stop seeing the scene and she has to stop him. So she leaves the axe sunk in his stomach. He's spluttering blood and wailing for help. Ada takes each girl by the hand and they check each other over to make sure they didn't get hit by a spurt of his disgusting blood. Then they go to the store and Ada buys them all those ice creams with the chocolate at the bottom of the cone, and they wrap themselves in blankets on the couch and watch cartoons and don't feel bad at all.

She almost feels like she might really kill him if she saw him and it scares her. She's still shaking and her breath is coming in and out in quick harsh bursts and her eyes sting. Her feet push the sidewalk away. She wants to drink tea in the kitchen with her mother or lie in bed and talk with her grandmother, but Joan is at work and Mattie needs to rest.

So where are you when I need you? Ada thinks to Pan. After everything with my Nan, and now this?

Pan hasn't called all week. Not that she should have. I mean, not that she owes me anything, Ada thinks. But Ạda's brain is full of heavy axes and thick blood and teeth-clenching disgust. She needs someone to be angry with, to share this injustice with, to shout with, and she needs to feel like there can be good touch. She wants to be held in a good way.

She goes, just walks toward Pan's house. I shouldn't have to call ahead, she thinks. She rings the bell and then remembers that it's broken, so she knocks.

Nothing.

Ada digs in her bag for a cigarette and lights it, sucks in. It tastes terrible. It's a prop. What am I even doing here? she thinks. A clamouring voice in her head tells her to knock again, to walk to the shop and look for Pan there, to check the café. But another voice says give it up, she's not your girlfriend. Go home, you're embarrassing yourself. Ada stands in front of Pan's door and feels a swell of tears rise. "Don't," she says out loud, and sucks hard on the smoke to stem the flow. Drops the burning cigarette into Pan's empty mailbox and leaves, smoke seeping out of the cracks like incense.

26

☘

August 1949–June 1951

The deep evergreen of the trees and the young greens of the ferns and fields blurred together through the window of the train as it rolled along steel rails toward Halifax. Mattie folded her hands, one over the other, and laid them in her lap. She crossed her ankles and pressed her knees against the wall of the train, away from the hot thigh two inches over in the next seat, sweating in thick blue jeans. She kept her face turned to the window to hide her leaking eyes. Ian wiped his beaded forehead with a crisp new handkerchief, embroidered in the corner with his initials—*ITC*. Mattie had received a matching set. *MLC*. A wedding gift.

Ian didn't seem to notice his new wife trying to make herself as small as possible in the seat next to him, staring out the window, avoiding conversation. Her avoidance wasn't necessary. He wouldn't have known what to say to Mattie if she were looking him straight in the face. He daubed his upper lip. He ate a salted peanut from the bag in his lap. He wiped the grease from his fingers on the handkerchief.

Mattie glanced at her childhood friend, fidgeting in his seat, and wiped her running nose with the back of her hand. Ian nervously smoothed the now smudged, damp piece of cloth in his lap. His toe tapped an erratic beat inaudibly on the floor of the chugging train.

"Can I have one?" Mattie asked.

Ian started at the question.

"Pardon?" he said, looking like he often had after school, when any attention he received from his classmates was followed by a blow.

Mattie nodded at the bag.

"Oh," Ian said, holding it out to her. "Here, take it."

"I don't want them all," she said, tipping a few into her cupped palm and passing it back. "We can share."

Ian timidly accepted the bag, looking relieved. It would be so easy to hate him as she hated her father, Mattie thought, looking at her compulsory husband as he chewed a mouthful of peanuts and tapped his toes. But Ian was nothing like her father. And this was as much a shock for him as it was for herself, Mattie was sure. She'd wondered about the logistics. Likely Ian's mother had expressed her concerns about him to Mattie's own mother long ago. Her soft, spineless son. What was to be done? Would he ever marry? Was he peculiar, as Mattie had come to understand she herself was? Doubtless Mattie's parents would not have offered their eldest daughter as a cure for Ian's queer nature when the topic was first broached. But in a panic, facing what appeared to be the same curse, they jumped. A convenient way to remedy the strangeness of their children, by binding them together.

On the train they spoke of Shubie and kids at school in generic pleasantries to pass the time, but not of Edith. They talked about their new house, bought for them by their families, and, Mattie had to admit, the excitement of moving to the city.

Ian had been accepted to Dalhousie and would start in September. And Mattie's mother had arranged for her to work in a women's clothing store run by her second cousin, who was more than happy to take on a bright young woman as a shop hand. It was she who had gifted them the handkerchiefs.

The store wasn't far from their new home, though when Mattie's back and feet began to ache at the end of long shifts spent ironing dresses, dusting hats, arranging gloves, and fluffing crinolines, she could always take the electric trolley coach. She took it more as her belly grew. Ian insisted.

It had only happened once. Mattie wanted a friend in Ian, not a husband, and he had been so painfully embarrassed during the event that it seemed unlikely to happen again. It had just felt like the thing to do. One child would be enough between a young student and a young store clerk. She would become their life, the one thing that kept them together when nothing about their marriage made sense.

Joan was almost a year old when Edith dropped the letter into the mailbox from nearly thirteen hundred kilometres away. She had learned to walk well enough to toddle over to her mother and tug on her skirt as Mattie stood by the window, reading and crying, holding the photograph of Edith to her heart.

"Do you want to come with me to Toronto, Joanie?" Mattie asked, her voice cracking.

"Up," Joanie said, reaching her small arms toward her mother.

Mattie lifted her up and swayed from side to side, her tears falling into her daughter's wispy hair. Could she go? Zip Joanie into her slicker, pack a few sandwiches and a change of clothing, take her secret fold of bills from the tobacco tin under the crib, and leave that afternoon on the train? She held the photo up to the light and traced the line of Edith's cheek with her thumb as Joanie fiddled with the clasp of her necklace. What would her parents do? Would they find her? Would they take her baby?

IN THE DARK TORONTO BAR with its sticky floors and loud music, Edith told the story of her first kiss.

"And where's she now, E?" Lil asked. "Married?"

"Married," Edith nodded.

"It's always the way," Mitch said between swigs of beer. "You woo so many straight women until you find a good femme, like this beauty right here."

She leaned in and kissed Iris. That kind of sweetness between women, open and in public, made Edith's heart ache.

"It's the same story every time," Lil agreed. "They'll let you make love to them and tell you you're their one and only. But when a man comes along…."

"They'll leave you lonely!" Pat jumped in from across the table.

"It's the truth, E, the sad truth," Mitch said, patting her on the back.

"Straight women. They'll break your heart, honey. You need to move on. Make some lucky girl happy," said Iris, squeezing Edith's hand.

Edith nodded in thanks. But she was sure she would see Mattie again.

27

January 28, 2008

L*ike a lot of other loner fourteen-year-olds, Ada discovered the thrill of* drawing on her skin with thin blades. Back when all those hormones were making her cry so much she'd pound her fists on her bedroom floor loud enough to make her mother yell upstairs for her to knock it off, the blades calmed her—a quick shock to snap her out of it, like sucking the breath out of a baby. And then later, when the chemicals and hormones and whatever else found their balance and she stopped crying altogether, she used them to feel pain again, even if just a little.

It seems to be a pretty common practice. Ada sees the thin silvery lines and the thick puffy pink and purple scars on the arms of drugstore cashiers, the girl she serves mango salad to at the restaurant, kids at music shows. Lots of kids, really, anywhere. Sometimes she wants to give them knowing, empathetic smiles, but since she's usually cold and wears long sleeves, the cut-up kids wouldn't know what her smile was trying to tell them.

Sometimes she wants to roll up her sleeves and compare scars. Ask them what they used and how deep they went. James has a thick, dark red one that he says went so deep, little white lumps of fat came out of the wound. Maybe Ada's fascination with piercing is connected, but she feels better about it because she doesn't do it to herself. Because she pays for it. It's professional, decorative. Artful maiming. Like those people who dream of having no feet and trick doctors into amputating them. Well, maybe not quite.

Her body feels like it's gone dormant, like her grandmother's. She hasn't sent a jolt through it lately to stir her nerves. She wants Pan to cut her into beautiful shapes and shadows like she cuts the blocks for her prints. To cut out her negative space and make what's left into something beautiful. Cut her into art. Fold her up and snip her into snowflakes. She wants Pan's attention. Since she's not getting it otherwise, she supposes she can go back to paying for it. Is that fucked up? Maybe.

"Would you do a special piece for me?"

Ada called the shop before thinking about it enough to decide not to. "Well, hey to you too," Pan says, sounding casual and amused. "Haven't heard from you in a bit. What's new?"

"Not much."

Silence. It seems to dismantle Pan's ease.

"Um, so, what was it you said? Something about a, uh, a special piece?"

"I was thinking," Ada pauses to suck in smoke, "that we could meet up to talk about it."

The smoking provides a rest in her fast, nervous speech, making her seem calmer than she really is. It's also a good way to feel self-destructive and romantic without slicing up her arms. But she has to smoke out the window and then brush her teeth and tongue and scrub her fingers hard after each one, because she doesn't like the stale bitter scent of it, and because her mother would kill her. She's heard citrus takes the smell out, so she drinks syrupy juice and rubs orange oil on her wrists and through her hair. It's a lot of work to maintain the ruse, but people seem to get more respect when they don't believe in their own mortality. Ada wonders if Pan will take her more seriously as a smoker.

"Okay," Pan says. "Let's meet for coffee. At six."

Ada blows smoke into the afternoon air. There's a bird hanging out in the tree by her window. Its song sounds so unpremeditated. Ada would like to whistle like that.

The second hand of her watch ticks delicately, indifferently. There's a couple drags left before she's smoking the filter, but Ada can see her mother walking up the street with her fast, determined stride. Joan walks everywhere fast, even when she has nowhere to go. Ada stubs out the cigarette on the outside windowsill and goes to the bathroom to flush it down the toilet. Stabs a swan-necked straw into a juice box, sucks it down in three long pulls, and drops orange oil onto her wrists and fingertips and runs them through her hair.

She decides to leave the house two hours early.

At the café, the thick-eyebrowed man gives her a smile and squints his eyes at her, like those people who call you trouble, old teachers and grandads. They say they're keeping their eye on you but really they want you to get away with whatever it is they think you're up to.

Her eyes run around the room, looking for empty tables and there, it's Pan, in her usual spot by the window, also almost two hours early. Pan sees her too and they both seem unsure of whether or not to be embarrassed. Ada walks over to the table and Pan folds her newspaper clumsily, crunching it where it won't crease. A frustrated child's origami. Pan looks at it and sighs.

"Hi," she looks up at Ada with a little smile.

"Hi," Ada says. "Do you want me to come back in a couple hours? I can sit at that table over there while you practice your folding."

"No," Pan grins. "Sit."

Pan looks at her like she can see something's missing. She looks at Ada's face—at her mouth and back up at her eyes.

"Are you okay?" she asks.

She holds Ada's gaze, but her eyes slip every now and then, like she's walking a concrete ledge around a parking lot and she loses focus, walking too fast. Her worn out shoes slip and she touches pavement, hot lava, alligator water. Her eyes slip to Ada's lips.

"Yeah, I'm okay," Ada says, none too convincingly. But Pan doesn't push it.

"So, what did you mean by a special piece?" Pan asks, leaning back in her chair. "Do you even have anything left to pierce?"

"There's always something more to pierce," Ada says. "But I meant something else."

Ada's fingers find the newspaper and work to arrange it back in order.

"You know how I love your prints?" she asks, eyes down on the paper she's creasing, getting its grey words all over her fingers. "Well, have you ever thought of doing a cutting?"

The question snaps Pan's eyes up from Ada's mouth.

"Like on skin? On your skin?" She breathes out. "I don't know, girl. I've never done one before. And it would be cool to learn but I don't know if I want to experiment on you."

"But I want you to. Will you think about it?"

"I don't know. What if I just drew on you with a magic marker or something?" she asks. "It'd hurt less."

"I can take it," Ada says.

"I know you can," Pan says. "I'm just not sure I can give it."

28

❧

February 11, 2008

As a kid, Ken was fascinated by big machines. When he first started getting into construction, working his way up to operating the hulking equipment, he never imagined how much he would grow to dislike tearing buildings down. He hadn't been in Africville when the houses were flattened, didn't feel what it was like to watch thick metal teeth bite into his family home. Though he's starting to feel it now.

He doesn't like demolishing buildings in his own neighbourhood. He knows the people who live there—who lived there. He's visited friends in these apartments, bought pop and beef jerky from these convenience stores. He could stop, he supposes. Just refuse to do it. But they'd replace him with someone else and Ken would miss out on a paycheque.

In the cab he sits still, staring at the building in front of him, trying to remember which window was his high school girlfriend's. He isn't sure, but it doesn't matter. They had each been someone's window, had been opened up by people to feel the ocean air, to call down to friends and neighbours on the street. And now he needs to take them apart to make room for a new building with smooth concrete walls and sleek glass panes, whose tenants won't know the people walking around on the sidewalk below, who will lock their windows at night. At least, that is, until they've run all the old residents from the area and pushed out the unseemly resources. No more drop-ins, no more needle exchange, no more legal aid.

"Ken!" the crew boss hollers at him, walking up to the cab. "What's going on, buddy? You tired or something? Get going."

Ken nods, waits until his boss is standing safely back, and pulls the levers to swing the excavator's head toward the building. He pauses, exhales, and sinks the steel teeth into the roof, tapping the brittle beams and letting gravity do the rest. He nudges the machine's head against the front wall, gently pushing it inward. It collapses loudly in on itself. Ken scoops up the broken planks with the shovel and transfers them to the industrial bin. His machine is elegant, for all its exhaust and grease and clanking metal. It's not brash and clumsy like a wrecking ball. The excavator taps, nudges, and pulls apart these old buildings, gingerly picking up after itself when it's done.

"This is not my fault," Ken tells himself as he works the machine. "This would carry on without me. If I don't tear it down, someone else will."

AND IT'S TRUE, it will carry on.

But in between classes, when Kiah's able to make a bit of room in her brain for something other than school, she's beginning to think that even if she can't stop it, she can do something. She keeps thinking of her grandma and her dad, predicting the future of their neighbourhood. They're right, she thinks. But what can she do? If only her mom were still around to tell her. It would have been so cool to organize something with her. So what would Leona do? Get on the phone, invite friends and family over to complain and eat cookies, and then make a plan. Kiah won't have to call her friends up to come over, though. They already all congregate in one place.

When Kiah gets to the Black students' centre, she's greeted warmly as always by Alice, the advisor. A few of her friends sit around at the computers, working on assignments, listening to music with headphones on. Nadine must be in class—her half-eaten, wilted salad abandoned on the table.

"How's it going, Kiah?" Alice asks. She's so good with names. One of those people who will remember you forever after the first time you introduce yourself.

"I'm good," Kiah says. "I've been thinking about something though."

"I'm all ears," Alice says, putting down her pen.

"I've been thinking about all the condos going up in the north end."

"Mhm," Alice affirms, nodding her head. "I think about them too."

"And I feel like I want to do something about it," Kiah says.

Alice smiles.

"Nice to hear you talking like your mom."

Pride blooms in Kiah's chest like a patch of yellow flowers, opening in the sun.

"But," Kiah admits, "I don't know what to do."

"Well," Alice says through a soft breath, "Kiah, it's tough because a lot of those condos are already sold, even in the buildings that haven't been built yet. It's a little late to be pressuring the developers for affordable housing."

Kiah nods slowly, disappointed.

"But you can be sure the condos won't stop there," Alice says, planting seeds. "For the ones that haven't been built or converted yet and the units that haven't been sold, like that junk shop on Gottingen, you could start getting the word out, getting people together. You know, pressure the developers to make at least some of the units affordable."

"You have the best ideas," Kiah says, brightening.

"Though," Alice continues, balancing hope with reality, "I mean, it could be useless. There's nothing in the City's development standards to make those suits offer affordable housing, even though there should be. Could be frustrating to organize people to push that message and then see no results."

"Yeah," Kiah says, looking down at her hands. "Well that sucks."

"I'm not saying you shouldn't try. Your mom did a lot of impossible things. Why don't you go pull Noah and Mel's headphones off and chat them up about it? I'm sure you'll figure something out. You're smart kids."

Kiah pulls up a chair between her friends sitting at the computers and taps each on the shoulder. They tug their headphones off and swivel around.

"Hey," Noah says. "What's going on?"

"Look at you," Melissa says, grabbing Kiah's hands and turning them over, like she's looking for something. "No book! Noah, do you see a book?"

"Nope," he says, scanning her over, peeking inside the hood of her sweatshirt.

"All right, all right, yep, I get it." Kiah laughs.

"So what's up?" Melissa asks.

"Well, okay, so I was talking with my dad about all the demolition and construction going on uptown, about all the condos being built, and you know, they'll just keep building and building, right? None of those units are affordable. Like, who's going to live there?"

"Not me, that's for damn sure," Noah says.

"Yeah, not me either," Kiah says. "And so all those condos make land more expensive, drive rents up, and you get what happened to the Carters—the landlord raises the rent or sells your house and you gotta move."

"Yep," says Melissa. "That fucking sucks."

"It does, right? So I dunno, I want to do something about it but I'm not sure what. I was thinking you might be down to brainstorm? It just feels shitty to sit around and do nothing while they creep into our neighbourhood all righteous and fancy with their giant billboards and bougie buildings."

Her friends sit for a second. Noah's music thumps fuzzily through the small speakers in his headphones.

"I mean, we could just spray-paint all over their billboards," he says.

"And their buildings," Melissa follows.

A loud throat-clearing comes from behind the desk.

"Vandalism isn't quite what I had in mind," Alice says. "Think you geniuses could come up with a plan B?"

Noah chuckles.

"How 'bout I call you both tonight," he says. "We'll meet up and figure something out. Nice to have you back in the real world, Kee."

29

✼

January 5, 1953

oanie was finally asleep in her crib, but Mattie kept instinctively swaying from side to side. Since the baby, she could never keep still. She rocked her hips back and forth like she was slow-dancing, but alone.

She knelt down beside her sleeping child and reached a hand under the crib, dislodging the tobacco tin from its secret place between the slats. She walked over to the window so she could read by the blue winter light. It had been over a year since the letter came. She'd read it many times. The photo was hidden between the slats of her own bed, since it didn't fit into the tin and Mattie wouldn't fold it. As Ian never made the bed, there was little danger of him finding it.

And suddenly she was sobbing. Silently, like she'd learned to. Her hand covered her open mouth and shut-tight eyes, leaking tears again. The persistent loneliness that trailed her like a shadow and chilled her like a sickness. What could her life have been? If they'd never been caught. If she'd refused her parents' plan and left Nova Scotia. She cursed herself for thinking Joanie out of existence. How selfish of her to wish for a different life. But she did. She wished an impossible life. Where she and Edith and Joanie lived together in one house. Where they cared for the child and read poems out loud and kissed within the walls of their home where no one could stop them. Surely they'd quarrel. Surely some nights they'd sleep back to back, not touching, as she and Ian did. No love is perfect all the time. But this love, built up in Mattie's mind from glances, a few words, one kiss, and a letter—it could just, it could just be so good.

Mattie pressed the tears from her eyes with her palms and expelled her held breath. She needed a pen.

In the living room, she lifted the handle of Ian's rolltop desk and found one exactly where it should be, resting in the groove that was carved for it. She sifted through his school notes to find a blank sheet of paper, and sat down heavily in the small wooden chair. A hazy veil welled up, obscuring the page, but she blinked it back. What could she say? Over a year with no response. How cold of her. How cowardly. What did Edith think of her now? Did she think of her at all, anymore? Perhaps she'd found someone else.

INDEED, EDITH HAD. OR RATHER, her friends had found someone for her. They had made it their mission to fix her up with a street-smart sweetheart who would treat her right, and after a few flops, someone had stuck. Someone whose curls spilled onto Edith's pillow, tickling her face and making her dream of dragonflies. Who both loved to hold Edith and be held by her, and didn't insist that she pick a side, butch or femme. And who listened to her. Listened to her tell stories of home, of school. Of the river. Though Edith was selective in her storytelling. She didn't talk about Mattie. It wouldn't be hard for her lover to tell that Edith loved her, and though most everyone knows you can love more than one person at once, not many like to admit it.

So Edith let her lover think that all the poems she wrote were about her and her alone. She once had a poem folded and slipped into an envelope for Mattie, her lips parted to lick the seal, when she finally decided otherwise. She couldn't do that to her lover. It felt cruel.

She wondered if Mattie got that first letter, if she had written back. Edith moved from her apartment not long after sending it, and had checked twice for mail with the gruff new tenant before telling herself enough. Mattie wouldn't know where to write to her now. Though perhaps that was for the best. They could live their lives instead of daydreaming.

But Edith couldn't bury her tenderness for her first love. Instead, she kept it in out-of-the-way places. Down a narrow mud path through bird-specked branches. In the pocket of an old coat. Places she could visit once in a while, where time kept moving but everything was different. An alternate world. Perhaps, she thought, that would one day shift. Her life now would be the one she kept in a tucked-away place while she stepped back into a story that had never really finished.

30

❧

February 11, 2008

oo dramatic. Too '90s. Too depressing. All Ada wants is a good dyke film with a hot sex scene, and she can't decide what sort of nonsense she's willing to sit through to get it.

For the past week she and Pan have done nothing but lie in bed and nap. The reverse of what they started with—sex and no sleepovers. Now it's no fucking and all sleeping.

Pan called her last week, called the house very late, and Ada was awake because she doesn't sleep much these days. Pan sounded sad, very tired and alone. Sounded like she was sitting in the dark. She had sent Ada home a few hours earlier from another dinner date where they hadn't actually managed to make dinner, and now she wanted her to come back. But she kept saying no, you don't have to. No really, it's no big deal, you don't have to come.

Ada did come. Pan must have known she would. Walked back with the freezing ocean breeze breathing on her face and down her neck, forcing her insomniac eyes wider. Walked to Pan's flat and came upstairs through the unlocked door. Pan was in the kitchen, slicing carefully into a sheet of linoleum with a cigarette between her lips. She looked up like Ada had disturbed her. Like she was fine and Ada had gone and made a big deal out of things by coming over.

"Oh hey," she said, with a casual laugh.

Ada wondered what was wrong but didn't ask. Pan hadn't said on the phone. So she sat down and watched Pan work and they didn't talk. Pan just cut and smoked and Ada watched, trying to breathe as evenly and quietly as she could, but she kept swallowing so loudly. She must have been producing more spit than usual, she had to swallow so much.

She wanted to go but didn't know how to leave. It was that thing where your whole body feels frozen, like that hand trick where you squeeze your fist tight and run your fingers over it and when you try to open it up again it's so hard, like all your joints have become rusted hinges. She kept making to get up, to say okay, well, I guess I'll go, but she sat there for about half an hour before she finally managed to squeak her chair back.

"Okay, well," Ada said, with an awkward smile.

"Are you going?" Pan asked, as if they had been having such a good time.

"Uh, yeah. I'm gonna go."

Ada picked up her bag, feeling like an idiot. Pan didn't seem to care. But as Ada was shoving her heel down into her shoe, Pan told her to stop, wait, finally talking in a voice that wasn't pretending to be fine.

"Okay," she said, like the jig was up.

Ada thought an apology was coming so she took the shoe back off with her other foot and waited. It looked like it took a lot of effort, but Pan finally came over to her and stood really close.

"I'm sorry I asked you back," she said with pleading eyes. "I was just lonely. You can go if you want."

"I don't want to go. I didn't want to go the first time I was here, either. But I figure you'll probably send me home again soon anyway, so I might as well leave of my own accord. Like I have some self-respect or something."

Pan looked wounded, like that had been an unfair thing for Ada to say.

"No," she said. "You can stay."

Her words were like a gift, and Ada was ashamed for feeling grateful.

"I mean, please stay. I want you to stay," Pan said, with her hands around Ada's waist and lips grazing her forehead. "It's just that I can't get too close, because I made an agreement."

"An agreement?"

"An agreement with my partner."

Ada stood still, turned to stone. Pan fiddled with the buttons on Ada's shirt and looked up at her through thick curls.

"She's out on the west coast. We're giving each other some space right now, but not too much. Not enough space for me to see someone more than a couple times a week. Or to have someone sleep overnight in my bed."

"This is maybe something you could have mentioned sooner," Ada said, feeling smaller than ever.

"I know. But I like you so much, Ada," Pan said. "I want you to stay."

So she did. They lay in Pan's bed, holding each other and breathing together. But when Ada tried to touch her, Pan brushed her hand away.

"Let's just go to sleep," she said.

FILM IS THE BEST REPLACEMENT for sex Ada can think of for now. But not that one. And not that one.

"That's a good one," a finger points from over her shoulder to a case on the top shelf. "They fuck in a treehouse and no one dies in the end."

Ada smiles. The tall blonde dyke from the bar. Small city.

"Perfect," she says, and thanks her for the suggestion.

"My pleasure," she replies. "Are you going to the bathhouse on Thursday?"

Ada's never been, but she's thought about it. It always seemed to her like some sort of secret society that you had to be invited into. And here's her invitation.

"I might," she says. "Are you?"

The blonde woman is going. With her partner, of course. These fucking women and their partners.

"I told her about you after that night at the bar," she says. "She thought it sounded pretty hot."

"Oh did she?" Ada grins.

So this is how you respect your partners, Ada thinks. Pan should take notes.

"I'm Dylan," the woman says, extending her hand. Those fingers.

"Ada," she says, shaking it with her own.

"So, if you happened to be at the bathhouse, I think me and Kate would probably be up for a little group session."

Ada blushes and fumbles her movie to the floor.

"Maybe," she says, grinning.

ON THURSDAY ADA HAS TO work a dinner shift until ten before she can go out. At the end of January when her boss was making up the schedule, he asked who wanted Valentine's Day off. Priority went to people with partners, he said, and he wanted no moping from the singletons.

"I'll mope all I fucking please," James said to her afterward. "Why don't you take it off so you and your girlfriend can make sweet lesbian love?"

"Fuck off, James," Ada said. "First off, she's not my girlfriend. And second, I've told you before, I'm not a lesbian. Third, we're barely having sex these days, and fourth, if I even thought for a second she would spend any kind of coupley time with me I would jump at the chance, but she's way too goddamn punk for that. Corporate Hallmark romance? If I even mentioned it you know I'd be cut."

Pan has made her disdain for Valentine's known, and Ada's not even sure sex is an option at this point. This open-relationship business is so convoluted. Ada doesn't even want to try to comprehend the rules that state Pan can fuck but not love and love but not fuck. As some wayward young thing with a crush, Ada was vetted for sex, but now that Pan "likes her so much" it seems that sex is off the table and the best Ada can hope for is a half-decent spoon and maybe a kiss on the neck before Pan drifts off. That's not to say Pan isn't seeing anyone else in town—a possibility Ada hasn't dared to try to confirm, lest her highly conformist dreams of ever-after love and monogamous marriage reveal themselves through her badly affected nonchalance.

Oh god, she thinks. I hope you won't be there tonight.

Surprisingly, she hadn't thought about it until now. What if Pan thinks Ada's trying to wedge herself into her scene? Ada doesn't even know if this is Pan's scene. Older dyke, bathhouse. Seems possible. If she showed up to see Pan and her ex-lover and all Pan's cool queer friends that she's never been introduced to, she'd feel like a stalker. Or a tagalong kid sister.

After her last table pays up, Ada brings a Singha to the tiny, humid bathroom that the cook showers in after his shift. It has no windows. She cracks the beer and sets it on the wet countertop. Peels off her salty shirt and pulls on a worn yellow one that lies loose over her belly and small tits. Anyone who kisses her body tonight will taste the sweat and spice of the kitchen.

She swigs the beer in long, cold gulps until she gives herself hiccups. Pulls her polyester pants down and inches into jeans. She wipes makeup smudges from under her eyes, her skin glowing from hours of slow sweating. Tips the piss of the beer down her throat and looks at herself in the mirror.

"You look cute," she tells herself. "I'd make out with you."

The bathhouse is humid and packed. Ada hadn't been so sure she would be able to walk around naked while trying to pick up, thinking it would compromise her confidence. But there's no way she'll survive hours in this damp labyrinth in her clothes. She stuffs her coat, shirt, scarf, and jeans into a locker along with her socks and shoes, leaving her hypochondriac feet to fend for themselves on the clammy tile floor.

I don't know any of these people, she thinks, although she's bought gelato from the cute queer in the corner who is busy making out with his pink-haired partner. A short, spunky woman bounces around the room, asking everyone for kisses. Her breasts hang heavy and soft and her shoulders look round and strong. Ada leans against the wall and pretends not to notice her making her way over, kiss by kiss.

Most of her awkwardness comes from not having any pockets. She's a hands-in-her-pockets kind of person and right now she has none. People always seem to need to do something with their hands—cross their arms, tangle their fingers together, cradle their chin, grasp a drink. Next to Ada, the tallest girl with the longest hair combs her fingers through her ponytail, and another person walks around gripping a shiny whip.

But Ada's hands don't feel safe anywhere but inside pockets when she's nervous. Someone hanging out by the hot tub wears red suspenders clipped to their shorts, and hooks their thumbs in the straps. Cute. Ada wishes she had suspenders.

The bouncy woman gives a quick peck to the tall girl leaning against the wall next to Ada and thanks her. She continues on her way.

"Hi there," she smiles, and somehow Ada feels special, as if she didn't already watch her make out with everyone else in the room. She decides she'll make herself exceptional.

"Can I kiss you?" she asks before the woman can, making fun of her a little and coming off more confident than she really is.

The woman grins. Ada kisses her long and full, sucking her lip and pausing to pull back. They look at each other for a second and start again. It feels good and friendly and her tongue is nice and soft without a bar through it, even though Ada misses Pan's, clicking against her teeth when she darts it fast into her mouth.

She feels the woman's hand on her naked back and their sticky bodies press together, the woman's soft breasts against her own.

"Do you want to go find a room?" she says, like she's asking Ada to play catch or go for a run. She reminds Ada of her eighth-grade gym teacher.

Ada follows her muscled back into a small room where they kiss on a plasticky bed. The woman bites hard and deep into the muscle of Ada's neck and Ada twists her nipple back. She hums pleasure into Ada's skin and pulls back to look at her.

"Do you want me to fuck you?" she asks, still playful.

"Yes," Ada says quickly, before thinking it through.

The woman grins and goes off in search of gloves, and Ada's left sitting on the plastic-covered bed in the tiny room with mirrored walls. She can see herself from every angle. Her hair looks gross from the back, she thinks. She wonders if Dylan and her partner are here, and if she'll miss her chance with them while the bouncy gym teacher has her fingers in her cunt.

Maybe I don't want this after all, she thinks, but here the woman is, snapping her gloves on and wrapping her hands around Ada's ankles. She yanks her down along the bed toward her and her sweaty skin sticks to the plastic, squeaking and stinging. Tissue paper is much better. The way Pan moves her much better—slow and certain, firm and authoritative.

But the woman pulls her down and climbs up on the squeaky bed and when they kiss again, Ada knows she's not into it. She wonders if the woman can tell.

All of a sudden the woman's spit is thick and slimy, no longer watery and sweet, and her tongue is an intrusion. She squeezes a packet of lube out onto her fingers and when she slides them in, Ada tells her harder. The woman fucks her so hard and Ada feels strange. Her moans are short uh uh uhs and she breathes sharp.

"Okay, okay," she says between breaths.

The woman slips out.

"Do you want me to go down on you?" she says seductively, like only a gym teacher could.

Ada loves to be licked but what is she doing? Am I doing this for you? she wonders to Pan. I am. Jesus.

"Yes," she says, and though she's sober enough to think to ask her to use a dam, the woman's mouth is already on her. Ada looks in the mirror and sees this stranger's body crouched between her legs, and all she feels is lonely.

She stutters out some excuse about being too sensitive and the woman comes up with wet lips and kisses her.

"That's okay, babe," she says. "Is there anything else you want?"

Really she's waiting for Ada to ask her the same, and it would be the polite thing to do but she just can't.

"No, I'm good. Thanks," Ada says, and gives her an insincere kiss beside her lips.

"You're welcome…?" the woman says, looking at her for an explanation. Getting none, she heaves herself up from the bed with a squeak, leaving the little mirrored room.

Ada tugs her underwear back up and takes a last look at herself in all the mirrors. Her reflection looks disapprovingly back from behind the glass.

Warm, damp bodies brush by her as she walks through the narrow, tiled halls, moist under her feet.

"Hey," a voice calls from inside a dark room as Ada passes by the open door.

She backs up. Dylan and her partner are sitting on the bed, side by side, sweaty and rosy-cheeked, sipping from water bottles. They rest their hands lazily on each other's thighs.

"We just finished a bit of an intense fuck," Dylan says with a laugh. "Do you wanna come outside with us for a smoke?"

"Me too," Ada smiles, tucking strands of her damp hair behind an ear. "And yeah, I do."

She grabs her jeans, shirt, scarf, and coat from her locker, wraps her body in the familiar fabric, and steps around all the laughing, sighing, chatting, silent, moping, kissing, excited, and awkward queers that line the hallway to the door. She emerges into the cold air trailing wisps of steam, and sees Dylan and her partner standing a few feet away. Dylan holds a glowing invitation between two fingers and Ada takes it, sucking in smoke to cleanse stranger spit from her mouth. She reaches her other hand out to Dylan's partner.

"I'm Ada," she says.

"So formal," Dylan's partner teases, but squeezes her fingers. "Kate."

"How's your night been so far?" Dylan asks. Ada mentions fast sex with the bouncy woman.

"She's intense," Dylan and Kate agree, nodding knowingly.

Dylan leans in to Ada and kisses her, slow and warm. She pulls her head back, grins, and turns to kiss Kate. They pull each other close, leaving Ada to finish the cigarette.

Ada likes watching them kiss. She wants to know about them—how they met, if they live together, if they get jealous, how they talk to each other when it's just the two of them, how they sleep. They wrap their arms around each other as they kiss. Ada takes a hard pull on the smoke and her head lightens. She looks up at the streetlight overhead, glowing artificially beside a pale moon. Across the street, she catches the eyes of three people looking back at her and the kissing, giggling couple who have possibly forgotten that she exists. One of them looks familiar, Ada thinks, pushing her hair out of her eyes.

31

February 14, 2008

A *few hours ago Kiah almost envied her brother for the first time since* they were kids, when Ken took Shawn fishing at Kearney Lake without her. Other than that one afternoon fourteen years back, she generally feels that, compared to her brother, she doesn't want for much. She got the brains, the drive, her mom's hair. Tonight it only stung for a minute or two when her brother took off to his room right after dinner, leaving her to clean up the dishes, and emerged in a wave of cologne so dense Kiah knew he had a date. Her scrawny little brother. Goddammit.

She shook it off. Whatever. Let Shawn go hold hands in the movie theatre, she thought to herself. Let him get a blow job in the back row for all I care. Shit, that's disgusting. Sometimes Kiah's brain goes too far. But for real though. Kiah's basement troll of a brother got a date and she didn't?

Most of her indignation was sucked down the drain along with soap suds and bread crumbs as her mind turned to her own plans for the night. She had better things to do than swoon for flowers and small talk with some Valentine's Day sucker. She had paste to cook.

Once her dad and grandma were settled in front of the TV in the living room with their can of beer and cup of tea, Kiah pulled a pot from under the oven and filled it with water to boil. The flour and water mixed up milky and she stirred it as it bubbled, measuring out sugar and lining up old yogurt containers on the counter. She poured in the sugar and left the pot to cool on the stovetop with a note:

School project. Do not eat.

After trying and failing to fall asleep, reading a chapter of one of the books Nadine prescribed, and having a quiet conversation with herself in the mirror about her impending scheme, with the tiny framed photo of her mother sitting on her shoulder as her conscience, Kiah creeps back down to the kitchen. She treads carefully alongside the wall where the steps are the least creaky, and quietly pours the lukewarm paste into three yogurt containers. It's two in the morning on a school night and Kiah is sneaking out of the house for the first time in her life. Ken probably would have supported the cause but would have been nervous about the method. Ask your mother, he would have told her if Leona had been alive. And Kiah had, sort of.

They decided to meet at Melissa's house, because her mom either doesn't notice or doesn't care whether Mel is at home or whether she has friends over at 2 A.M., as long as they aren't being too loud. Mel lays the neon stack of posters out on the old coffee table in the basement, still stuck with shiny fragments of stickers from when she was a kid—unicorn heads and half smiley faces and purple panda bear paws.

"*Wasn't one eviction enough?*" Kiah reads from the fluorescent yellow pages. "*Condos out of the North End. Learn from Africville. We need affordable housing.*"

"Right on," Noah says.

The headings stand out in bold black ink, a different one on each page. Below, Mel has written about the lack of affordable housing in the area, the jacked-up land values, the eviction of people and community services, and added an email address, set up specifically for the cause.

Tell these developers they're not welcome in our neighbourhood, the posters read at the bottom. *Contact us to get involved.*

"These are awesome, Mel," Kiah says. "All I did was get the spray paint and cook the paste."

"That's impressive too, Kee," says Noah, reclining in a sagging orange armchair with his hands behind his head. "I didn't do anything. I'm just your bodyguard for the night."

"Yeah right," Kiah says. "We don't need a bodyguard. You're here to spray and glue. I'm not the only one getting this nasty porridge on my hands."

She hands him a yogurt container full of warm paste and a paint brush. Mel splits the pile into three and hands a stack to each of her friends. The pages, paste, a brush, and a can of paint fit perfectly into Kiah's carefully chosen messenger bag, where they'll be within easy reach. She slips on a thin pair of black gloves that she can toss when they're through, to keep spray paint residue off her fingertips. You know, *evidence*. She's been thinking about nothing but this for four days. Doing some discreet Googling. Surreptitiously watching her grandmother's crime dramas from the kitchen doorway. She's ready.

But out on Gottingen, she starts to feel nervous.

"God, we look so fucking sketchy," she says to her friends.

"No," Mel says. "It's cool. We'll just say we're coming home from a late-night study session at a friend's house."

"Oh yeah? And what if they search our bags?" Kiah asks. "How do we explain the paste and paint?"

"We'll say the spray paint's for a school project," Mel replies.

"And the paste?" Noah asks.

"Uh," Mel takes a second to think. "The paste is our late-night power snack. Wheat gluten. Lots of energy."

Kiah laughs.

They walk down the sidewalk past abandoned buildings, keeping an eye out for cop cars.

"How 'bout here?" Kiah says. "Let's post some on these empty buildings. Maybe the developers who buy the lots will read 'em and think twice."

They pull out their posters, one of each, and quickly slap the sticky paste on the dark, dirty windows of the abandoned club and smooth out the paper, sealing it in with another coat, so fast. And then they move on.

"That was fucking great," Kiah whispers. She can't stop smiling. "Don't get too excited," Mel says. "We've got a lot of street left."

A block away people sway and lean into each other, pulling on cigarettes and breathing out smoke and vapour, subtly trying to blow into each other's mouths for want of a kiss. Valentine's Day proper is already finished but clusters of people linger, holding onto the dwindling beats escaping out through the insulated walls of the bar and floating tinny in the frigid night air, waiting for any potential love to reveal itself in the final minutes of the night before their eyelids get heavy and the tips of their fingers freeze.

Across the street, from behind frosted windows, bodies bundled against the cold emerge in a cloud of steam. Skin flushed, fingers brushing hair from eyes through the cut-off tips of gloves, laughs ringing out down the street. Who is that girl? Kiah wonders. Is that her neighbour?

"That's a gay sex club, y'all know that?" Noah says, glancing back at the giggling queers over his shoulder.

"As if that's legal, a sex club on Gottingen. And we can't put up a couple of posters in our own neighbourhood without risking a criminal record?" Mel shakes her head.

"Aw whatever," Kiah tries to redirect where she sees the blame heading. "If they want to do that, I don't care. It's not my business, or yours."

Mel pulls a poster out of her bag as she eyes a smooth, graffitied concrete wall.

"You don't care, huh?" she glances back at Kiah. "Maybe you should join them. I know you haven't been gettin' any."

The cold February air blows sharply up from the harbour and Kiah's glad for it, cooling her hot cheeks. What the fuck is Mel's problem, saying that in front of Noah?

"You don't know shit," Kiah says to the back of Mel's head. "You don't know a thing about who I do or don't sleep with, so shut your mouth."

"Testy," Mel assesses her friend as she slops a coat of paste on the wall. "Are you saying you won't confirm or deny that you would actually go to this club?"

"No," Kiah says, frustrated. "I like *men*. I'm just not telling you which *men* I am or am not sleeping with."

"I mean, some of those girls kinda look like men," Noah interjects, trying to make a joke to break the tension. But Kiah's glare lets him know he failed. "Just sayin'," he says, lifting his hands to show they're empty of prejudice.

"Whatever," Kiah says. "You're both being assholes. Can we just get back to business?"

Kiah pulls a stack of posters out of her bag and pushes them against Noah's chest. "Here," she says. She dips her brush into the sticky plastic bucket and paints a cloudy square on the concrete wall next to Mel's.

They seal posters onto newspaper boxes, boarded up windows, road signs, and billboards advertising new condo units for sale. *A dream home for a dream price*, one billboard reads over a giant image of a white woman meditating against an ocean backdrop. Noah crouches down so Kiah can get her feet on his shoulders, and Mel holds her hands as Noah slowly stands up. Kiah teeters and almost falls forward, the metal bar at the bottom of the billboard right at mouth level. But she grabs onto it before her teeth connect and catches her breath. She reaches in her bag for the can of paint and scrawls *WE NEED AFFORDABLE HOUSING* over the woman's lotus legs.

"Let's move," Mel says, once Kiah's feet hit the ground. "That was fucking conspicuous."

"We should head home," says Noah. "We've pretty much covered the street."

Their fluorescent yellow posters beam back at them from either side of the empty road. Kiah can't believe they did it. Her whole body buzzes with possibility. This was just one thing. She could do way more. She'll make the time.

The neon posters seem to flicker—yellow, green, orange. Noah spins around fast and books it up Cunard, his long legs carrying him up the hill before Kiah can call after him. By the time she's turned back from her fast-departing friend to see the source of the lights, it's too late.

32

February 23, 2008

Flossing is a commitment. It hurts so much for the first few days, when your gums bleed and your teeth feel loose in their sockets, shifting while you chew.

The last time Ada made up her mind to change her dental habits was because she had found an old thing of floss in the bathroom cabinet, but it ran out before she got past the bleeding gum stage. It was so disappointing, all that pain for nothing. She could have walked a few blocks to the drug store and bought another spool, but she figured it wasn't meant to be.

Pan's a bit like floss, Ada thinks. Even though it hurts, she feels like she'll toughen up after a few more tries and it'll be worth it. As long as

Pan doesn't run out. As long as she doesn't cut this short before it gets good. So she keeps trying. Maybe this time Pan won't push her out or push her away, leaving her feeling unanchored, floating. A loose tooth uncertain in its socket.

The premise of this hangout is that Pan is going to teach her how to make a print. They sit at the kitchen table, Ada in the same chair she came in a month ago. It's hard to keep her mind from drifting as Pan describes positive and negative space.

"Like in film negatives, you know?" she says.

"Yeah. Light is dark and dark is light. Sounds pretty simple."

"It does," Pan says, patient, slow, but a little agitated. "But there's more to it than that. You should stick with bold shapes and lines, and remember that your print will be a mirror image of your linocut."

"Makes sense," Ada says.

"And I'd suggest you draw it out first," Pan says. "It's easier to plan where to cut away."

She hands Ada a permanent marker with a thin, delicate tip and pulls the cap off her own with her teeth. She holds it poised over a piece of linoleum, thinking.

Ada reaches for her mug of coffee with the marker between her fingers and accidentally grazes Pan's hand with the liquid tip, leaving an inky line that bleeds across the surface of her skin.

"Shit, sorry," she says, but Pan's already retaliated with a swipe across her arm.

"Hey!" Ada protests. "That was an accident."

"Well I can't think of what to draw," Pan says, "So I might as well draw on you."

"Yeah," Ada says. "You might as well."

She eases her shirt up over her head and sits facing Pan with belly and breasts bare.

"Turn around," Pan says.

Ada swivels on the slippery wood seat and sits up tall, straightening her spine. She can feel Pan's warm hand hovering over her skin.

"Don't think so hard," Ada heckles, and Pan brings the tip of the pen down, drawing a line just under Ada's shoulder blade. It feels good. No pain and only pleasure, and the feeling of Pan's complete attention.

"What are you drawing?" Ada asks.

"Canvases don't talk," says Pan.

She lights a cigarette. The steady tracing of the pen on Ada's skin begins again, trailing lightly just along her spine, gliding across her lower back.

"It's kind of abstract," Pan finally offers, lisping from the cigarette between her lips.

Her left hand curls around Ada's ribcage, holding her still. Ada tries to calm her breathing.

"I'm drawing around the curves of your body."

Pan's pen slows. She sucks once more on her cigarette and puts it out. The smell fills Ada's nostrils, bitter and warm, as Pan brings her face close to her neck.

"You're beautiful," she says, cupping Ada's shoulder with the palm of her hand and sliding her fingers down her arm.

Ada watches over her shoulder how Pan looks at her body, so close. She kisses freckles and brushes her lips along the thin scars on Ada's arms. Ada is sure this crosses some line in Pan's agreement with her partner but isn't about to stop her.

"Beautiful," Pan says again.

LATER THEY LIE IN PAN'S BED, all lines crossed like they never even existed. Ada wonders if she should feel bad. Does Pan? She kisses Pan's neck and lets her eyes travel around the room as she breathes in the smell of her hair. Her eye snags on a photo on the dresser, half obscured by a stack of burned CDs and a bottle of lube.

"I wish you could meet her," Pan says, when she realizes what's caught Ada's attention.

"Think about that," Ada says. "The thing you want most is for us to meet?"

"Not most. The thing I want most is…not physically possible."

"Why don't you explain it," Ada says, as her eyes remain penned inside the frame. Wandering across the glossy surface of their three faces, Pan and her partner and their dog, squished in self-portrait. Her eyes pace around the four walls with no gate out. Look at her, Ada thinks to Pan. She's so in love with you.

Pan turns Ada's chin toward her with her thumb, always moving her with hands instead of words. She places Ada's hand on her chest, over her heart. But it's a clammy fist. Ada clenches it but Pan pries her fingers open, laying her palm flat against her body.

"My heart," Pan says, "is an amoeba."

Ada laughs through her hurt.

"It's split. It pulled apart into two hearts. And one's yours. And one's hers."

"Hm," Ada says suspiciously, split between smiling and crying.

"If I could split the rest of my body, I would."

"But you can't."

"No," Pan says. "I can't. But if I could, it wouldn't be so weird if you met her. We could go on double dates."

"Funny," Ada says, pulling her hand back.

But Pan is stronger. One by one she stretches Ada's fingers back out so she can feel their five points around her heart—a warm, lopsided starfish.

"It's just hard," Pan says. "It's like two different lives."

She holds Ada's face in her rough hands and kisses her warm with eyes open. They lie together, side by side on the bed, looking up at their hands. They couldn't think of anything else to say so they lifted them up and held them above their faces. Pan's fingers wander down Ada's wrist, grazing her skin, drifting to the soft crease of her elbow and back up again. They watch their hands touch each other as if they aren't connected to their brains and their stupid, complicated feelings.

"Look at our skin together," Pan says. "It looks beautiful, brown and white."

Ada's not sure what to say. She has convinced herself that the best way to make sure she isn't being racist is to pretend she doesn't see colour at all. Isn't that the most PC thing? She scolded herself hard when they moved into the new house and she saw they had Black neighbours. No, you fucking racist, you have *neighbours*, she silently chastised herself. Why does your brain have to register that they're Black? Can't you just see that they're *people*? When she was in grade twelve French she was convinced that when she finally became fluent, she would just hear all the French words in English. Her educated brain would make the translation for her. Likewise, Ada is sure that when she finally figures out how to be not racist, she will cease to see colour at all.

So she says, "Your skin is beautiful."

"It looks so dark compared to yours," says Pan. "You're really white. Even kind of pink. Like a baby mouse."

She grins and nudges Ada.

"A pudgy, hairless little mouse," Ada agrees, keenly veering off this nerve-wracking acknowledgement of race onto an easy, self-deprecating tangent. "I burn so fast in the sun."

"I don't," Pan says. "I'm made for heat."

"Sometimes I hate being so pale," Ada says as they continue to wind their fingers together.

Pan raises her eyebrows.

"White privilege not quite doing it for you?"

"No, that's not it," Ada mumbles, reddening at the word *white*. "I just meant I'm all pasty and pink. Your skin's so brown and...glowing."

"So you wish you had brown skin because it looks nice?"

Pan rolls over and props herself up on one elbow.

"Maybe you should get a spray tan and wear a bindi," she says, touching Ada gently between the eyes.

Ada winces.

"No," she says, thinking about it. "I wouldn't wear a bindi. I don't know what they mean."

Pan nods.

"Yeah," she says. "And you wouldn't get called dot head like my mother was when my folks moved from India to Vancouver. Tanned white girls don't get followed around shops like I do."

"No, probably not."

"Definitely not," Pan says, and pauses. "Have you dated a person of colour before me?"

Ada smiles.

"Are we dating?" she asks.

"I don't know," Pan sighs. "Pretend I didn't say that. Have you?"

Ada wonders what the right answer is.

"No," she says. "Why?"

Pan lies on her back and stares up at the ceiling.

"I've just dated white girls before who I know were with me to get back at their parents. You know? I could see it when they introduced me. Like they were challenging their authority. It made me feel like a fucking bellybutton ring," she says, touching one of Ada's.

Her fingers trace their scratchy tips across Ada's belly. Warm shivers bloom at the top of her head and spread down through her body.

"I guess I've never dated a Black person before," Ada says. "And I feel like I should."

Pan pulls her hand back.

"Sorry," she says, "you feel like you *should*? Why? So you can tick it off some liberal white girl list?"

"Uh…no," Ada says as she scrambles to sit up. "No. Shit. That's not how I meant it."

She leans against the wall and puts her hands on her face, drawing them back through her hair, trying to clear her head.

"I just meant…I meant that…this city's really segregated. I don't even have any Black friends."

"The city's segregated. And what part of the city do you live in again? Could you remind me?" Pan asks.

"Uh, the north end."

"Yes, the north end. Who do you think lives on your block? Or goes to church around the corner from your house? Or uses the same library as you?"

"I know but—"

"And are you incapable of saying hi to people on the sidewalk, or introducing yourself to your neighbours? Is there a bylaw against interracial friendships?"

Ada's cheeks burn.

"Is there? Because you don't seem to have trouble talking to me."

"No," Ada manages.

"You can't blame it on the city, Ada. You're part of this. This is your history and your present. You get the privilege, so you get the responsibility of learning how to be accountable for it."

Ada's throat sticks and she holds her eyes wide, trying to force her rising tears to dry. She was sure she had this all figured out, was training herself so hard on this colour-blind thing.

"No no," Pan says. "You don't get to cry about this."

Ada nods.

"I'm sorry," she says. "I'm really sorry."

"Don't apologize to me," says Pan. "You're smarter than this, Ada. And you've gotta figure this shit out, 'cause I'm getting tired of teaching it."

33

March 24, 2008

The blade of the paint scraper sticks as Kiah tries to slide it between the papier-mâchéd neon page and the rough concrete of the empty building. Why the hell are they even making her do this? All four sides are already covered in spray paint and you know some thirty-something dude with a popped collar and an Escalade is gonna buy it up and hire her dad to knock it down in a month or two. She chews her lip and throws another glance at Mel, who's attempting the same impossible task a metre away, rigid with cold and resentment. She's barely looked at Kiah since the cops picked them up, and Noah's been walking around on his fast fuckin' legs like he never even met the two of them.

For a few days now Kiah's been coming after school to scrape paper for an hour in the dusk. They'd have made her stay longer but the probation officer sent to babysit has to be home for dinner, so this shit will just drag on and on until all their righteously pasted propaganda is removed. And until Kiah can come up with the money for the fine she was offered in place of a criminal record.

The cop who arrested them told her and Mel they could go to Burnside for two years for all that property damage. No joke. They could go straight to jail. He's just trying to mess with us, Kiah told Mel while they waited in a cell for what felt like forever before they finally got to call home. They can't send us to jail for this, she said. No way. But she wasn't so sure.

Mel's mom, contrary to her reputation, showed up right away and sober as the day she was born.

"Jesus Christ, Melissa," was all she said through tight lips.

Mel hung her head as she followed her mother out the door, wiping snot and hot tears on the sleeve of her coat.

And Kiah sat alone in the cell. Her dad hadn't answered his phone. Probably couldn't even hear it over his own snores. Sure as sin if the kids who pasted that goldfish on the bus shelter by the south-end Sobeys were caught in the act they'd have got a warning. How was she even here? She should be home sleeping—sleeping or studying.

When they brought her to the phone again an hour later, Kiah called the house line and Betty answered, her voice rough with sleep.

"Hello? Who's this?"

Kiah almost hung up. She tasted tears in the back of her throat. How could she tell her grandma she was at the police station? But when she finally managed to talk through trembling lips, Betty was all business.

"Kiah, you tell them I'm coming to get you right now. I'll be there in five minutes. Five minutes, Kiah. I'm putting on my boots."

Betty didn't wake her son. She didn't want to have to soothe two stressed-out kids at once. Kiah sounded scared enough, and Ken could scold the girl when she got home. No need to make things worse now. But putting her granddaughter in lock-up for a little graffiti? Betty had something to say about that.

"You're trying to tell me it's necessary to keep a young woman in a dirty cell for painting on some billboard? For putting up a few posters? You've got to be kidding me," she said to the clerk. "You know my granddaughter is an honours student at Dalhousie? This is absurd."

The clerk shrugged.

"It's not up to me, ma'am," she said. "The arresting officer wanted confirmation from a parent or guardian that she'd appear in court before we let her go."

"My granddaughter is an adult. Are you suggesting she can't be trusted?"

"She was just arrested for committing a crime, ma'am. If gangs of young people are running around at night damaging property, we want the assurance of a parent or guardian that they'll show up for court."

Betty bristled.

"Gangs? How dare you talk about my granddaughter like she's some criminal. Where is she? I'm here to take her home."

The woman behind the Plexiglas pushed her glasses up her nose and peered at Betty.

"If you want to take her home tonight, *ma'am*, she'll have to agree to show up for court, and we'll need your assurance that she'll be there."

Betty sucked in air like she was fortifying her defenses. She readied herself to preach all of Kiah's credentials and a political history of street art and resistance. But she knew her monologue would bounce off the Plexiglas and never reach the clerk's ears. She breathed out.

"Fine."

KIAH HAD TO MISS CLASS to show up in court. She thought her dad might have gone with her. But no, Ken refused. He was in shock. He could barely talk to his daughter without reprimanding her. Without telling her how disappointed he was. And Shawn didn't say a word at the dinner table—the only place where he could be close enough to his sister to glance at her quickly from under lowered lids. Who was this person? He knew Kiah was passionate, even that she thought of herself as mildly revolutionary. But the girl had gone guerilla.

Dinners have been nearly silent, save for the scraping of forks on plates. If Shawn dares to even ask his dad to pass the salt, all he gets is a grunt and a glare, and Betty has to reach over plates to retrieve the shaker and keep some semblance of decorum and peace. Shawn didn't do a thing wrong. All this time Kiah's been trying to frame him as the bad one and now she goes and gets herself arrested, and the tension in the house is so thick Shawn can't even gloat.

34

⚘

March 24, 2008

"**C**ap for me, cap for you," James says, gently placing a dried mushroom top in the withered brown pile in front of Ada.

They sit in James's kitchen, listening to his roommates getting loud, playing video games in the next room. A bigger pile of trail mix sits between them, the kind with M&M's, to eat in between the musty shrooms.

James doesn't do synthetic drugs anymore, he tells Ada. Now it's mostly just weed, plus mushrooms on special occasions. You can trust them a bit more, he says, but God knows what they've been sprayed with. These ones came from his cousin's best friend who grows them on PEI and knows his shit, so James isn't worried.

They touch their fattest stalks together as a sort of cheers and pop them in their mouths, chewing them up with salty almonds and chocolate.

"Chew them up really good," he tells Ada.

"I know," she says.

She hasn't done mushrooms since eleventh grade with the prettiest loner, who stayed at her high school for only half a year. But she knows. The boy had moved to Halifax from Wales, which has the best mushrooms, he told Ada. Apparently the local ones they did together in the public school playground on a sunny Saturday were no comparison. Ada liked them though, aside from the acid stomach clenching and the way they made her legs feel wild, like she couldn't move them fast enough.

She hadn't done them since then because she thought she would never have such a good trip again. But lately her dreams just aren't enough of an escape. She was hoping they might merge with those of her sleeping grandmother so she could finally talk to Mattie again after all these weeks of rest and recovery, but so far it hasn't happened.

James thought Ada seemed pretty low, and told her on their last shift together that he had mushrooms and they were going to do them, no questions. Not that it's a great idea to do drugs when you're already fucked up, but here they are, chewing up the fungi, trying to ignore the pungent pulp stuck in their molars.

They're preparing for a good trip. They have a playlist going and James has a cat, and he's telling his roommates to chill out and shut up before the drugs hit.

They wait, not sure if it's working yet. Ada keeps checking in with herself: Would she be this into a song usually? Do cats always feel so soft? How much does she normally rock back and forth? They confer and agree that it's starting to kick in.

"I feel sick," James says.

"Nope. Just ride it out. Hold the cat," Ada tells him. He's a great cat, she thinks. He makes this face where at first you think he's just like any other cat, but if you look closer you can see that he smiles a little, and smiles more on the left, like a cat smirk. And he winks. He winks at her.

If she shifts from side to side in her chair she can feel the warm metal bead pushing against her clit. She feels it so much. Usually her attention is spread across all the senses in her whole body but now her powers of concentration are so great she can block everything else out and only feel this one thing.

"If I tried to meditate right now I bet I could make my mind so clear that I could split from my body and finally look at my face with my own naked eyes," she says.

"What?" James asks, petting the cat.

"Well actually I'd probably just float over to Pan's house to see what she's doing."

James looks up at her.

"You're high," he grins.

Ada forgets about the meditation and shifts right and left, shifty shift, rolling over the warm bead. James is petting the cat so fast, brushing his fingers back and forth along his spine. The cat looks worried, tail twitching.

"So tell me more about things with Pan. I want to hear all the dirty details," James says, saucy.

"There are no dirty details, or barely, anymore," Ada says, propping up her head with her hands, elbows on the table. "I could tell you some depressing details, but not many dirty ones."

"Oh," James says. "Shitty."

"I know, right? Because the sex was so *good*."

"So what's the problem?" he asks.

Ada leans forward, walking her elbows across the table toward James.

"Her partner," she says.

James cringes like a cartoon, eyes wide, sucking air in loudly through pursed lips.

"Damn, girl. Does that seem like a common tale or what?"

"Doesn't it?"

"Does her partner know about you two?"

"Nope. Plussss," Ada says reluctantly, closing her eyes as her ego deflates through her teeth, "I said something stupid. She must think I'm an asshole. I'm trying to fix it, but I don't know if it's something you can fix."

She looks at James but he is curled overtop the cat, examining his fur like it's braided with mystical secrets. The cat leaps out of James's lap and pads away across the kitchen floor.

"Let's go outside," Ada says.

"Okay," says James. "No more Pan talk, cross my heart."

Everything is beautiful outside. James and Ada talk about nature and feel like genius philosophers. All the things they say sound so true. The trees are exquisite. Adorned with new green buds, they look like wise queens dressed by handmaidens. The crocuses push up through the dense crust of spring snow like baby birds hatching, their butter yellow and velvet purple noses insisting it is time. Every year it feels like winter will last forever. That we've finally fucked the climate up so badly we don't deserve the thaw. But here they are again, after waiting in the cold and hard-packed earth, waiting in the dark, weighted down by heavy snow and stepping boots. How do they do it? Escape, grow up through the dirt without light to feed them? From somewhere in her brain, Ada remembers—it's the challenge of the soil itself. Their slender stems thicken. They transform under pressure, become exactly strong enough to break up and out, drawing on their last reserves of energy to sustain them before they can open, finally, to the sun. Ada turns her own face to the pale light, a small coin sinking low in the sky.

She feels James's hand in hers, he gives her cold fingertips a squeeze.

"How's your Nan?" he asks.

"I don't really know." Ada shakes her head slowly. "She's so tired. So so tired. She's been in bed for months. It just seems like she never wants to get up. And when I wake her to take her pills she barely opens her eyes. It's like she's permanently asleep."

"Do you think she's having good dreams at least?" James asks as he runs his fingers along the bark of a tree.

"I hope so."

"Do you think I should climb this tree?"

Ada smiles.

"Yeah. I will too. You go first."

They perch in the tree, two birds looking to the setting sun.

IN AN ATTEMPT TO MAKE the house feel less empty when she comes home late, Ada flips on the television. She needs to hear voices talking. Being in a house with someone who is never awake is maybe worse than being completely alone.

The last person to turn on the TV was probably Mattie. She watches awful soap operas.

Ada flips through channels, searching for a soothing voice. It seems like it might be a difficult thing to find. Everyone is so excited to sell her something. She clicks and clicks and stops on a channel where the colours look worn, an old documentary. The jovial narrator is telling the story of the last pearl fisherman in Scotland. It sounds romantic.

The last pearl fisherman pushes off the riverbank with one foot in a flat boat made from reeds, like a big matchbox, and lies on his belly, leaning his body over the front. He breaks through the skin of the water with a metal pail and puts his head inside. The narrator explains that the pail has a glass bottom so the fisherman can search the riverbed for mussels.

His head dips below the water's surface without getting wet, and it sounds like a minor miracle if you just say it like that and don't explain the logistics.

And there, look: he's found one. He pulls the boat up to the bank and steps out, the narrator explains, in case he should slip and fumble the pearl into the river. And also probably, Ada thinks, so the cameraman can get a better shot.

The fisherman takes a knife from his pocket, slides it between the mussel's mossy lips, and twists, cracking the hinge and wrenching the shell open. He pushes his fingers through fishy flesh and there it is—a pearl. He holds it up and smiles, sunworn skin crinkling like rippling water that spreads out from his grin.

The phone rings, and as Ada hoped, always hopes, it's Pan.

"Hey Ada," she says softly. "What are you up to?"

Her gentle voice is a balm on Ada's buzzing brain. She's been trying to make up for the last twenty-some years with a few short weeks of reading and research. Strategic Googling. "What's white privilege," she asked of the internet. How had she missed that one? She supposed that was the true mark of it, not even knowing you had it. "Explain systemic oppression," she demanded. And, "Am I the worst?" She's been trying to make up for history by learning it, and quickly discovering that that's the point—you can't.

She moves these heavy thoughts to the back of her mind so she can tell Pan about the last pearl fisherman in Scotland in shell-cracking detail. Pan loves it. She loves it so much that the way she talks back to Ada about how amazing it is makes Ada feel like she herself was only pretending to love it. Like she doesn't understand it well enough to love it like Pan does. It makes her feel so young.

"You should come over," Pan says.

Ada's heart floats up from the riverbed where it's been burrowed. "Thank you," she almost says out loud. She heads to her room to pack her bag, writes her mother a note and leaves it by the stove, slips on her shoes, and heads out the door. This walk to Pan's house, she knows it so well.

Do you even know where I live? she wonders to Pan.

She's told her before, but she's not sure it registered. She's asked Pan over, explained how her mother is really more like a roommate than a parent so it wouldn't be weird. But Pan always shakes her head like Ada's silly to suggest it.

"Naw, man," she'll say. "I think that'd be a little too real for me."

Fine.

Ada opens Pan's unlocked door and shuffles up the stairs, suspended somewhere between self-conscious guilt at her political failings and an adolescent desire to pout as Pan calls all the shots, writes all the rules of whatever sort of relationship this is—if Ada's allowed to call it that.

She drags herself into the kitchen and lets her bag slump to the floor. That art she used to love so much, on the table under Pan's careful hand. Pan's so focused on it that she doesn't even look up from the square of lino to say hello. And now Ada's jealous of it, that art. She wishes Pan would cut her with such care. She pierced her carefully but it was always over too soon. Ada wants Pan to bend over her for hours, pursing and pressing her lips, looking at her like she has such potential, touching her like she knows how to bring it out.

But if Pan cuts her into art, how will Ada ever be her own?

She sits down in the chair beside Pan.

"Hi," Pan looks over with a gentle smile. "It's good to see you."

Oh god, that mouth. Those beautiful teeth. Pan leans in and how could Ada not kiss her?

"I'll make you some coffee," Pan says.

Ada watches Pan boil the water and grind the beans. She wants to tell Pan that she's been reading, been trying to fix her fucked-up framework, trying to be better. Wants to ask Pan if she told her partner about her split heart. Is half of it still for Ada? She'll take half over nothing. She stares at the back of Pan's neck and her hands as they stir soy milk into a mug, fingers threaded through with steam. Pan sets the mug on the table in front of her and all Ada can manage to say is "Thank you."

Pan settles back down in her chair and picks up the blade, and Ada fishes in her bag for a book she's been wading through. She tries to finish the page she left off on but keeps having to start at the beginning again. Halfway through, she wanders off to the sounds of Pan's precise slicing.

You grab me by the shoulders and push me up against the wall, biting at my skin, holding your blade between the fingers of the hand that grasps the back of my neck, pulling it to the side so your teeth can get at my flesh. Your hand appears in front of my face and I see a metallic glint, like you just performed a cheap magic trick, pulled a coin from behind my ear. You draw the sharp silver down the front of my shirt and peel the cut fabric off me, laying me out on the table. Now I'm your canvas, a blank surface of skin whispering potential. You look at me intently, almost like you're intimidated by the task, but you bring your hand down and draw your blade across my chest in stinging strokes.

And then she starts at the beginning of the page again, trying this time to pay attention. It's hard to find a book that competes with her imagination.

When Pan's ready to go to bed, Ada lies down inside the curve of her body. Pan slides her hand around Ada's soft belly and pulls her close.

"You can blow out the candle," she says.

Ada leans up on her elbow. She hates blowing out candles. It's so sad. She usually falls asleep with them burning and Joan will creak into her room and snuff them out. Ada blows too gently at first, like she's lulling the fire to sleep. But it doesn't work. She has to kill it quickly, so she puffs it out with a decisive breath. The wick of this one has burned down low and the ember glows through the golden wax. Ada closes her eyes before it goes dark and imagines it flickering through the night.

35

April 3, 2008

When Shawn gets home, Kiah's sitting alone at the kitchen table, reading.

"Hey," she says, glancing up at her brother.

Shawn saunters to the fridge, messing her curls as he passes.

"Don't touch my hair!" she says, rearranging her ringlets from the attack. "What's wrong with you?"

"Relax. You want a pop?"

"Sure," Kiah says, turning a page and eyeing her sibling. Her hands are still dry from all that scraping. Even through her wool mitts the cold sucked moisture from her skin, and she hasn't yet been able to restore it. She's been taking Nadine's advice. She rubs lotion on her hands while holding the pages of her poetry book down with her elbows, savouring the words, barely noticing her brother pulling out a chair and sitting down beside her. She hadn't even had to go to the library to get her hands on most of the titles on Nadine's list. She found them on the shelf in the living room, nestled in amongst nursing texts and children's books. Why hadn't she noticed them before?

"What're you studying?"

"Huh?" Kiah says.

Shawn passes her a pop.

"I said, what are you studying?"

"Oh," Kiah says, reaching for the bottle and twisting the cap. But her oiled palms can't grip the plastic. "I'm not studying. Can you open this?"

Shawn cracks the seal and the soda fizzes.

"Man, now I have your girly lotion all over my hands."

Kiah takes a sip of her brother's favourite drink and looks at his face. She can't remember the last time he sat down beside her by choice. She studies his narrow jaw and the tiny patch of stubble up by his ear where he missed a spot. Huh. Stubble. Kiah can't think of the last time she'd been close enough to notice he was old enough to grow any. He looks at his palms and rubs them together.

"Actually this stuff smells kinda good."

Kiah passes him the bottle.

"Shea butter. It's Mom's. Remember?"

Shawn pops the lid open and inhales the scent. It's his mom getting ready for bed. It's her, first thing in the morning, leaving fingerprints on his cereal spoon as she set his breakfast down in front of him before school. It's her coming into his room at night and rubbing lotion on his elbows in the winter until he turned nine and wouldn't let her do it anymore. It's the smell of her hair from when he was small and she would carry him to bed from the couch, when he was still awake enough to walk but pretended to be sleeping so she would scoop him up.

"Whoa," he says, opening his eyes. "Mom."

In the warm light of the kitchen, Kiah can see the shine of welling-up tears as her brother tries to blink them away, and she reaches over to squeeze his shoulder. Shawn clears his throat.

"Listen," he says, reaching into his pocket. "I know you only have a month left to pay your fine or whatever, so I'm helping you out."

He tosses a creased envelope onto the table between them.

"What's this?" Kiah asks.

Kiah's been trying to think of ways to get that money. She had a couple babysitting gigs and shovelled a few walks on snowy weekends, but just hasn't had much time to work, what with all her classes and exams coming up next week, plus all the e-mails still arriving from folks who saw the posters before she scraped them to a pulp. She's been planning, working to set a date and place for everyone to meet as soon as these tests are behind her. But the deadline for her fine is creeping up.

She opens the envelope and thumbs through a stack of bills.

"Shawn, what is this? Where'd you get this?"

Shawn leans back in his chair and smooths his lotioned palms over his hair.

"Sold a few games I don't really play these days. It's no big deal."

Kiah peers into the envelope and looks at her brother.

"This is like four hundred dollars."

Not wanting this to turn into some sentimental family sitcom, Shawn pushes his chair back and gets up.

"It's not a big deal," he says again.

"You sold your games? I—wow. But I can't take this from you. I'll figure it out. I mean, thank you, Shawn, really, but I can't take it."

Shawn rinses his pop bottle out and tosses it in the bin.

"Kiah, just take the money. If you're gonna be getting yourself arrested for graffiti and I get to brag about it, I should at least support the cause."

36

�

May 18, 2008

Ada likes the smell of her own wounds. She always has. When she was little she used to peel back Band-Aids from her scabby knees and breathe in deep through her nose. After a bath, when the scabs got soggy and soft, was when she could smell them the best. Sweet and sour milk. A human smell.

Her mother saw her do it once and didn't even reprimand her.

"You're a weird kid," she said, and that was all.

Maybe it is a weird thing—in a bad way, a masochistic way. Like she likes the smell of her own weakness. Like she's a wild animal travelling in a herd, and these cougars or wolves can smell her wounds and they hunt her out because she'll be the easiest to catch, and she likes that or something. Or maybe it's that she knows there's something good about that blood clotting and scabbing. Maybe it's that she likes the smell of her body healing.

She still does it. She's doing it right now. Her swollen wrist was wrapped up in a cool wet cloth that softened the huge shell of a scab on the heel of her palm, and she unwrapped it and smelled.

It smells better now that the antiseptic Pan rubbed on it last night has worn off. Ada expected that Pan would have had iodine, since that's what she usually swabbed her skin with at the shop, but the stuff she brought from the bathroom smelled like yellow mouthwash and bad aftershave, and when Pan mixed it with water in a clear drinking glass it looked like milk. She soaked a cotton ball in it and drew it across Ada's bleeding palm. It looked sweet. Like Pan was anointing her or something. Like Pan was holy and Ada was a leper and Pan didn't even care.

Ada was so drunk she could barely hold her head up and had to concentrate really hard to speak. She did think it was milk for a second.

Is that how milk is made? she thought to herself. Is this condensed milk?

She decided it wasn't because it smelled so awful, like a hospital. That sterile smell—the iodine, the rubber gloves, the tissue paper. It really used to do it for her, but now it seems so cold.

Vodka has that smell, too. Antiseptic. It probably would have worked just as well, but when Ada fell she was already running away from James at the bar, running to Pan's house. She could have stumbled back and ordered another vodka shot to pour on her bleeding hand, but the bartender probably wouldn't have liked that much.

Really, Ada should have gone home and saved herself the embarrassment. But she had decided she would see Pan once more before Pan left town, and she was hammered. When Ada makes decisions to do things while drunk, failure is not an option, no matter how stupid or difficult or juvenile the thing might be.

"I'm moving," Pan had said over the phone earlier that day.

"New apartment?" Ada asked. "One that doesn't smell like pizza 24/7?"

"No. I'm going back to Vancouver. I can't hang out today. I gotta pack."

So they didn't hang out as planned and Ada drank vodka in the park with James instead. They got cheesy microwaveable bean burritos and slushy drinks from the convenience store, mixed their vodka in, and drank and talked until it was time to go to the bar, where they danced and drank some more. Ada couldn't stop looking around, looking for Pan's face, her lean, her grey-clothed form in the corners of the room. All Ada knew was that Pan was solving things by leaving, solving their relationship that Ada wasn't allowed to call a relationship, and the fact that Pan missed her partner, who filled the space Ada fell through.

"I have to see her," she yelled into James's face. Picked her way through the crowd, left the bar, and took off running.

She fell a few blocks later. Drunkenly loping with flopping feet and flailing arms until she tripped on a curb and flew forward. Palm driven into concrete, followed by bare knees and cheekbone. Knocking Ada's righteous determination right out of her. Seeing her own blood made Ada feel sort of serene. The blood looked the way it always had, when she'd brought it to the surface on purpose to ease her hurt.

"I fell," she said when Pan opened the door, her injured hand palm up, like she was offering her something.

While Pan cleaned the cuts, Ada looked blurrily around the flat. Cardboard boxes lay open on the floor like homely paper flowers, petals open to the fluorescent ceiling light.

"You're packing already?" she asked.

"I'm leaving in three weeks," Pan said, eyes fixed on Ada's hand. "But I like to get a head start."

"Wow."

Pan looked into Ada's wound like she could see her future, like she was reading her palm.

"You've got some tiny stones stuck in your skin," she said, and reached for one of her blades, not packed away yet. She swiped it with milky antiseptic-soaked cotton and used its sharp point to dig out a bit of gravel.

"Ow," Ada flinched, closing her hand over the rest of the stones.

"I have to get them out or it'll get infected," Pan warned, stern.

"It's fine," Ada said. "I'll do it."

At the door, Pan kissed her antiseptic fingers and touched them to Ada's lips, a replica of a kiss she came up with since she decided they weren't kissing anymore.

"Thanks," Ada said, and Pan blinked at her, slow.

She left one in, a stone. A tiny grey shadow under her skin. She wanted to keep it, the small, sharp memory.

37

✿

June 2, 2008

"Go without me," *Leona told them.*
But there was no way they could. It was the summer before she died. She wanted her family to go to the reunion, to get outside and see old friends. But no one wanted to leave her alone.

Friends came by after the sun had gone down and the music had stopped, smelling of the sea. They brought Leona flowers and fruit, but she was so sick by then that she could barely eat. Ken stayed by her side as much as he could, stroking her head, kissing her face and hands, sleeping curled around her thin and frail form. Betty cooked and prayed. Shawn stayed out late with his friends. Kiah read in her room or in the dim corner of her parents' bedroom when Ken was out.

They didn't go to the reunion the next year, either. When July came, Ken knew he couldn't handle being there without her. Her warm voice and electric energy were what got him up and out the door when his aching body protested. Now his body ached and he was alone.

"Everyone would love to see you," Betty told him. "And it would be great for the kids."

But Ken couldn't. He drank too many beers and fell asleep in front of the TV instead.

"SO ARE WE GOING THIS YEAR?" Betty asks when Ken comes home from work.

"Going where?" Ken asks, as he takes off his boots and puts his lunch bag down on the counter.

"To the Africville reunion," Betty says. She keeps her eyes on the fish frying in the pan, not wanting to seem too eager and not wanting her son to think she's judging him.

Ken looks over his mother's shoulder into the pan.

"Do you want me to make a salad?" he asks.

"Sure son," she says. "Maybe with an oil and vinegar dressing. That'd be nice with the fish."

Ken opens the fridge and pulls out arugula and lemon juice. He takes oil, vinegar, and garlic from the cupboard.

"Where's your protegé?" he asks.

"Out with friends I think," Betty says. "I gave him the night off."

"And where's Kiah? Out burning cop cars?" Ken asks, voice low as he tosses the wilting leaves into a wooden bowl on the counter. "I still can't believe that girl."

Betty flips the fish and the butter sizzles in the pan.

"Kenneth, give your daughter a break. I know you're having a hard time. We all are. But you can't punish her like this for so long. She's a good girl and she had her heart in the right place. Don't tell me you and Leona wouldn't have done the same at that age."

At the mention of his wife's name, Ken shakes his head.

"Hm. At that age. What were we doing at that age?"

"You were going to the reunion, that's what you were doing," Betty says.

Ken looks wearily into the wooden bowl.

"I don't think I can go this year, Mom."

His mother turns from the stove.

"You know your friends would love to see you, son. Ray called again for you today. Why don't you call him?"

Ken chops the garlic, slowly and deliberately, trying to concentrate on the task. He takes a few breaths.

"We have to move," he says.

Betty turns around to look at the back of her son's head. Ken continues chopping.

"What's that?" she asks. "Kenneth, turn around and talk to your mother."

Ken turns.

"As you guessed, the landlord's raising the rent in September. We knew we wouldn't live here forever and I want to own my own house again, so we have to move."

"That greedy man," Betty says, prodding the fish.

"Yeah well, history repeats itself I guess."

Betty nods.

"We'll find a place," she says. "A good place with a nice yard."

"But it'll be farther away," says Ken. "Everything's so expensive now."

"So we'll do it," Betty says. "We'll make it work. Always have."

Ken pours the oil and vinegar into a glass with the garlic and lemon, salt and pepper. He stirs it up and watches it separate.

"So are we going to the reunion this year?" Betty asks again. "It'll be the twenty-fifth, you know."

Ken covers the cup and shakes the dressing.

"I don't think so, Mom. I'm too stressed about this moving business. This wasn't something I thought would be happening so soon. I don't want to have to leave this house."

Betty turns to look at her son.

"And who could understand that feeling better?"

38

June 10, 2008

Last night Ada re-dreamed her dream from eight months ago, but this seemed to be the extended version. In the beginning Ada lost her teeth and Pan swallowed them, as before. When she first dreamt this, she consulted her dream decoder to find that it symbolized a loss of power, of strength. Ada had lost her bite to Pan. And this made sense, she was reluctant to admit. She truly was losing it—losing her teeth, her tongue, and the quiet corners of her brain to the exquisite form and amazing mind of a person who, in turn, grew only up up up on the pedestal Ada built for her. In the extended version, the shining ivory shell still spread across the surface of Pan's skin but as Ada's lips touched her cold porcelain head, the carapace cracked back into teeth that clattered to the ground. *You fed them to me,* Pan told her. *You dreamed this shell.*

At the kitchen table Ada sits and studies her decoder, flipping through the index, looking for hints to help decipher Pan's message. *Shell, crack, feed.* Ada murmurs the book's interpretations, shaking her head because nothing quite fits. Joan scrubs a pan in the sink, moving her cloth in rhythmic circles and not really listening to her daughter's quiet mumbling. She's too distracted by the sounds coming from Mattie's room. Another in a long string of moans comes from down the hall and Joan smacks her rag against the countertop.

"It's nice to hear they're back at it," Ada jokes, looking up from her book.

But Joan doesn't find it funny.

"No, it's not," she says, bracing herself against the counter. "Your Nan has barely been able to get out of bed. Whatever she's doing in there, her heart can't handle it."

Ada closes her book.

"I don't think Edith would do anything to hurt her," she says.

"Please stop entertaining your Nan's dementia," says Joan, pushing the words out through the tiny cracks between her clenched teeth.

Ada sips honeyed tea from her favourite mug as she watches her mother's back, the warm ceramic soothing her still-tender palm.

"I guess," Ada begins, not intending to sound quite so snotty but sometimes unable to shake the speech patterns she developed for addressing her mother when she was thirteen. "I guess," she says, "that it's a lot easier to believe Nan has Alzheimer's than it is to believe she has a ghost lover who's good in bed."

Joan looks at her, exasperated.

"Her doctor says she has Alzheimer's. It's not something I made up. And yes, it is much easier to believe."

She turns back and resumes scrubbing.

"Well Nan didn't make Edith up either," Ada says. "Maybe you could try a little harder to believe her. Why can't you just let her be happy?"

Joan jerks back to face her daughter, dropping the rag in the sink.

"Are you finished your tea?" she asks coldly. "I'm almost done the dishes. Give me your mug."

"No, I'm not finished," Ada replies, like tires on gravel. She lifts the mug to her lips and stares at her mother.

"Finish it," Joan orders.

Ada drinks and they stare. She sips so slowly, letting the cooling tea seep through her slightly parted lips. Part of her thinks she is making some kind of point with this display, but she can't remember what it was supposed to be. Soon she runs out of tea and they're still staring, but she continues to swallow, mug tipped back.

Joan strides over and snatches the mug out of her hands and from between her lips. Ada yelps in surprise.

"You're finished."

Joan turns back to the sink and starts to wash the mug.

"What the hell, Mum?" Ada shouts at her mother, incredulous. "You can't just grab things out of my hands. You're acting like a child."

"Actually Ada, you're the child," Joan spits, leaning in as the words shoot out of her mouth. "You don't always get to be right and you don't get the last word. If you want to believe in a goddamn ghost that's fine, but I don't need a lecture from my *child*."

"That's great, Mum, real mature. Go ahead and pull the grown-up card on me. You're just bitter because your closed mind can't understand that someone doesn't live in your boring world. Actually, I think you're jealous."

Mattie moans again from her room.

Turning away from her daughter, Joan starts to cry.

"She is sick. My mother is sick," she shakes. "She's doing this to herself because she doesn't know who she is or what's going on. She's sick!" She turns back. "How many times do I have to tell you this?"

A louder moan now. Mattie doesn't sound far off.

"She's not sick!" Ada yells. "You're just mad because no one loves *you* like that!"

Joan screams like a car crash and throws Ada's mug hard onto the floor. It smashes into thick pieces as Ada shoves her chair back with a screech and stands up.

"Get out of my kitchen," Joan orders, pointing to the front door.

Ada stands still, looking toward Mattie's bedroom.

"No!" Joan shouts. "Outside!"

"Did she come?"

"What?" Joan asks, her voice still in shouting pitch.

"Did you hear her come?" Ada turns to her mother. "I didn't hear her. She sounded close—she always sounds like that right before."

She runs down the hall.

JOAN AND ADA GET HOME from the hospital a little after ten. They're both hungry but neither wants to put the effort into making food. Even canned soup seems like too much, and Ada's always felt awkward eating and crying at the same time. Her nose gets plugged up and she has to chew with her mouth open in order to breathe, and everything tastes salty and sticks on the way down.

It had been another heart attack. Mattie's narrowed artery had ruptured and clotted again.

They left her in intensive care overnight, with a breathing tube and a beeping heart monitor. The doctors weren't sure surgery was a good idea, considering her age and the fact she was still recovering from the last attack. It was awful to leave her, but the nurse said the best thing would be for them to go home, get some rest, and come back to see her in the morning.

Joan puts her hand on her daughter's back as she walks past her on the way to the kitchen.

"Tea?" she asks, in an underwater sort of voice.

Ada makes similar sounds, gurgling yes.

In the living room, they leave the lights out because it's softer that way. The streetlights project glowing squares onto the laminate floor. Joan sits on the old green couch beside her daughter and Ada wraps her arms around her mother's neck. Joan makes such young sounds when she cries, her voice high and cracking.

The electric kettle bubbles in the kitchen and clicks off, but they don't get up. Ada will sleep on the green couch tonight. She doesn't like the idea of sleeping on one side of the wall if her Nan's not sleeping on the other. It's like looking into a mirror with no reflection, which is the loneliest thing Ada can think of.

The next day Joan calls in early to see if she might be able to take work off to sit with Mattie, but another reporter has called in sick and beat her to it. Now Joan needs to cover the event he had been preparing for all week while she's been so concerned about her mother's health that she'd barely scanned the media release about the ceremony. She skims the schedule as she walks out to the company car—honouring of survivors, opening prayer, crossing over, pipe ceremony, letting go. She wishes the cameraman was coming with her so he could drive while she read it more thoroughly, but there are no cameras allowed. She'll have to keep her recorder off too, her boss told her. And she's late. Sixty kilometres away and it's already nine in the morning. She doesn't want to be disrespectful. If only she'd had more notice. Joan checks the map.

"Cross the bridge to Dartmouth, then take the 118, the 102, take the turnoff to Shubenacadie and find Indian School Road. Okay. Got it."

THE HOSPITAL WOULD HAVE BEEN so much better with her mother around, Ada thinks. Even after their fight last night, she misses her. It's scary to sit with Mattie in the sterile room. Worse than before. This time there are more tubes, more wires, more beeping machines. Last time Mattie was breathing on her own and it was reassuring. But the sounds the ventilator makes are unnerving, and Mattie lying there with a tube down her throat—Ada's sure her Nan would find it undignified.

After an hour of sitting, her legs falling asleep and a headache creeping up on her from the fluorescent lights, Ada decides she needs to go outside. And though she's not so sure it's a good idea, she calls Pan from the phone in the waiting room. It's her last day in the city.

"It's nice out," Ada says. "Do you wanna get a Popsicle with me?"

"Sure," Pan says. "I need to get out of the house."

They meet in the south-end convenience store where Ada had been buying cigarettes, and peer together into the freezer at the Popsicles. Ada picks an orange one and Pan opts for pink.

"I'll pay," Pan says.

They wait in line behind a man in a leather jacket. He talks angrily at the cashier, who has just run out of his favourite cigarettes.

"Sir," the cashier says, "I'm sorry, but we should be getting more in tomorrow."

The man is still grumbling, but the bell on the door breaks the tension as four young Black girls walk in with their hoods up.

"Can I help you ladies?" the cashier asks loudly.

The girls shake their heads and walk around the store, checking out magazines and candy. The cashier watches them closely.

"Boy, are they in the wrong end of town," the man in the leather jacket says to the cashier, and the two white men nod in agreement.

"I'll be back tomorrow," the man says as he leaves.

Pan and Ada stand at the counter, but the cashier's eyes are on the girls.

"You like magazines?" he asks them.

They look up at him, unimpressed and unintimidated, the blank stare teenage girls have perfected for stupid adult questions.

He glances down at the Popsicles on the counter and punches them into the register quickly, his eyes darting back up fast enough to catch sight of the tail end of a Kit Kat as it sinks into a deep pocket.

"HEY!"

He explodes with the rage he'd been preparing since the girls walked in and runs out from behind the counter. But the girls are fast and book it out the door and around the corner. The cashier gives up, not wanting to run on creaky knees for a chocolate bar.

He puffs back into the store and behind the counter.

"I knew it," he spits. "What else do you expect from those kids? That's $5.10 for the Popsicles."

"Well," Pan says, her voice hard like Ada's never heard it. "If that's all you expect of them and you're gonna treat them like it, why *wouldn't* they live up to it? Wouldn't want to disappoint you."

"Get out of my store," the man says, eyeing Pan up and down.

They turn and leave. Ada's impressed to have heard Pan deliver the comeback she wouldn't have thought of herself until days later. But she did think to grab some candy and stuff it in her pocket when the clerk ran out of the store after the girls, her hands quicker than her mouth.

"Fucking racist asshole," Pan fumes as they walk down the street. "He's just going to see that as a way to prove himself right, instead of seeing how he's part of the problem."

"Here," Ada says, pulling the candy out of her pocket and handing it to Pan. "Those Popsicles were too expensive anyway."

Pan shakes her head.

"Of course he didn't even notice you did it."

She looks at the candy Ada swiped—bright red, corn-syrupy goo in neon-wrapped baby bottles.

"This is some gross looking shit," she says.

"Yeah, it looks a little toxic."

They walk down the street, toward the park.

"I'm sorry for the way I told you about leaving," Pan says. "I've been so mixed up. I didn't mean to drag you into it. I was lonely and I let this go too far."

Ada is quiet as they stroll along the sidewalk, shocked to hear the apology she'd been imagining for weeks as she pushed her fingers against the small stone embedded in her palm. Though this isn't quite how she'd hoped it would go. The script was supposed to read: "I've been so mixed up—I thought leaving was the right thing to do, but now that I see your face I know...." But now that Ada sees Pan's face, she knows. Pan's not a character whose dialogue and intentions Ada can compose. Not some shiny effigy she can idolize. And their romance, it isn't a story she can tailor to her desires. It was a real thing, Pan's a real person, and she's leaving.

"It's not your fault," Ada finally says. "I dreamed the shell."

"Pardon?" Pan looks over at her.

"I mean," Ada says, "I mean it's okay. You didn't drag me."

Pan takes Ada by the hand and they walk into the park, palm to palm.

"I hate this park," Pan says. "They should have a plaque by that statue that says who Cornwallis really was."

Ada nods.

"I read about him and his Mi'kmaw scalp bounty. I can't believe so many things in this city are named after him."

Pan looks at the bottle of glowing goo in her hand.

"You know what I'd like to do with this shit?"

They unwrap the bottles and look around. The sticky red syrup is the most perfect fake blood, covering the statue's hands and running down his cape. Pan uses what she has left to smear across the engraved *FOUNDER OF HALIFAX* below his name. They toss the bottles in a trash can on their way out of the park.

"So, now that you've committed petty theft and some mild vandalism, what are you doing for the rest of the day?" Pan asks.

"I'm going back to the hospital. My Nan's in there. Heart attack, again."

Pan puts her arm around Ada as they walk.

"I'm so sorry, I had no idea," she says. "I'll walk you there."

JOAN DRIVES FAST AND MAKES it in forty-five minutes. It's already 9:45 and she still needs to find the old school grounds. She parks in the muddy field at the bottom of the hill with all the other cars and gets out. She's already missed a lot, but she might make it in time for the pipe ceremony.

The road is narrow. She begins to follow it uphill, passing a house and a dying tree. The school burned down over twenty years ago. Joan can see nothing that marks its history—no sign, no statue. At the top of the hill in the field she sees a large tent. But by the time she reaches it, the pipe ceremony has already begun. She decides to wait outside.

Inside the tent are over two hundred people, seated in rows. The south end is open and a sacred fire burns nearby. At the north end sit the elders and survivors of the school. The people who did not attend sit at the south, farther from the circle in the centre where the elders go to speak and lead the ceremonies.

When the pipe ceremony finishes, Joan finds a spot just inside the fabric wall and sits down. The air smells of sage and sweetgrass. She searches in her bag for a pen and pad of paper, but when she brings it out, a woman sitting near her shakes her head no.

Into the centre circle steps a man. He begins to speak, telling the people in the tent that he is going to call the spirits of the children who disappeared from the school. The sick and beaten children who were sent to the infirmary, never to return. Never to be given a proper burial. People sing in Mi'kmaw, calling the children to the tent. The smoke from the sacred fire blows in through the open southern side and billows above their heads.

Then the singing changes. The man has called the children and now he is telling them to leave. The Creator will take care of them, he says. They can go.

Mi'kmaw girls in red skirts lead the group to where the train station used to be, where they listen to stories of children torn from their families, scared and crying on the train to the school. And they dance. Joan stands to the side, hugging her arms around herself, watching as the group forms three concentric circles and pounds that history into the dirt with their dancing feet.

Back on the reserve they eat bologna sandwiches while they watch the Prime Minister, with his silver helmet of hair and eyes like icebergs, say his sterile sorrys to the TV cameras. Joan looks around at the old and young faces. Some angry, shaking their heads. Some crying, staring at the screen with tears shining on their cheeks. Some refusing to watch.

"They're just words," says a young man sitting beside his grandfather. "He looks like he doesn't feel a thing."

AND AT THE HOSPITAL, Mattie wakes up alone.

What is this thing down her throat, these sounds around her? Where are Ada and Joanie? Where is Edith?

"Right here, Sparrow," Edith says. "I'm right here."

Edith pulls the ventilator out of her mouth, and Mattie smiles.

"Hello, my love," Mattie says. "Did you eat my Jell-O?"

"They didn't bring you any Jell-O, you silly thing. You're too sick for Jell-O."

Mattie wishes she could move around, but her body won't cooperate. Her chest aches.

"Do you want to get out of here?" Edith asks.

Mattie nods.

"Let's go," she says. "I'll go anywhere with you."

"Except Toronto," Edith says.

"I should have come. But you came back to me, my darling. Take me anywhere."

"All right," Edith says. "I'm ready to go too."

39

❦

June 16, 2008

oan and Ada haven't talked much in the few days since the funeral.
J They haven't been cooking either, so the house doesn't smell like
anything. It's an accidental funereal ritual they've created, of sensory
deprivation. Is it out of respect for Mattie, who no longer has a body
with which to see, taste, touch, hear, or smell?

Ada hasn't cried yet today. She might be empty, at least for now.
There's probably some kind of refractory period where your body
replenishes its stores of salt and the chemicals that make you sad, that
you have to squeeze out through your eyes so you can feel better. She
must be out, because she doesn't feel much of anything right now. She
feels like an empty house.

Ada flicks on the kitchen light as she walks into the room and sees Joan sitting at the table.

"Oh, hey Mum."

She wants to run into every room, turning on every light. But Joan glances at her daughter and taps her temple, looking pained.

"Headache," she says.

Ada clicks the switch off and turns on the small bulb over the stove. It's softer, yellower. Makes this scene look like a snapshot from the seventies.

During the service Ada had felt disappointed with her mother. How could she have let that minister speak about Mattie? He hadn't even known her. But Ada knows how tired Joan is. It would have taken a lot of energy to plan the perfect funeral, and they're both so sapped. Tapped like trees and bled out. They weren't prepared. So there were biblical stories as allegories for a life the man who read them never knew, and bouquets of white carnations with petals like tissues found scrunched in a pocket. If Ada had had the foresight, she would have sat down and planned the funeral out with Mattie. Mattie would have liked to have her say.

Ada wouldn't have let anyone speak who hadn't loved her Nan well enough to know the charm of her lipsticked tooth. She would have let the friends Mattie and Ian used to play bridge with talk about how bossy she was during card games and how she was such a sore loser. And Ada would have spoken, though right now she can't think of what she would have said. The flowers would have been ones that grow here, that Ada could have picked with her own hands. Buttercups maybe, lupines.

At least they had her cremated, because she had made it very clear when they buried Ian that she would not be purchasing the adjacent plot; nor did she want her name on a headstone, waiting to be engraved with the date of her death.

"You don't have to buy the plot beside him, Mum," Joan had joked. "We can save money and put you on top. Like bunk beds."

Mattie raised one sparse, grey eyebrow.

"I'd rather be cremated, Joanie. It's awful to think of his body in the ground. I don't want it to happen so slowly. Better to go out with a bang."

"Okay, Mum," Joan said, patting her hand. "Of course. Whatever you want."

Mattie never said what she wanted Joan and Ada to do with her afterward though, so they brought her home. They haven't talked about it yet. Might put her on the mantle. She's still in Joan's bag in the hall.

At the kitchen table, Joan sits with fingertips to temples, rubbing clockwise. She's dehydrated from all the crying, and hungry too. Ada puts a glass of water in front of her, poured from the tap because Joan likes the fluoride. She rubs her mother's back but they're both so numb there's not much comfort in her touch.

Out of the purse Joan brought to the funeral, still sitting by the front door, Ada lifts the cool metal urn. It feels like a Thermos—stainless steel to keep the heat in. Ada wonders if, inside, Mattie's still hot from the oven. Bits of bone and teeth smouldering, glowing embers pulsing, their life hidden and kept safe in soft grey ash. She's heavy for a Thermos but so light for a grandmother.

Even though Mattie would probably be more comfortable on the couch, Ada places her ashes on the mantle. Ada needs to sleep. But where? In the living room, close by what's left of Mattie, or in her own room, against the wall they no longer share?

What if I put her in her room? Ada wonders. But this isn't her. I know that.

And yet it is her, sort of. It is her because Ada needs it to be.

They go together down the hall.

"Let's go to bed, Nan," Ada says. The metal is brushed steel that obscures her reflection and makes a sound like shh shh shh when she runs her fingers along it.

This is the first time Ada has opened Mattie's door since her heart attack and the room still smells like her. She bends down to switch on the nightlight and lays the urn on the pillow, in the centre, where the old feathers are still pressed down from Mattie's head. People say you should get a new pillow when the feathers don't spring back, but wouldn't you rather sleep on a pillow that remembers you?

Ada wishes she could cry. She feels like she should. In her mind she goes through a slideshow of remembering. She thinks of Mattie's bright eyes, her knobby hands and soft skin. She breathes deep the smell of her room. Thinks of Mattie's teasing voice and sees the halo of thin hair around her head, tilted to one side when she was listening. She always listened to Ada. Ada sucks in air, tries to breathe fast and uneven to start the tears. She clenches her teeth, knits her brow, closes her eyes, but nothing comes. She can't.

In her own room, Ada feels better than she thought she would, now that the Thermos is resting in Mattie's imprint. Ada's pillow remembers her too. She fits herself into it and sleeps.

"SHE WAS SUCH A BOMBSHELL," says Joan.

In her closet she found a shoebox full of old photos, and she and Ada are hanging up the best ones on their still-bare walls. Mattie looks back at them through the pane of glass, hands on hips, her body wrapped in a shiny cocktail dress. Lips pale and iridescent, hair piled high.

"I would've been three here," Joan says. "She loved to dress up and go dancing with her friends."

"I didn't know that," Ada says.

"Oh yeah," says Joan with a smile. "Such a beauty. I can see why Edith came back."

Ada stares at her mother. What an offering.

They crouch over the pictures on the living room floor, sifting through them and fitting some into frames. Joan grabs the hammer and stands, picking a spot on the wall and driving a nail in without knocking. It sinks straight into the drywall, all the way up to the head.

"Shit," she says. "I was trying to be impulsive."

Ada stands up to help her, rapping along the wall to find a stud.

"Here," she says. "Right here would be perfect."

Joan hammers and Ada returns to the floor, picking a portrait of her grandparents and her mother as a tiny child. She's probably four years old, with baby teeth and baby bangs, one chubby little hand caught in the act of brushing them off her forehead.

"Can we hang this one too?" she asks.

Joan peers closer to it and smiles.

"I love that one," she says. "I actually remember that day. They gave me a doll between pictures to keep me busy, and then they would take her away for the photo and I would throw a fit. So they let me hold her behind my back. That's her shoe peeking out from behind me."

There it is, a tiny Mary Jane.

"Did you ever have portraits taken of me?" Ada asks.

Joan hooks the wire on the back of the frame over the nail in the wall and stands back to examine her work.

"Your grandad took some," she says. "I don't think it's in this box, but somewhere there's one of you and Mum and I. It's really funny. I'm holding you in my arms and she's holding me in hers. Just like she did when she carried us to the ocean."

Joan hasn't mentioned that story in years, and just now she said it like it was true.

A knock at the door pulls them back to the present.

"Who could that be?" Joan wonders out loud as she stands up and leaves the room. Ada stays on the floor, sifting through photos. Joan opens the door.

"Hi," says Betty. "I'm your next door neighbour."

"Oh," Joan says, embarrassed. "I'm so sorry we haven't come over yet to introduce ourselves. I've just been so busy with work and, well, my mother's been quite sick." She feels tears welling up, stinging. "She passed away just a few days ago, actually."

"Yes, I'm so sorry," Betty says, "I heard, through the neighbourhood grapevine. I met your mother—a lovely lady," she adds, giving Joan a sympathetic nod. "My grandson and I made you stew with dumplings, in case there's a night you can't manage to make dinner. I always found that food was the most helpful thing when a loved one passed."

Joan takes the heavy dish in her hands, its rich smell rising up through the foil.

"This is incredibly kind."

On the floor, Ada pushes glossy pictures aside, uncovering an eye that looks softly out at her from below layers of faded photos.

"You're welcome," Betty says. "I'd better get back home to pack."

"Are you going on vacation?" Joan asks.

"No. We're moving."

"Oh?"

Betty doesn't have the energy to explain.

"I'd better get home," she says again. "My condolences to you and your daughter."

She leaves Joan standing in the doorway, holding the warm dish, and licks a drop of stew that slid down the ceramic and onto her palm. Shawn's got a real knack for cooking. Just the right amount of salt. You can bet she'll be talking up her grandkids to everyone who will listen at the reunion next month. The flakiness of Shawn's perfect pastries, the righteousness of Kiah's delinquence. And she'll be standing by to clasp her son's hand each time someone asks how he's been. When they say, Oh Ken, I'm so sorry, you must miss her so much. When they say, And now you have to move? What a sin, what a sin.

In her room, Kiah carefully wraps the oval-framed photo of her mother in a sheet of newspaper and nestles it in a cardboard box beside poetry books and her cousin's tarot cards. Shawn, her dad, her grandma—over the past few days they've all been slowly uprooting. Her father is going to have to fold up his bedsheets. He will lose Leona's impression, Kiah thinks, and wipes away a tear with newsprint-smudged fingers. She can't believe they're leaving the north end. But Kiah will be back—in a week, actually. She'll catch the bus to the library for the second meeting. Mel has agreed to take minutes this time after missing the first one, and Shawn will make snacks again. "Bet you didn't see that coming," Kiah says to Leona's picture in the box. "Your kids hosting neighbourhood meetings together." And from somewhere between the drum of her ear and the root of her tongue, Kiah hears her mother reply, *Oh, I saw that coming from miles away.*

In her hands, Ada holds a photograph of a woman with a gap-toothed smile and shining dark hair. She traces her finger along the line of her cheek. *To Sparrow*, it reads across the back in faint blue ink. She pulls a wooden frame from the pile and pries off the crumbling cardboard back, pressing the picture against the glass, and places the portrait beside the urn on the mantle holding her grandmother's burned body. Small bones smouldering with luminous love.

This near to the longest day of the year, time feels slow. The summer sun won't set until nine. It glows through westward windows, except where the houses are very close. Where they're close, and before the blinds are drawn, you can see into the kitchen next door as if you were over for dinner, or into the living room like you were invited for tea. You can see your neighbours packing and unpacking, folding and unfolding. Almost as if you were there.

AUTHOR'S NOTE

The easiest place to start is by writing a fictional version of yourself. Write what you know. You don't have to do any research and it doesn't get any more authentic. So the young, queer, white woman in this novel is loosely based on me at that age, because these are some of the things I know best: falling in love, feeling insecure, navigating family relationships, and starting to learn about systemic oppression and my own privilege.

This story is about many things: love, family, community, death, sex, age. It is also an attempt to contribute to the growing body of media that draws critical attention to racist, colonial histories, and that encourages white people to acknowledge our role in racist and colonial oppression historically and currently, take responsibility for our unearned privilege, and begin to learn how to act in solidarity with Indigenous peoples, Black people, and other people of colour.

I live near Halifax, or K'jipuktuk, in Nova Scotia/Mi'kma'ki—unceded and unsurrendered Mi'kmaw territory. It's a beautiful oceanside city in a lush province with an intensely racist past and present: the colonization and genocide of the Mi'kmaq and enslavement of Black people by white settlers, the brutal and deceitful treatment of Black Loyalists by white Nova Scotians, the abuses perpetrated by white staff of the Shubenacadie Residential School and the Nova Scotia Home for Colored Children, the eviction and destruction of Africville by Halifax

City officials, and the present-day segregation and gentrification of the peninsula, racial profiling by police, environmental racism, and more. In this city and province, race and racism are hard to ignore.

But because so many people with privilege still resist acknowledging it, I think it's vital to talk about systemic privilege and oppression. And I think it's necessary for people with privilege to do the work of educating other people with the same privilege. When someone is faced with an idea over and over, in different forms and forums, it becomes harder to deny. So I wanted to write a story that, among other things, includes a white character who is starting to learn and think about race, racism, and white privilege.

It would be difficult to write about these issues in a story solely populated by white people. And when the setting is a real place where Indigenous peoples, Black people, and other people of colour live, writing a book that only features white people would feel to me like a racist erasure. But I also know it can be problematic, offensive, and culturally appropriative for white authors to write Black characters, Indigenous characters, and other characters of colour.

In writing characters who are oppressed in ways that I am privileged, I've tried to be responsible and accountable by doing research and soliciting criticism. I watched documentaries, read books, essays, blogs, articles, and poems; attended talks, plays, poetry readings; and art openings; and listened to friends, partners, neighbours, classmates, teachers, and coworkers to better understand experiences I will never have. African Nova Scotian, Mi'kmaw, and South Asian friends, and African Nova Scotian and Mi'kmaw sensitivity readers engaged by Vagrant Press read the manuscript and shared insightful feedback and invaluable knowledge about cultural accuracy and respectful characterization. My most sincere thanks goes to everyone who has spent time and energy reading this book—especially Michael Davies-Cole, Cheryl Maloney, Andre Fenton, Tiffany Morris, Lindsay Ruck, Rebecca Thomas, Okanta Leonard, Balraj Dosanjh, Anne Bishop, Mynah Meagher, Steve Hart, Whitney Moran, Patrick Moran, and my editor, Stephanie Domet. This story is so much better than it ever could have been without your help. Thank you in particular to Okanta for sharing your experience of attending the letting go ceremony at the site of the former Shubenacadie Residential School for inclusion in this book. And thank you to Elder Dr. Bernie Francis for reviewing the Mi'kmaw words that appear in the story, which are written according to the Francis-Smith Orthography. Finally, thanks again and much appreciation to Whitney Moran, managing editor at Vagrant Press, for supporting this project and believing strongly in the necessity of, and working toward creating, an accountable editing process.

Of course, this does not mean I got it right. Any issues remaining in the text are due to my own failing. And while I understand that as a white author, it is vital to consult with people who share the identities of Indigenous and Black characters and other characters of colour in your stories, and compensate them for this work, I also know it's not possible to consult with everyone who shares these identities. The reviews of the people who read this story do not function as an unofficial or official approval, and cannot represent the views of the entire identity-based communities the reviewers are part of. Communities are complex and heterogeneous. As a member of "the queer community," I know how vastly different the politics, values, and opinions held by people in a community can be. I've considered these things and attempted a respectful process, and I will continue to listen and learn.

Thank you to my partner, Jesse, my friends—especially Jane, Okanta, Claire, An, Emily, Rebs, Tamara, Gems, Nasha, Kay, Balraj, Katrin, Esher, Jo, Sarah, Mary, David, Michael, Rosy, Su, Gavrel, Mynah, Elly, Jesse, Caitlin, Ned, and Tate; my parents, Kathy and Richard, and my sisters, Alex, Samantha, and Mackenzie, for your support of my creative life and my life in general. Thank you to Clove for coming into the world and making everything sweeter and more wonderful. Thanks to my employer for a supportive mat leave that doubled as a writing sabbatical. And thanks to the Cyberpunk Apocalypse writers' collective in Pittsburgh for hosting me as a resident to work on this novel back in 2010. The time I've spent writing this story—twelve years, on and off—feels both so long and too short, and I could probably keep editing and changing it forever as I encounter new ideas and come to more complex understandings of the issues addressed in it.

I encourage everyone who reads this story to learn more about some of these issues by going to the source. I have learned so much about Mi'kmaw histories, communities, culture, and issues through the work of Elder Dr. Isabelle Knockwood, Elder Dr. Rita Joe, Elder Dr. Daniel N. Paul, Donald Marshall Jr., Elder Catherine A. Martin, Elder Dr. Bernie Francis, Patricia Doyle-Bedwell, Dr. Pamela D. Palmater, Naiomi

Metallic, Ursula Johnson, and Rebecca Thomas, and about African Nova Scotian histories, communities, culture, and issues through the work of Dr. Sylvia D. Hamilton, Dr. Burnley "Rocky" Jones, Senator Dr. Wanda Thomas Bernard, Dr. G. Lynn Jones, Michelle Y. Williams, Angela Simmonds, Robert S. Wright, Dr. George Elliott Clarke, Gloria Ann Wesley, Wendie L. Poitras, El Jones, Shauntay Grant, and Andre Fenton. I will always have more to learn from the work of these and many other people who are fighting for justice, building community, and creating beautiful and powerful things.

All profits I receive from this book will be used to support organizations, initiatives, and scholarships run by and for Indigenous and African Nova Scotian peoples.